CAME A
GENTLE WHISPER
a Novel

by

REBECCA A. CATHEY

This book is a work of fiction. All of the characters,
organizations, and events portrayed in this book are either
products of the author's imagination or are used fictitiously.

PRAISE FOR

CAME A GENTLE WHISPER

"Cathey's yarn steeps readers in a richly textured panorama of Ozarks culture and folkways. The author explores this world with a homespun lyricism, but also gives her characters a grit that she brings out in evocative, sinewy prose…A beautifully written saga of love, loss, and belonging that turns trauma and grief into hard-won wisdom." – *Kirkus Reviews* (Starred Review)

"The great virtue of this book is the vanished world it evokes. An impressive amount of research has gone into portraying the setting, and countless small details… accumulate to lend the story a sense of verisimilitude… Cora Lee's escalating misfortunes sustain interest till the very end. This is a fine work of historical fiction with a strong moral center." – *U S Review of Books*

"Rebecca A. Cathey's *Came a Gentle Whisper* is a quietly powerful exploration of love, endurance, and moral integrity…Cathey's prose evokes the era with vivid authenticity—the rough beauty of the land, the cadence of ridge talk, and the quiet dignity of ordinary people making their way through extraordinary times…Cathey writes with deep affection for her setting and characters…It's a story that lingers long after the final page, reminding readers that faith and love, like the hills of the Ozarks, endure in their own quiet way. **It is unreservedly recommended!**"

– *The BookViral Reviews* (5 Star Review)

For

Iva Tempest White, my grandmother,
the orphaned mountain girl who's spark
ignited the idea for this story,

and

My beautiful sisters,
Deborah, Karen, Tamala, and Lara,
the women who fanned the flame,

and

All the members of my writing group,
the people who kept the fire going.

CHAPTER 1

The winter of 1912 gripped the landscape in a sudden, terrible fist. Bitter, hard frosts covered the earth and seemed to slow its spinning as a great blue norther moved over the hills of Missouri's Ozark Plateau. While some argued that the cold was as bad as the Great Winter of '05, the Old Residenters had lived through it and remembered. They knew better.

"No! Not even close!" they'd argue as they tucked in around their fires while wind and snow battered their cabins. "Why, in 1905, the mighty Mississippi River froze solid up near Saint Louis. But I'll give ya—this one's bad enough!"

Plenty of signs indicated this winter would be a hard one. Goose bone prophets predicted heavy snows after studying the thickened sterna of geese. Hornets' nests hung low in trees, and an unusual number of squirrels gathered an abundance of acorns and walnuts that fall. Old Man McDaniel's lilac tree bloomed late in October, a phenomenon that had only happened once before back in that hard winter of 1905.

The howling wind tore at travelers approaching Bennett's Ridge, but the icy blasts did not deter their progress. A young man, his hat tied down with a bandana and huddled deeply in his coat, held the reins of his horse in the frozen fingers of one hand, the other shoved deep in his pocket. Riding pillion, a young girl hid her face against his back, pulled her stockinged legs tight against the horse's sides for warmth, and shivered.

"Will it be much farther?" she asked, but the wind either swallowed her question or, as likely, the young man chose to ignore it.

The rarely used road they were on wound its way from the train depot in town where Silas Bennett had collected the girl, past the sawmill and frozen mill pond at a logging camp on the river, and into a thick forest of pine, oak, red cedar, and chinquapin. Leaving the main road, he turned his horse onto a steep dirt track that led up into the hills and along a ridge. The wind here grew less fierce among the trees and rocky ledges that overhung the path, and the girl lifted her head to survey their surroundings.

They passed a small burial ground, its boundaries defined by a split-rail fence. A painted wood sign that read "Beautiful Gate Cemetery" swung noisily from the crossbar above a turnstile gate. Some of its inhabitants rested there in unmarked graves, others were pinned down by newly-chiseled, wooden headstones. All were the ancestors of the residents of Bennett's Ridge who had lived for generations among the timbered peaks rising above the town of Endurance in the valley below.

A few miles farther, past the McDonald's, Dobson's and Campbell's farms, Mae Clarey's one-room cabin huddled against a low rise as if to protect its rickety back from the winter storm. The resident of the shack, Granny Mae as folks called her, lived simply and clung to her farm with a sort of stubborn inertia reminiscent of her ancestors' ways. It was here with the old woman that the young man, at last, deposited the girl.

Silas reached to take the child from the saddle as she craned her neck to take in her new surroundings. He sat her on the ground and steadied her as she gained her footing after the long ride from town. Saying nothing, the taciturn young man clamped a hand on the girl's shoulder, moved her up onto the porch, and knocked on the door.

The old woman took the girl into the cabin and removed the child's coat and mittens as Silas closed the door on the storm outside. Swaddling her in a heavy quilt, Mae sat her granddaughter on the floor next to the warmth of a wood stove. She poured steaming water into a cup from a kettle on the stove, added a splash of milk and a few herbs, and handed the warm drink to the child with a biscuit for her dinner.

Mae turned to Silas who still stood at the door. "Have a cup of coffee to warm yerself." The offer was more a statement than a question.

"Thanks, but no. Don't wanna get too cozy 'fore I have to go back out in this mess. Don't have much more to go. Pa wouldn't want me to linger."

"Well, Silas. I thank ya kindly fer fetching the young 'un fer me."

He nodded, turned, and departed out into the winter storm without another word.

Mae bustled around the cabin for a moment as the girl nibbled the biscuit and watched her. There was no fear in the child's eyes, only an alert curiosity and quiet demeanor as she waited for what might be expected of her next.

Mae finally settled into a pine-wood rocking chair next to the stove pulling her knitted shawl tighter around her rounded shoulders. Her hands, calloused by hard living and wrinkled with age, busied themselves with bits of cloth and a needle. The orphan, a thin-faced girl of about the age of nine, sat at the old woman's feet as Mae finally spoke.

"I'm yer granny. Did they tell ya that?"

The child nodded. "Yes'm. I'm Cora Lee McMillan, your grandchild."

"I suppose you be tired after that long ride in this terrible weather?"

The girl shook her head. "No'm. I'm just happy to be warm and out of the storm."

The two sat quietly for a time before the child braved a question. "How come you to live in such a far-off place as this?"

The old woman chuckled. "I ain't always lived up here. I lived in a different place when I was yer age."

"How come you to end up here, then?"

Mae thought for a moment and settled more comfortably before launching into her story.

"I was just a girl when the War of Northern Aggression broke out. Ma and Papa farmed in these mountains up near Bear Creek, and the minister of their church announced he was refugeein' to Little Rock when the fighting came to Missouri in '61. That caused quite a bit o' panic among the folks. Most of the congregation declared to go with him, so Ma warted and fussed to go, too. Papa wouldn't go 'til we was ordered out by General Ewing in '63.

"Oh, of course, me and my girlfriends all thought it would be a great lark, but turned out not to be so. My dearest friend, Bessie McFearon, had an uncle up in Springfield who refugeed to his plantation on the Yazoo. Bessie was sent up to him fer her safety, but she drowned when the river flooded later that year. You see, when the Good Lord calls, Ol' Death is gonna find ya no matter where you go."

The old woman cleared her throat and raised her hand to a charm string tied at her neck. Her fingers sought and found a button in the collection hanging there. She rubbed it thoughtfully for a moment. "She was such a bonnie lass—so good and so gay," she murmured. She was quiet for a moment, her fingers moving from one memento to the next. She dropped her hand and cleared her throat. "Where was I?"

"You were talking about leaving with your church folks and pastor…"

"Yes! Well, weren't long 'fore we was refugeein' again and again to stay ahead of the Yankees. Went to Camden, but it was flooded with so many homeless people—all desperate, and some were dangerous folks. Papa wanted to go to Texas. Ma wouldn't have that—nothin' but snakes and Injuns and dust there, she claimed. Ma was set agin' it, so Papa didn't take us down to Texas."

Granny Mae shook her head, dropped the sewing in her lap, and sat still as memories of the past flitted behind her faded green eyes. After a short spell, she picked up her needle and quilt patches with a sigh and resumed piecing the squares of cloth together with tiny, expert stitches. Light from a kerosene lamp flickered across her weathered face casting shadows that softened its hard lines with the smudges of bygone days.

"But what next, Granny?" the child at her feet whispered, tugging at the old woman's skirt.

Mae smoothed wisps of the girl's light brown hair from the pale, upturned face and continued. "Oh, youngin', we lost near ever single thing we didn't carry with us. I still have my Ma's iron skillet and my

Papa's old guitar—that's it o'er in the corner by the bed." Mae pointed with her needle.

"I can play that thing a little and used to could sing, too, 'fore my voice got too old and wore out. I'll learn ya to play and sing songs when yer a little older if you've a mind to take it up."

The child looked at the object in the corner certain she would never master such a feat, and then settled closer to the warmth of her grandmother's knees.

"The Yankees burned out the farm—barn, house, fences and all," Mae continued. "Nothin' to go back to, couldn't pay the taxes on the land and it was confiscated, so we lived in the wagon fer months."

The old woman adjusted herself to an aria of creaks and groans from her wooden rocker and settled again. Pulling the kerosene lamp on the shelf on the wall a bit closer, she again bent over her work.

The only sound in the room was an occasional pop from the fire in the stove and the rattle of sleet blowing against the oilcloth-covered window behind her. Cora Lee sat still, afraid that any motion or word from her now could break the spell her grandmother was under and put an end to the story.

After a short time, the woman continued. "Pa passed away, and Ma did the best she could to raise me to be God-fearin' and decent. She passed on about a year after Pa. I made my own way fer a bit, then met a merry man who made life seem better than it was and soon became his wife. I was almost twenty-four by then, and I thought I might end up an old maid.

You see, there weren't many young men left fer marryin' after the war.

"Yer Grampa Nelson saved me from a long life of lonely, bless him. He moved us up here to where his family had this fine land. He built this cabin, and we took up farmin'. Been here 'bout forty years, now."

Cora Lee finished her biscuit and drained her cup. "Thank you for my dinner, Granny. And did you like living up here, then?"

Mae nodded, took the cup from the child's hands and set it on the shelf next to the oil lamp.

"Been a good 'nough life, I reckon. Never went hungry. Lost three babies, but raised up yer ma and had four fine boys, too. My boys were killed by nature or died by disease 'fore they was fully grown. Yer Grampa Nel died from a bad heart 'bout six years ago.

"Yer ma was my youngest. It took a long while fer me to learn she had passed on and to find you. Awful time you had in that orphanage, I reckon."

"It wasn't too bad. I had lots of friends at Saint Anne's, and at Christmas we got apples and new sweaters. A man from the St. Louis Auto Club would come with his machine and take some of us for rides around the park. I liked that."

The girl thought for a moment. "But, I didn't have anywhere to go home to. Some of my friends at the orphanage got to go home to their folks on the weekends and holidays, but some of us lived at the place all the time. Family and a belonging place is all I ever wanted."

8

Mae flashed a gap-toothed smile and placed a gnarled hand on the girl's head. "Well, I'm yer family, and this is where ya belong. It were mighty lonely up here fer a time 'til the Good Lord sent you to me. Ya know, 'God works in mysterious ways' as the Good Book says, and that's surely a true thing."

"Tell me about my ma, Granny Mae." Yawning, Cora Lee leaned her head against the old woman's knee and gripped the woman's homespun skirt in her fist. "Was she pretty? How come she died so young?"

Granny Mae shifted in her rocking chair and, frowning, struggled to rise. "Oh, child, time enough fer all that story on another night. Time you was in bed."

The girl whimpered a half-hearted protest but tucked her hand into the work-hardened palm of her grandmother and allowed herself to be led to the bed in the far corner of the room. Shivering, she removed her dress, changed into the nightgown she had from the orphanage, and climbed beneath the covers. Swaddled in the quilt-laden rope cot she would share with her granny and warm against the chill night air, she watched the old woman shuffle about the room until sleep, at last, closed her eyes.

The urgency of her bladder woke Cora Lee to a room cold and dark. Her body tensed in confusion at her strange, new surroundings, but her grandmother's soft breathing next to her brought reassurance, and she relaxed. Realizing the necessity of climbing out of her cozy nest to make a trip to the outhouse in the night through the wind and sleet, she briefly wrestled with the impossible thought of wetting the bed instead. She drew a breath, steeling herself against the miserable cold, and carefully crawled out of the blankets.

Granny Mae reached out a hand and stopped the girl. "What is it, honey?" she mumbled.

"I have to go to the outhouse," Cora Lee whispered.

"Here, child," Mae said as she rose. "We keep a chamber pot handy fer night visits."

Sliding a covered enamel pan out from under the bed, the old woman helped the girl lift her night dress and waited as Cora Lee relieved herself.

"Better than wading out through the dark and the haints to that old outhouse, heh?" Mae chuckled as she returned the pan to its place, and the two climbed back into bed. Shivering, Cora Lee snuggled close to her grandmother and, once again, drifted off to sleep.

The winter months passed away with many such nights filled with stories of long ago, stories Old Ones had passed down, and stories of her grandmother's youth. Cora Lee loved them all. At the end of a day laboring on the small mountain farm in the Missouri Ozarks that had become her home, Cora Lee curled up on the floor next to the rocking chair by the warmth of the cook stove waiting with eager ears.

"Mary sent word 'bout you. I was so pleased to have a grandchild at last, and I hoped she would bring ya up here to meet me. I didn't hear about their passin' fer quite some time. Mary passed on to Glory

10

Land a few years after you was born. A fever set in—they told me she got the pneumonia from the flu. Then yer Pa died, too—gone within a week of each other. It's only God's mercy that they didn't take you with them, I reckon, and His blessin' that brung ya to me.

"I learned that they passed you around the lumber camp fer quite some while 'fore someone finally took ya to the orphanage over in Saint Louis. Mary and yer Pa, Joe, hadn't neighbored with folks in Pine—lumber folks never settle long. Nobody knew where else to send ya, and you was too little to know or tell.

"A few years later, that old peddler that passes through here from time to time gave me the news about Mary and Joe. When I asked about ya, he said he didn't know where you was.

"Our neighbor, Mr. Bennett, sent his son, Silas, out searchin' fer ya. It took him a long time to find you. He ended up goin' all the way to Saint Louis and made arrangements fer them to send you here on the train. It took a while, but you finally got here, and he rode down to town to bring ya here. He brung you home to me."

CHAPTER 2

Cora Lee stood leaning against the corner post of the porch, a puzzled expression on her face. She watched the sow pushing leaves and other brushy debris into a pile near the chicken coop. When the pig picked up a fallen branch in its mouth and carried it to the mound, she ran to the cabin door and called, "Granny! The hog is being peculiar! Come see!"

Mae wiped her hands on her apron and came to the door. Stepping onto the porch, she put her hands on her hips and watched the hog continue building its heap.

"Storm comin'," Mae said after squinting at the sky and noting a few broken patches of grey clouds scuttling along ahead of a gusty north wind. "Could be a big one. Best put the chickens up fer the night and gather in the wash 'fore it sets in to rain."

Mae turned to go back into the cabin, and the rooster began to crow. "'Cock crows at bed, chickens rise with a wet head' as the sayin' goes," she said as she stepped through the door.

"How do you know rain's comin'?"

"Oh, lots of signs tell it. Whirlwinds in the road, my achin' bones, pig buildin' a poke like that 'un's doin'. Our coffee boiled over this mornin'. Those are all signs fer rain. After you bring in the wash and the chickens is settled, best help me with another load of firewood."

Cora Lee ran to the chicken yard and, waving her arms, herded the hens into the coop. A few of the birds ran away, clucking and flapping their wings in protest, but Cora Lee managed to get them settled at last. She shut and latched the door of the enclosure then ran to take the wicker basket off the porch where it hung on a peg outside the door. She hurried to where the washing hung on the line.

Nervously glancing at the sky as clouds rolled in, strong gusts of wind began to whip the clothes on the line madly about. She removed clothes from the line as quickly as she could and managed to put the last apron into the basket as rain began to fall. She dashed back to the porch and rushed inside.

"Do you want me to bring in some more wood, Granny?" Cora Lee went to the door and looked anxiously out as fat, dark clouds overhead unleashed their cargo in blinding sheets, and wind blew rivulets of water across the yard.

"No, child. Come back in and shut the door. We'll make do with the wood that's in here."

Flashes of lightening split the air, and thunder shook the house. Gale-force winds howled about the cabin. The doorlatch rattled and shook, but held fast as gusts of wind forced themselves between chinks in the walls and lifted shingles off of the roof.

Rain dripped in several places from the ceiling, and Cora Lee hurried to put pans and bowls on the floor to catch the water. A corner of the oilcloth over the window blew loose sending rain across the room, and Mae rushed to tack the covering back into place.

The two of them finally settled next to the warmth of the stove as the squall leveled off and then finally began to subside. Damp, but safe against the storm outside, Cora Lee begged for another story.

"What was it like when you were a girl, Granny?"

"Oh, well, I was considered a pretty girl in those days. I had a beau when I was a young girl back 'fore the war. I met him at a dance, and I thought he was the finest young man ever made. Dancin' with him made me think that the waltz was the finest dance ever made, too," she laughed, then sighed. "He got killed in the fightin' up at Wilson's Creek. So many, many of our boys—gone."

Stories like that sometimes ended in long periods of silence as Granny Mae drifted back to bygone days in her memory. Shaking her head, Mae continued her tale as she played absently with Cora Lee's wispy, light brown hair.

"We spent most of '63 livin' in a chicken shack on Ma's cousin's place down near Bald Knob. Papa got some middlin' work at the salt mine there fer a time. We had to move on again when the Yankees came and busted up all the boilin' pots, and the fightin' got too close fer comfort. We traveled around from pillar to post—saw nothin' but burnt-out farms... sad and solitary chimneys standin' where homes used to be and gloom everwhere.

"Them war years was tough, but the Good Lord brought us through."

Cora Lee nodded, and looked around the room as Mae's story wove pictures in her head. The cabin was wet and drippy with pans and bowls strewn about the floor. The furnishings were sparse—just this old rocker, the kitchen table and chairs, and a small table next to the bed in the corner—and there were no fancy paintings on the chinked, log walls like there had been at the orphanage, but this, at last, was her home. She leaned against her grandmother's knees with a smile.

***

The rains leveled off after the first, intense burst to a steady, persistent drumming for the next few days. The storm cleared away the remaining winter snow where it had lain in patches down in hollers, in the shade of trees, and under rock overhangs.

Mud made the ridge road and river path impassable for several days. "Road's so muddy it'd bog down yer shadow," Mae said when Cora Lee begged to go for a walk. "Best wait a bit."

Disappointed, Cora Lee meandered around the cabin, too restless to sit still for more than a minute.

"Cora Lee, yer gonna wear the smooth right off'n them planks. Come over here, and help me with sortin' these rags."

Cora Lee complied and plopped down on the floor at Mae's feet.

"These here are good enough for cuttin' into squares for a quilt; these have holes but are big enough to cut patches out of; these is rotten and ain't worth keepin' for more than cleanin' rags."

Cora Lee half-heartedly picked at the rag pile and tossed a few into the three piles her grandmother had specified for each purpose. After a few minutes, she stopped sorting and begged a story.

"Granny, tell about my ma. How did she and my papa meet?"

Mae laughed. "Yer ma met and married yer pa back in the summer of '01. She turned sixteen and was so anxious to marry. Yer pappy was a teamster— had his own wagon and mules and made a good livin'. He came up here with a surveyin' crew come to buy timber off'n Old Mr. McDaniel's land. Them two younguns got one look at each other, and they weren't no keepin' 'em apart after that. They married right quick."

Cora Lee smiled, happy to learn that her parents were actors in a real-life, fairy tale love story. "Love at first sight, Granny?"

"Sure was! They moved to a timber camp down near Pine. That's where they was livin' when you came into the world in yer pa's wagon. Some folks believe bein' born in a wagon is a fortunate thing."

Cora Lee grinned, her mood lifted, and dove with more enthusiasm into the rag pile.

It took a few days of warming spring sun to eventually dry out the land enough that farmers could work at spring plowing and planting. Children roamed the woods, once again digging for sassafras root and herbs to make tonics, ginseng root to sell or trade, and young pokeweed leaves, wild onions and dandelions to put fresh greens on the table.

Mae, not immune to the rising sap of spring, looked forward to calling on her neighbors to catch up on news. She stood at the table with her hands on her ample hips as she took inventory of the things in the wicker basket in front of her.

"Candles!" she said aloud. "Mean to take 'em a few of those, too—and some of them peach preserves I put up last summer."

Mae rummaged around the room locating the named items and adding them to the few gifts she had already placed in the basket on the table. "Cora Lee, honey, we're gonna go pay a call over to the Campbells' place. Their gal, Amanda, got engaged to the oldest Bennett boy, Silas. You 'member him.

We're gonna take her a few things fer her hope chest. She'll be havin' her weddin' soon, I reckon, now that winter's done over.

"I 'spect, after the school term is over this summer, they won't be any more schoolin' fer young'uns," Mae continued. "Amanda will be too busy takin' care of a husband and raisin' her own babies to be a teacher to other folks' kids like she's been doin'. But at least you'll have a little dab o'learnin' 'fore she moves in with her new husband and starts a family."

Excited over the prospect of an outing to meet neighbors, Cora Lee clapped her hands and scrambled to fetch her bonnet and shawl. She loved her new home, but the isolation of her grandmother's mountain cabin was often lonely. She had almost begun to miss the orphanage and the companionship of the children there.

Mae picked up the basket after donning her own bonnet and shawl and started out the door with Cora Lee close behind her.

"I don't mind about school. I can do a little reading and ciphering from my time at the orphanage. But I think going to school for a little while this summer will be nice, too."

Mae and Cora Lee walked along in silence. The Campbell farm lay about a mile from Mae's place, and the older woman became a bit breathless about halfway down the road. She sat down on a tree stump to rest.

Thousands of wildflowers covered the roadside meadows in a brilliant, multicolored spring quilt, and Cora Lee became immediately drawn to them. Unable to resist collecting a few blooms, she busied herself by gathering a colorful fistful of white yarrow, yellow tickweed, bright blue chicory, and purple columbine while her grandmother rested and caught her breath.

"These are sweet, don't you think, Granny?" she asked as she dropped the bouquet into the basket on Mae's lap. She noticed her grandmother's pale face and troubled breathing and reached to take the basket from the older woman's lap. "Do you want me to carry this?"

"No, no, honey. I'm fine. Let's just walk on." Mae stood, took a deep breath, and restarted the journey. "I guess I'm a little out of sorts after being holed up in the cabin all winter."

Passing a small path that led from the road down to the river, Cora Lee spotted a boy standing by the road. He poked at a mound of dirt with a long stick, then he began to attack a bush with the stick as if he fought a fierce battle. His long hair fell over his face. The sleeves of his homespun shirt, rolled up to his elbows, exposed his gangly arms, and a rope belt held up pants too short for his long legs.

"What are you doin' there, Walter Douglas?" Mae called to him.

The boy dropped the stick and turned to greet Mae. "Howdy do, Miz Clarey?" he asked politely while tugging the shock of black hair that fell over his forehead. The corners of his gold-brown eyes crinkled as he grinned in embarrassment at being caught fighting his silly war game.

"I'm just playin' with that old ant bed, ma'am," he answered. "Them ants make a powerful army."

Mae eyed the boy and noted his unkempt hair, dirty face and ragged clothes. "I haven't seen you in quite a while. You've grown almost tall as me now. How old are ya this year? 'Bout twelve?"

"I'm turnin' thirteen this fall, ma'am."

"And how's yer mother and sister?"

"They both fare well, thank ya."

Mae reached into the basket on her arm and produced a crock of peach preserves. Handing it to Walter she asked, "Can you take these to yer mother fer me? It would save me the walk down to yer place in the holler, and I'd be much obliged."

Walter accepted the gift readily, his eyes wide, and thanked her again. Cora Lee peeked out from behind her grandmother's skirts.

"Howdy do. I'm Walter Douglas."

Mae pulled Cora Lee from behind her. "Manners, child! Walter, this is Cora Lee McMillan, my daughter, Mary's, girl. She's come to live with me, and I'm mighty thankful to have her here."

Cora Lee mumbled a greeting and dipped a quick curtsy as she'd been taught to do at the orphanage.

"Well, it's a pleasure seein' ya, boy," Mae said. "Give yer mother my regards, and be sure to give her them preserves, hear?"

Walter nodded, "Thanks, Miz Clarey. It's been a awful while since we've had sweets!"

Mae and Cora Lee watched as he ran into the woods toward his home in Poke Holler clutching the preserves to his chest as if it were a precious treasure. Cora Lee turned to her granny to ask, "Why did he call you 'Miz Clarey?' My name's McMillan, and isn't that your name, too, Granny?"

Mae chuckled. "No, child. My name was same as my papa's—Murphy—'til I married Nelson Clarey. Then my name became Clarey like his. Yer ma's name was Clarey 'til she married yer papa, Joe McMillan. Her name became McMillan, and that's yer name now, too. When you marry someday, yer name will change and be the same's yer husband's."

"Sounds like a woman doesn't have much of a name for herself at all," Cora Lee said indignantly, "if a man can just keep changing it!"

"That's the way of things, honey—God's order of things in this life," Mae laughed.

The pair continued along toward the Campbell farm in silence. Cora Lee considered the unfairness of having no name that sticks and finally decided that God did, indeed, work in mysterious, if sometimes rather disagreeable, ways.

A bit farther along, the ridge road curved at the point that a rail fence marking the Campbell farm began. Blackberry bushes grew along the fence line, and a small but well-kept cabin came into view. The yard was swept clean of leaves and debris. A hard-packed dirt path lined on each side with large rocks led from the road to two wide steps and a porch that ran the length of the house, and smoke rose from a chimney made of sticks and clay. The cabin, built from hewn logs tightly chinked and daubed with mud from the riverbank, looked sturdy, solid, and welcoming.

A pigsty and chicken coop were tucked into the far corner of the rear yard, and on one side of the house near a firepit over which hung an iron cauldron, a nanny goat grazed. Most of the rear yard had been tilled, and small green shoots of corn were emerging in neat rows. A plow leaned in an untilled kitchen garden near the corn field.

"Are they rich folks?" Cora Lee asked, wide-eyed.

"Oh, child, I reckon they may appear so to some, but they's always those that have more or less than others. What's important is whether they's decent people, not how much or how little they have. The Campbells is good folks, and we're blessed to have them as our neighbors."

"And how did they come to be livin' in such a fine place as this?"

"Well, I reckon some is luck, but it's a lot because they's hard-workin', Christian folks that don't fritter time nor money away on foolishness. Mr. Campbell has a grist mill down on the river, and he works that and this land with his older boy, Roy Dale. Miz Campbell keeps a clean house and raises her children with a stern hand. Their girls, Amanda and Alice, help out, too."

A barrel-chested, red-faced man with sandy hair and a thick beard that covered his chest stepped out of the house and onto the porch. "Miz Clarey! What a nice surprise to see ya!" he bellowed. "Come on in this house and sit down."

"Good to see you, Luther," Mae called back. "Is you all doin' well?"

Luther nodded. "We're doin' fine." At that, the man turned and yelled through the doorway, "Ada! Ya got company!" Then he turned and hollered for his son. "Roy Dale! Let's get down to the mill, boy! Time's a'wastin'!"

A sandy-haired, loose-limbed boy of about fourteen came loping into the yard from around the back of the house. Luther strode from the porch and met his son in the yard. "Got a pile of work to do 'fore dark, so let's get a move on." With a friendly wave to Mae and Cora Lee, the two of them crossed the yard and disappeared into the woods toward the river.

Mae and Cora Lee walked up the dirt pathway to the porch as Ada Campbell stepped to the door, a smile lighting up her moon-shaped face as she greeted them. Her pale-blonde hair, tucked into a bun, sat low on her neck, and she wore a clean white bib-apron over her blue gingham dress. A baby that looked to be about a year old sat on her hip.

"Oh, lands! What a blessin' to have visitors today!" Ada exclaimed. "Come on in here and sit. I'll just bedpost the baby and put a fresh pot of coffee on fer us so's we can ketch up with each other."

Cora Lee followed the two women into the cabin and stood by the door as Ada sat the baby on the floor near a bed in the corner of the room and pinned the tail of the child's dress under one of the bedposts. She handed the baby a set of wooden spools strung on a string and offered her visitors a chair at the table.

With a huff, Mae set her basket on the table in the kitchen and took one of the chairs. "The baby's lookin' mighty well. Have ya named him, yet?"

Ada smiled and shook her head. "Luther wants to call him 'Phineas,' but I'm kindly set on 'William' after my pa. I guess when one of us gives in, it'll be settled, and Luther's awful stubborn. I reckon I am, too, but I do tend to give Luther his way on things."

Mae laughed. "Well, I reckon they's no rush about it. He ain't walkin' yet, is he? I brung a few piddlin' things fer Amanda's hope chest. She'll be getting married soon, I 'spect?"

"Well, she and Silas wanna wait 'til he has his place built first. I reckon they won't wed 'til sometime next year—maybe even after next year's summer school term. Adam Bennett give Silas a few good acres up by the cemetery. Silas's buildin' them a place on it. Mr. Bennett likes to keep his family close by, ya know, and who can blame him?"

Mae nodded at the basket on Ada's table. "Well, I reckon she can add these few things to her hope chest to help set up her new home, if she can use any of 'em."

"That is so kind of you to think of her! She'll be so pleased. And who have ya brung with you, Mae?" Ada asked and extended her hand in invitation to Cora Lee. "Is that Mary's girl? Isn't she sweet!"

"Yes, Mary's girl. She finally come home to me this past winter, and she sure did brighten up these last few dreary months, I'll tell ya."

"Well, she looks like how I remember Mary did when we was that age! She's about the same age as my Alice, isn't she?" Ada got up from the table and went to the door calling out for her youngest daughter, "Alice! Come on in here and meet—" Ada trailed off, turning to Mae with a question on her face.

"This is Cora Lee McMillan."

"Come in here and meet Cora Lee!"

Within a few minutes, a young girl dressed in a tidy gingham dress and white linen apron appeared at the door. She looked Cora Lee over taking stock of her new playmate. Cora Lee smiled, and Alice grinned back at her, grabbed Cora Lee's hand, and pulled the two of them through the door.

"Come and see our new baby piglets," Alice said in a torrent of excitement. "They's born a few days ago. They's twelve of 'em, and they sure can squeal! Do you have piglets at your place? I bet not. I bet you only have chickens. Do you have any baby chicks yet

25

this spring? How old are you anyways? I'm ten years old and three months. I bet you're not ten, are you? 'Cause you're not as tall as me."

Cora Lee tried to answer that she had already turned ten, but the flood of conversation coming from her new young friend made it impossible to say anything. Laughing, Cora Lee went along willingly and did Alice's bidding. From the pigsty, the girls went to the barn, then to the vegetable patch. Alice continued her stream of friendly chatter naming each of the vegetables that had ever been or would ever be planted there.

"This is where Ma always puts bush beans. I hate beans, but she continues to plant 'em year after year anyways. You'd think she'd pay more attention to what I like—tomatoes, too. I hate tomatoes, too, don't you? What do you like to eat? I bet you like the same things I do. I love blackberry cobbler. We have blackberries out by the road. Do you have any at your house? I bet not. I bet you only have peaches, huh? I know you have peaches 'cause we trade fer 'em sometimes. Peaches are good, too, but I like our blackberries better…"

And so, the afternoon went until the girls were called back to the house where Mae had donned her bonnet and shawl and was ready to return home. Mae watched Alice and Cora Lee walking arm-in-arm across the yard.

The two girls could not have been more different. Alice, with her round blue eyes alight with humor, her blond curls bouncing in excitement, and chattering non-stop. Cora Lee, her straight brown hair coming loose in undisciplined strands from her plaited pig tails and blowing into her almond-shaped green eyes and across her olive-skinned face. One quiet and shy and the other a font of activity and chatter, Mae wondered if they would be good friends as their mothers had been.

On their walk back home, Mae pointed out a narrow path on the south side of the ridge road that led to the schoolhouse. The square building was nestled back off the road a short way in a clearing surrounded by tall pines and chinquapin.

"The elder Mr. Bennett built that on his land several years ago as a meetin' hall and school. He wanted the children who live up here on the ridge to get some education. The Campbell's oldest girl is gonna teach some this summer, and maybe some this winter if the weather ain't too cold fer it. She may even teach some next summer if she ain't married 'fore then. You'll like to go to school, won't ya?"

Cora Lee considered the prospect. "Yes, ma'am, I believe so. Will my friend, Alice, be going? If so, I believe I'll like it just fine. I had a little learning at the orphanage, but I don't remember it all."

They walked a bit in silence, then Cora Lee asked, "Granny, do you think that me being an orphan will matter to the others in school? I mean, do you think they'll look at me different like I'm strange?"

Mae stopped and pulled her granddaughter to her in a hug. "The Bible says we're to 'forget the things behind us and reach for the things to come.' Whatever ya was before, yer my child, now, and I love you. You ain't gotta worry none about that. Yer God's child, too, and He's gonna keep you in His hands. Just trust in Him, and do yer best."

Cora Lee nodded, relieved to hear she belonged somewhere and to somebody that loved her. Still, although she was excited to know she would be going to school, she couldn't help but worry about whether she would fit in with the other children.

"Well, I'll try, Granny. I just know I'm different 'cause I grew up in an orphanage, is all."

"First of all, you ain't growed up yet. Still have a bit to go 'fore then. Second of all, you ain't no orphan, anymore, 'cause ya have me. Yer gonna be fine as snake feathers. You'll see."

CHAPTER 3

The few weeks before school opened for the summer term flew by filled with the business of spring planting, spring cleaning, and a visit to the ridge community by Peddler Man Dan—an event that caused much excitement on the mountain.

As the peddler's mule-drawn wagon came up the road, the music of copper pots and utensils rang in the air like a clunky windchime as they swung together in his open-sided vehicle. The noise alerted Cora Lee and Mae to gather items for trade.

Peddler Man Dan shouted a lusty "hullooo the house" from a few yards away and pulled his mule to a stop in front of the cabin. A bewhiskered, middle-aged man with long, stringy-black hair jumped to the ground and held a hand up in greeting as Mae and Cora Lee came to the door. He wore a deer-skin vest festooned with buzzard feathers and beads, and his beaded leather moccasins were fringed up to his knees.

His flat-topped box-wagon, painted a bright green with yellow trim, had black lettering that read "Peddler Man Dan—You Need It, I Got It" on the side. Several brooms, standing bristle-end up, rode in a cluster at the rear of the wagon. Bolts of factory-made cloth, bonnets, gloves, fans, buckets, wicker baskets and tinware filled racks behind the driver on one side. The opposite side had drawers for sewing notions, hair combs, straight razors, and other small sundries.

The flat-topped roof of the wagon held barrels of sugar, flour, molasses, coffee, and a small trunk that contained packets of spices and glass vials of medicinal concoctions packed in straw. Bundles of pelts, bunches of dried yarbs, and straw-lined boxes holding mason jars full of moonshine the peddler had taken in trade completed the wagon's inventory.

"Miz Clarey," the old man sang out. "Good to see ya again! Yer lookin' plum lolliper!"

"And yer lookin' as wampus as ever. Don't think yer about to come 'round here and arkansas me with sweet talk." Mae ambled out to the brightly-colored wagon in a disinterested fashion as she exchanged banter with the peddler. "Can't think of a single gewgaw that I might want."

"Oh now, Miz Clarey!" Dan returned with a mock-wounded air. "You say that ever time I stop by, but I can always tempt ya with some little somethin' or other. 'Sides, I'm sure that young'un needs something', now don't ya, gal?"

Dan turned his attention to Cora Lee who stood close behind her grandmother. "Maybe some fine gingham fer a new frock?" He grinned, bent over, and leaned down to the girl. "Ribbons fer that pretty hair? Come on out here, young'un, and see what Old Dan has to trade."

Overwhelmed by the peddler's boisterous manner, Cora Lee shrank behind her grandmother.

"She's fine where she is," Mae said. "I don't need a thing, but I'll see what ya brought, anyhow. I might could use a new tuckin' comb fer my hair—a toddick o' sugar and some coffee as usual, and a new pair of shoes fer my girl. Otherwise, we're pretty well fixed."

Mae turned to go back to the cabin to fetch the items she had assembled for trade—some dried yarbs, some sang root, and the quilt topper she stitched over the winter. Cora Lee grabbed onto Mae's skirt and stayed close behind, glancing over her shoulder at the strange man who stood in the road by his wagon.

"Don't worry about Peddler Man Dan," Mae said once they were safely back in the cabin. "He's mostly bluff and bluster, but no bite. Stay in here while I go finish tradin'. I'll get you some material fer a new dress out of the bargain, too."

Cora Lee hid by the open door, peeking around from time to time to watch as her grandmother finished her business with the peddler. True to her word, Mae also managed to barter a few yards of light-weight, sky-blue denim to make a new dress for her granddaughter.

"He gave me this to give to you, too," Mae said as she held out a small stick of peppermint candy. "Said he wanted ya to know he's a friend."

A smile spread across the girl's face as she eagerly accepted the treat. "I'll have to be sure and thank him proper next time he comes around!"

The exciting production of a new dress to wear to school kept Cora Lee in high spirits for the next week. She could hardly stand still long enough for Mae to measure and fit the garment.

When the first day of school finally arrived, Cora Lee danced about and twirled in a circle. Finally allowed to wear her new dress, loving the fashionable drop waist and the way the pleated sky-blue skirt belled out around her knees, her excitement made her green eyes dance as much as her feet.

Her grandmother even managed to crochet a little "lace" to edge the simple, rolled collar of her bodice. Some of the leftover material fashioned two bows for the ends of her pigtails. Delight in the new frock she wore and the new moccasins she held in her hand almost dispelled her nervousness at starting school.

She finally calmed down, put on her bonnet, picked up her lunch bucket with a hard-boiled egg and a biscuit carefully packed inside, and stood in the doorway. "I'm ready to go, Granny."

"Oh, honey, you'll be fine. Walk on up the road and take that little path I showed ya earlier. If you walk all the way to the river path, you've gone too far." Mae laughed and gently pushed the girl out the door. "Behave and make me proud."

Cora Lee stepped off the porch and, with a small wave, walked to the road and turned left toward the path to the school house. She looked back at her grandmother to make sure she was headed in the right direction. Mae nodded and smiled, and squaring her shoulders, Cora Lee walked on with more confidence.

When the building came into view, Cora Lee let out a sigh of relief that she hadn't missed it. Sitting down on a tree stump, Cora Lee brushed the dust from her bare feet. She put on the moccasins she had carried to keep from getting scuffed and dirty during her walk. Patting her hair, she was assured that her tight braids were still neat and tidy, but a mixture of anticipation and nervousness still made her worry that something would go wrong.

She didn't know if she would do well here, and awareness of her own lack of education caused her to doubt her ability to manage this new endeavor. What if she had forgotten what little she learned at the orphanage? What if everyone knew more than she did? What if no one here liked her because of her past?

"Hello, Cora Lee McMillan!"

Alice Campbell's cheery voice spun Cora Lee around on her perch. Alice, dressed in a pink dress and white pinafore, her gold curls pulled back from her face and tied with a pink bow, skipped up to Cora

Lee. Awash with sudden relief at seeing her new friend, Cora Lee jumped up and gave Alice an enthusiastic hug.

"I'm so happy to see you! I was afraid I would have to go in there all by myself. I've never been to a real school—just Bible classes and a little schoolin' at the orphanage. I don't know anybody else, so what a relief that you're here!"

Alice laughed and pulled Cora Lee along to the schoolhouse. They passed a group of four boys playing marbles in the dirt. The smallest, a white-haired boy, lay on his stomach with a large glass ball perched on his thumb. He squinted in concentration, then shot at the smaller balls in the center of a ring, successfully knocking one out. He grabbed the prize and added it to the pile at his elbow as Alice steered Cora Lee around them at a distance.

"Better stay clear of the boys," she warned sending a glance their way. "That Lucas McDaniel, the black-haired one, is mean enough to bite himself, and that Jacob Bennett thinks he's the biggest toad in the pond 'cause his family owns all this land. And because he wears shoes even when he don't have to. The one in the blue shirt is Robert Dobson. He ain't worth a lick. The little white-haired one is Joshua Oakley. He ain't so bad. His folks live at the far end of the road, and they's moonshiners. But most of the girls are nice.

"You never been to a school? I bet you hated livin' in that old orphanage, didn't ya? Or maybe not.

34

I been to school last year, but not fer very long. My sister, Amanda, be teachin' it again. She done taught Roy Dale to read, and now you can't keep a book out of his hands. You have any sisters? Oh! No, you don't. Wish you did? I bet not…"

The two girls approached a group of girls huddled together near the door of the school house, and Alice introduced them to her friend. Cora Lee bobbed a quick curtsy and, smiling silently, allowed them to continue chattering. Then she noticed another girl standing off to one side.

The girl appeared to be a little older than Cora Lee and Alice. Her carrot-colored hair fell about her face in unruly tangles. The dress she wore seemed to be made out of a flour sack, and her feet were bare and dirty. She studied the girls in the group in a detached fashion.

"Who's that girl?" Cora Lee asked in a whisper. Alice glanced at the outcast and curled her lip.

"Don't go near that one," Alice sneered. "Her mother is an old suggin slattern that lives down in Poke Holler. Decent families don't neighbor with 'em. That girl has a nerve showin' up here."

Cora Lee's protest at her friend's harsh description of the girl was cut short as Amanda Campbell stepped to the schoolhouse door and rang a brass bell.

Amanda, like her younger sister, Alice, was quite beautiful—flaxen-haired and blue eyed. She was tall and thin with small breasts and wide, straight shoulders tailor made for the softer silhouettes coming into fashion. She wore a modest, high-necked white blouse and a dark-grey, A-line skirt that reached the tops of her button-up boots. Her hair was tucked up in a chignon at her neck.

Alice pulled Cora Lee into the school room amid the small crowd of still chattering girls, hung their lunch pails on a peg on the wall, and found a seat together on one of the long split-log benches that filled most of the room. The red-haired girl came in last and, largely ignored, stood awkwardly at the back of the school room.

Cora Lee surveyed her surroundings. The one-room school, built of unpainted pine boards that were beaded in several places with hardened amber sap, still smelled of freshly cut lumber. A pot-bellied stove sat in a back corner, unused at this time of the year. Pegs for hanging coats and lunch pails lined the walls on both sides of the room.

An over-sized oak desk dominated the front of the room, and a small upright piano sat against a corner behind the desk. A large blackboard with chalk scribblings sprawled across it hung on the wall behind the teacher's desk.

The center aisle between rows of split-log benches divided seating for boys on the right and girls on the left. Four open windows, two on each side of the room, allowed in a slight, cooling breeze that carried the scent of newly-mown hay. The smell of the open fields made Cora Lee almost want to get up and flee, but she thought of Granny's reassurance that she would be fine and managed to calm her rising panic.

Amanda, scanning the school yard first to make sure all of the children were in the building, closed the door and walked to the front of the room. She wrote her name on the chalkboard and clapped her hands to quiet the children and get their attention.

"Ruby Douglas, please find a seat," Amanda instructed the odd girl still lingering at the door.

Alice leaned toward Cora Lee and whispered loudly enough for everyone to hear, "*Ruby!* Humph! A fine name fer a bit of trash like her!" Cora Lee shook her head at Alice's rude comment as the red-haired girl moved away from the door.

Ruby took a seat on the back row amid snickers from some of the students. Two girls who were already sitting there quickly moved to another bench as Ruby settled herself on the hard seat. Ignoring sneers and barely suppressed giggles from the other children, she boldly raised her head and steadfastly trained her eyes on Amanda who stood at the head of the room.

Amanda rapped the desk with a long, thin stick and called for quiet in a sharp tone. Once the room had settled, the lessons began with recitations followed by reading aloud and arithmetic. Cora Lee watched as Amanda assessed and sorted the children according to their abilities. She was moved to the second bench from the front and assigned a seat next to Ruby.

"These are to be your assigned seats," Amanda announced as she handed out writing slates and chalk to the students. "Those of you who return next term will be reevaluated and moved according to your progress. If any of you are unhappy with your seat mates," she said giving Ruby a sympathetic smile and turning a stern eye to Cora Lee as she handed them pieces of chalk, "work hard on your lessons to earn a more pleasing placement when you return next term."

Girls broke out in giggles behind them, and Ruby trembled, gripping the bit of chalk in her fist. Cora Lee slid closer to her seat mate. Ruby set her jaw in a hard look as if expecting to hear a rude remark. Instead, Cora Lee touched Ruby's arm and smiled at her.

"I'm glad I'm not the only big girl who has to sit up front with the little ones," she whispered to Ruby. "It's nice to have a friend in the same spot to share learnin' with, don't you think?"

Ruby nodded but said nothing. She managed to keep her seat even though she looked uncomfortable and shifted around on the hard, wooden bench. When Amanda finally released the children at the end of the day, Ruby slipped away into the shadows of the woods.

Cora Lee watched the red-haired girl walk into the woods and, breaking away from Alice, followed.

"Hey," Cora Lee called.

Ruby stopped and turned to face her seat-mate.

"I'm glad we'll still get to sit together tomorrow," Cora Lee said as she caught up to her. "I don't think school is too hard, do you?"

Ruby, expressionless, answered, "I ain't comin' back. I had enough of learnin'."

Cora Lee's face fell. "Oh. That's too bad, then." She brightened a little as she added, "But I bet we'll get to see each other, though. Don't you think? I mean, since we both live around here?"

Ruby nodded. "I reckon so."

The two stood in awkward silence, and then Ruby turned away and walked on.

"See you sometime, then," Cora Lee called after her then turned back to rejoin Alice in the school yard.

The other children had gone, and Alice sat on the steps to the entrance of the building. Cora Lee walked up to her and sat down beside her friend.

"Where'd you run off to?" Alice asked.

"I just went after Ruby to tell her goodbye."

"Why on earth would you? She's just a nothin' girl. Nobody likes her."

"Well, I like her just fine, and there's nobody that's a nothin' in God's eyes."

Alice snorted. "Well, do as you like, then. I'm certainly not goin' to be caught dead bein' a friend to the likes of her."

The door to the school house opened, and Amanda stepped out. She had a short stack of books in the crook of her arm, and as she exited, Cora Lee and Alice stood.

"Cora Lee, you did well today," Amanda said as she came down the steps. "I hope you will continue to attend class. There is so much to learn, and I'm eager to share what I know with you."

Cora Lee smiled, pleased with the compliment. "Thank you, Miss Amanda. I'm real happy to be comin' to school. It wasn't near as hard as I was afraid it was gonna be."

"Well, I may be able to move you to a higher level in a few weeks if you keep up the good work in class."

"Oh, I wouldn't want to move too fast, Miss Amanda. I don't want to miss out on anything I might be learning where I'm at if I move up too soon."

"I'll make sure that doesn't happen, then."

The three of them walked to the road together, then Cora Lee turned left toward her cabin while Amanda and Alice turned right toward theirs.

"We'll see you tomorrow," Alice called.

Cora Lee waved, and skipped down the road, eager to tell her granny about her first day.

"It went really good, Granny. I think I'm gonna like school just fine."

CHAPTER 4

Cora Lee ambled along the river path swinging the wicker basket by its handle and humming a hymn that her grandmother had been singing earlier that morning. The heady scent of pine and damp earth filled the air with summer's perfume. Cora Lee's spirits rose in the warm weather after having spent another long winter and lingering cold spring cooped up in the cabin.

"Fine day to go hunting for shells on the riverbank," she had suggested hopefully to her grandmother. "Probably find plenty, and I could take 'em up to Mr. McDaniel or Mr. Oakley to carry to the button factory when they go to town, or we could trade 'em to Peddler Man when he comes again."

Mae had paused, thoughtfully wiping a plate with her drying rag, then agreed. "I reckon yer growed enough to go alone." She looked at her granddaughter as if she hadn't seen Cora Lee in a while or realized how much she had grown over the winter. Hard to believe that a year and a half had gone by since the girl had come to live on the ridge; harder to believe there ever was a time when Cora Lee wasn't with her.

"Take care near the water, and don't go fallin' in. The river's gonna be swollen with snow melt and rain."

"Granny Mae, I'm eleven years old now—goin' on twelve! I reckon I'm smart enough not to go and get myself drowned," Cora Lee laughed and kissed the old woman on the cheek.

Grabbing the wicker basket from the peg on the wall outside the door, Cora Lee jumped off of the porch and skipped down the ridge road. The path that cut between her granny's farm and the Campbell place led down to a tributary of the Big River in the valley below. Bucket Run Creek, as the locals called it, was more river than creek and frequently flooded and overran its banks in the wet season.

The water ran easterly along the north side of the highlands through Fellowship Gorge to where it joined the river and turned back south flowing past the lumber mill and mill pond before cutting westward again through Endurance. Bucket Run Creek provided a treasure trove of fish, shells, pelts, yarbs and plants, and it collected run-off from snowmelt and spring-fed streams on Bennett's Ridge.

Cora Lee walked along the narrow path that wound through the pines and led to the creekbank below. The air was scented by the evergreens that towered overhead and by the damp, mossy earth beneath her feet. She loved this walk. There was always a new discovery to be made—a new fern sprung up among the ankles of an oak, a stone tumbled from the ridge above, the fresh print of a deer in the soil, an unopened pine cone.

She shivered in the shade of the woods, eager for the warmth of sunlight and hurried down the path to the creek. She could hear the lap of the water on the bank and caught sight of a large, white crane as it spread its wings and flew away into the cloudless, blue sky.

"Peddler Man better have lots of new gingham and ribbons for Granny and me," she sang aloud to the tune she'd been humming. "And he better come soon, too!"

The sound of the water grew louder. Cora Lee quickened her step in anticipation, but a boy's laughter up ahead brought her up short to listen. Curious but a little apprehensive, she walked a bit farther down the path, rounded a slight corner, and stopped short. Surprised to see three boys standing in the woods about a stone's throw from the river path, Cora Lee stood frozen for a moment, confused by the scene before her.

It was Lucas McDaniel, Robert Dobson, and Jacob Bennett, her schoolyard tormentors.

All during the school term they had taken great delight in tormenting the girls. The three of them had chased the girls with snakes and toads, hid rocks in their lunch biscuits, and pulled the girls' hair.

Lucas had also made sport of trying to pull up the girls' skirts to get a look at their undergarments, an event that finally led Cora Lee to report his conduct to her teacher. After Amanda suspended Lucas, the boys labeled Cora Lee a "snitch." She became an even bigger target for their hateful derision and was tormented unmercifully anytime they could catch her alone, mocking her for being an orphan.

"Yer nothin' but a stray dog," Jacob had taunted.

"She ain't exactly a stray. Her granny had to take her in and feed her. Does she make ya sleep under the porch, dog?" Lucas had jeered. "You got fleas?"

The rest of the school term would have gone as well as the first day if those boys had only left her alone.

When the scene in the woods in front of her became clear and she realized what they were doing, shock and disgust stunned her. The boys stood in a circle facing each other, and their pants and skivvies pulled down around their ankles left their bottoms bare. Shock gave way to fear that the boys might see her.

Cora Lee turned to run back up the path when one of the boys shouted, "Hey, fellas! We're caught! Get after her quick!"

Fear exploded into terror as Cora Lee ran. She dropped her basket and veered off the path diving into the safety of the woods. The boys could run much faster and, even though she had the advantage of a slight head-start while the boys scrambled to pull up their pants, Cora Lee knew she had no chance of getting away from them on the river path. She hoped their larger sizes would slow them down in the undergrowth. She desperately began to search for shelter among the low branches and brambles that tore at her bare legs and feet as she ran.

"Split up, boys," shouted one. Cora Lee recognized Lucas McDaniel's rough voice. "Don't let the little snitch get away!"

Terror flooded Cora Lee anew. She ducked and dove through the thick woods. She ran downhill into Polk Holler and stopped to catch her breath. She turned about trying to find her bearings, fearful she might lose her way in the dense forest around her.

I have to make it up the hill to the ridge road and the safety of my cabin, she thought.

"There she is! Over this way," Lucas screamed.

Cora Lee let out a shriek. She spun around frantically hoping to find a place to hide. Sliding down a small slope into a shallow ravine with a trickling rill below, she waded to the other side and fell to her knees in the mud. She crawled to a large fallen tree limb on the bank and rolled into a small depression underneath. Covering her face with shuddering hands, her body shaking, she gasped for air.

"Please, God, don't let them find me," she whispered a prayer and lay as motionless as she could, barely daring to breathe and willing her thundering heart to beat more quietly. She listened intently for sounds of the boys, and then she froze as she heard the boys sliding down the ravine near her hiding place.

"She ran down here," said Lucas. "She can't 'a got far. Find her, and we'll make sure she don't go rattin' us out fer what she seen."

"Here she is! She's crawled up under this here log. Let's drag her out!" yelled Jacob Bennett, his face, twisted into an ugly mask, suddenly appeared inches from Cora Lee. She struggled to back farther into the hole where she desperately sought safety.

Jacob's hands tore at her and grabbed the hem of her skirt. Yanking on her dress, Jacob began to laugh. "Come on out, ya little dog," he sneered.

"Drag her out! Get her outta there!" Lucas ran up to where Cora Lee now struggled wildly in Jacob's grip. Lucas, quickly followed by the third boy, Robert Dobson, grabbed the girl by the front of her blouse, ripping her collar and jerking her to him. She clawed at his face and beat him with her fists, but she was no match for the older boy. "Grab her arms," he ordered the other two boys, "and hold her still."

Cora Lee, nearly mad with the horror of her situation was unable to move with her arms pinned behind her. Her knees began to buckle. She opened her mouth to scream, but the hold that Lucas now had on her neck strangled the sound. The world began to spin away, and her vision blurred as he squeezed and finally released her.

Falling to her knees at his feet, Cora Lee looked up into Lucas' face and gasped for air. The four of them stood frozen in place like some macabre tableau. Lucas bent and extended a hand to Cora Lee, grinning wickedly. Cora Lee stared at him as her vision slowly began to clear and the wave of dizziness that engulfed her faded away.

"Here now!" a woman's brassy voice rang through the holler. "Jacob Bennett, what are you boys up to? What kind of devilment is goin' on here?"

Jacob and Lucas spun to face the woman. Robert turned and ran away.

"I see you, too, Robert Dobson! Don't think I don't!" The woman yelled at the youngest boy's retreating back.

Cora Lee crawled away from the two boys who still stood over her and struggled to rise from her knees. Lucas and Jacob turned and quickly followed Robert into the gloom of the woods. Cora Lee locked eyes with her rescuer, a woman she had never seen before.

A woman stood at the top of the shallow ravine Cora Lee had escaped down. A brace of cotton-tailed rabbits hung from the woman's waist, and she carried a shotgun broken open over her arm. Her faded red hair, streaked with gray, hung in a loose, untidy braid over her shoulder. One corner of her skirt, pulled up and tucked into her belt, revealed hob-nailed boots covered in a thick layer of mud, grass, and weeds.

"Come on up outta there," the woman said as Cora Lee weakly climbed up the incline. "What kind of games was ya playin' with them boys out here in the woods, heh?" Peering closely into Cora Lee's pale face she continued, "Yer Mae Clarey's little granddaughter, ain't ya? You ought to know better than to be messin' around out here like 'at. Shouldn't have been down here in the first place."

Cora Lee, still an innocent, was too traumatized to understand the meaning of the woman's scolding words. Struggling for breath, she simply nodded and hung her head in shame and confusion as she coughed and fought to regain her composure.

"Come along, then. I'll walk ya home, and I won't say nothin' to yer granny about these goin's on out here. Just don't be lettin' it happen again, ya hear?"

Cora Lee, relieved to have an escort, nodded mutely. Remembering that she had lost her grandmother's basket, she gasped, "My basket! I dropped in on the river path!"

"Don't worry none 'bout that basket. I'll pick it up and bring it by. I need to stop in and say hello to yer granny, anyway."

The woman deposited the girl at Mae's gate and turned to walk to the river path to retrieve the basket. "I'll be back by in a bit. Let yer granny know I'm comin' to see her. Best tell her you fell. That won't be a complete lie, just not the whole truth. No need to hurt the woman who's taken you in to raise by lettin' her hear about the shenanigans I came across down in that swag just now."

Luckily, Mae was out of the cabin. Cora Lee hurriedly began to clean up and change her shirt before having to explain her disheveled state. She put her torn blouse into her mending pile and had re-plaited her braids when Mae came back inside carrying a handful of potatoes from the root cellar.

"How did the shell huntin' go, honey? Did you find very many?" Mae said as she looked Cora Lee over. "Managed to get yerself muddy and scratched up enough fer havin' found a wagon load!"

Cora Lee simply shook her head and mumbled, "I met a woman who said she wants to come by in a bit."

"Well, I had a sign of a visitor this morning. Dropped my dishrag on the floor, and my left eyebrow's been itchin' me. Here, peel these tatties, and I'll put the coffee pot on."

Cora Lee, glad to have something to occupy her trembling hands, took the potatoes out onto the porch to peel them. Her mind was reeling as she replayed the trauma she had just experienced. *How could those boys have been so horrible? Did Lucas really try to kill me, or was he just bein' awful as usual?*

She shook her head to clear it and bent to concentrate on peeling the potatoes in her lap. She had just finished the task, taken the peelings out to the chicken yard and returned to the porch when the woman from the woods walked up to the cabin with the rescued basket.

"Thank you, ma'am," Cora Lee said taking the basket and hanging it back on its peg outside the cabin door. "Granny's making coffee. You can go on in."

The woman leaned her shotgun against the wall, wiped her boots on the rough wood of the porch, rapped on the door, and stepped inside. Cora Lee followed with the bowl of peeled potatoes.

"Howdy, Miz Clarey."

"Well, hello, Pearl Douglas! It's been a good month of Sundays since we've seen you. How are you and them two kids of yers?"

Mae carried two mugs of steaming coffee to the table and offered a chair to the other woman. Cora Lee set the potatoes on the table and retreated to the bed in the corner. She drew her torn blouse from the mending pile, took a needle and thread from her sewing basket, and began to repair the garment while the two older women visited with each other.

"We're fair to middlin', I reckon," Pearl answered shaking her head at the chair. "Can't stay. I wanted to stop in and thank you fer the peach preserves ya sent with Walter awhile back. Folks all say you grow the sweetest peaches around, and we sure enjoyed 'em."

"I'm only glad the Good Lord gifted our trees with such wonderful crops the last couple of years, and that by His grace I'm still well and hearty enough to can 'em. Sure ya won't sit a spell?" May offered the chair again, but Pearl again declined.

"I brung these here rabbits to thank you. I'm pretty sure they's edible. It's still early enough in the spring fer the meat to be good."

"Well, I'm sure they're fine. Thank you kindly."

Pearl took a small knife from her pocket and cut the brace of rabbits from the rope around her waist. Laying the game on the table, she continued, "I best be headin' back. My Ruby's been feelin' a bit off today. She flowered her dress fer the first time and has the misery with it. I left her with some horehound tea."

Mae clicked her tongue in sympathy. "Women are born to suffer," she said thoughtfully. "I reckon Cora Lee'll be comin' into womanhood pretty soon, too. Here, take Ruby some of this red yarn to tie around her waist," Mae said rummaging for the scrap of yarn in her sewing basket. "It'll help with her misery, too."

Mae pulled a chair from the table and sat down. Pulling the yarn from her sewing basket, she looked up at her visitor and continued as she wound the string into a small ball, "And how's Walter? Cora Lee tells me he didn't go to school with the other boys."

"Couldn't make him go," Pearl answered, taking the yarn with a nod of thanks. "Says he ain't got no use fer readin', and he says he can already cipher a little, and he ain't gonna be cooped up in a stuffy school room on a warm summer day. He's been helpin' build that new place fer the Bennett boy and Amanda Campbell fer after they's married."

"Should be getting close to that day, I hear," Mae said. A spasm of coughing overtook her, and she held her apron to her mouth fighting to breathe. "Sorry," she managed to croak once the coughing fit had passed. "The ragweed and cedar must be bad. It has really got to me this year more than most. Sure ya can't stay fer a cup of coffee?"

"No, thanks, again, Miz Clarey. I best be headin' back." Pearl walked to the door, then turned, "I'll mix a little sumac and sorghum into that horehound tea I made fer Ruby and send Walter over this evenin' with it. It'll help with that cough—whatever's causin' it."

CHAPTER 5

Walter arrived later that evening with the promised tincture. Stepping up on the porch, he pushed the hair out of his face and knocked on the door.

"Ma sent this fer yer granny's cough," Walter said handing the bottle to Cora Lee. "She said she thinks it'll help some."

Cora Lee took the medicine from his hands. "Thanks kindly. Granny says I'm to invite you to come in, so, do you want to come in?"

Walter nodded and stepped across the threshold. "I reckon I should pay respects to Miz Clarey."

Cora Lee stepped back and let her visitor into the room. "I've seen you a couple of times down near the river, haven't I?" she asked. "We met on the road when Granny and I walked over to the Campbell's place awhile back, but you're taller now than you were back then. You're Ruby's brother?"

"Yup. Ruby's big brother, and we seen you down by the river, too."

"Come on in, Walter, and eat some supper with us," Mae called. "Sure appreciate you bringin' that tonic from yer ma."

"Well, I'd be tickled to share supper with you, Miz Clarey. Thank you! Food's about my favorite thing!"

Mae laughed. "Well, boy, I'm happy to be able to share it, then!"

Cora Lee and Walter sat down while Mae dished beans and ham onto plates for the two young people. Placing a round of cornbread and some fried potatoes on the table with a pitcher of fresh water, Mae sat down but did not serve herself. She leaned back in her chair and watched as the two younguns tucked into the food she had prepared.

"I hear ya been helpin' Silas Bennett build his new place, Walter. How's that goin?' Will it be done so him and Amanda can get married this summer? We all thought those two would be married last year. Long engagements is unlucky, ya know."

Mae lapsed into a small coughing fit. Wiping her eyes with the corner of her apron, she drew a shaky breath and laughed. "I guess you bringin' that medicine just in time! This old cough has been bad this year."

"Pleased to do it, Ma'am," Walter answered as he reached to tear off a chunk of the cornbread and continued, "Hope Ma's elixir will do some good fer it."

"Granny Mae, aren't you eatin' tonight?" Cora Lee asked. "You didn't have breakfast and didn't even eat so much as a boiled egg and coffee for lunch."

"No, honey. I'm fine. I'll fix me a little buttermilk and cornbread later. Go on, Walter. You was about to say about that new house yer workin' on."

"Well, yes'm. Me and Amanda's brother, Roy Dale, is helpin' Silas build it. It's gonna be fine. It's got a big, wide porch with a screen door, and the kitchen is a whole separate room with a pump right inside at the sink! I guess Miss Amanda is too fine in Silas' eyes to be luggin' water in from a wellhouse or the creek."

Walter laughed, and his voice broke with a squeak. Turning red, he cleared his throat and continued. "One of these days I plan to find a gal that's 'too fine' fer me, too. But first, I wanna travel and see the world."

"Well," Mae said, "they's an awful lot of world to see. Don't know if they's a lot of world worth seein', though. I been lots of places. The best place I ever been is this place right up here on our ridge."

"All I ever seen is St. Louis, but I don't remember much about the city. I reckon I like it here best, too," Cora Lee agreed.

"Sure," Walter answered. "This place is fine, and Ma and Ruby are here. I only said I wanna see more of what's to see. I didn't say I didn't like it here. I especially love the river and fishin'. Cora Lee, you ever go fishin'?"

"Sure I have! We used to go when I lived at the orphanage 'cause we had a big pond there, and Granny has taken me lots, too."

"You wanna go with me and Ruby sometime?"

Walter surprised himself by making this impulsive invitation. Fishing was an activity he enjoyed on his own or, on occasion, with his sister. He didn't stop to think if he'd enjoy his solitary sport being intruded upon. He didn't know if Ruby would enjoy fishing with this kid, either. He immediately began to regret asking her to come along with them.

Cora Lee hesitated a moment, still shaken from her experience in the woods earlier. Then remembering how her schoolmates had shunned Ruby the one time the ostracized girl had shown up at school last summer, she took a breath and said, "Yes. I'd like that very much—" but added a little fearfully, "—if you can come by and fetch me, that is."

Walter, surprised at her request, stopped chewing for a moment, swallowed and consented to the detour. He could hardly refuse the request, as inconvenient as it might be, since he was sitting at her granny's table and eating her granny's food.

"Sure," he said a little reluctantly. "I'll come 'round in a few days when I can take a break from

Silas. It'll be dark of the moon, so that's the best time fer fishin'."

True to his word, Walter came by the cabin as the week ended to take Cora Lee to the river. He carried a bucket in one hand, and his other held two cane poles balanced over his shoulder. His black hair, lightened some by the summer sun, stuck to his forehead with sweat, and his shirt clung to a wet patch on his back.

"We're getting' a late start. Ruby's already down on the sandbar. Might have caught all there is to ketch 'fore we get there," Walter said grumpily. He regretted his promise to come and fetch his timid little neighbor, but he was duty-bound to honor his word.

"Oh, I reckon the river still has plenty of fish to be caught, Walter. I sure appreciate you coming to fetch me, though, even if it did delay you some," Cora Lee said as she tied on her bonnet.

Following the boy through her gate and down the road, she skipped a little with high spirits and eagerness to spend time on the river. Her moody companion walked alongside her in silence. When they reached the river path and turned off the road onto the tree-shaded lane, the air turned cooler. Walter relaxed a little, and he began to whistle a tune that Cora Lee recognized.

"I like that song," she said. "You can whistle it real fine, too." She began to sing some of the words as he continued his accompaniment.

Walter stopped his tune and sheepishly apologized for his bad mood. "I guess I'm always in a hurry to be where I wanna be. It ain't nothin' about you askin' for me to come fetch ya."

Cora Lee nodded. "I guess I just haven't ever been in any hurry to be anywhere," she said. "I always seem to be happy right where I'm at. Like being here on this little walk with you is just as fine as being on the river with a worm in the water to me."

She caught his arm and turned him to face her. Smiling at him, she said sweetly, "Thanks, Walter, for letting me come with you. And thanks for stopping by to fetch me. It was awful nice of you."

Walter, embarrassed by his earlier resentment toward the girl, only nodded and said "Sure. It ain't nothin'. Say, you sure talk different from the rest of us. Kind'a fancy. How come?"

"Oh, I didn't realize that. I expect it's because I was raised at the orphanage. The nuns there didn't let us use slang words or bad words. They'd wash out our mouths with soap if we didn't talk like they said we should."

"Glad I ain't never been to a orphanage, then. I reckon yer glad you ain't there no more, too. How long did ya have to be there?"

"Almost five years, and, yes, I'm glad not to be there anymore. I'm glad to have Granny as my family. And, Walter," Cora Lee quickly hugged him, "I'm awful glad to have you as my friend, too."

Walter nodded and walked on quickly causing Cora Lee to scramble to keep up with the long-legged boy. When they rounded the corner and reached the spot where Cora Lee had seen the three boys with their pants down, she hesitated, then ran to catch up with Walter. She passed him at a run and didn't slow down until she reached the shoreline at the end of the path.

Ruby stood about ankle-deep in the water at the edge of a sandbar about twenty feet from the shore. Her back to the beach, she didn't turn when Cora Lee came running out of the woods with Walter following a short distance behind. The hem of Ruby's skirt, pulled between her legs and tucked into her skirt's front waistband, left her legs bare, and her red hair was braided and wrapped around her head in a coronet.

Cora Lee was taken aback by the change in the girl from the slovenly child she had met at school a year earlier. Ruby had grown taller, and her body had filled out into that of a young woman. Seeing her so beautifully silhouetted against the shining ripples of the silvery water, her movements graceful as she swung her fishing line into the river, made Cora Lee feel awkwardly out of place and even younger than her eleven years.

Walter let out a shrill whistle to grab his sister's attention. "Ruby!" he yelled. "Ketch anythin' yet?"

Ruby turned, a grin lighting up her face as she yelled back, "Got about all of 'em. Sorry you wasted yer time comin' down here fer nothin'. Might be a few minnows left fer ya, though."

Walter laughed, baited his hook with a worm from his bucket, and waded out to the sandbar. Cora Lee reached into the dirt in the bucket, pulled out a worm, and baited the hook of the second pole. She stood apart on the grassy bank and swung her hook into the reeds at the shoreline.

"She afraid she's gonna ketch cooties if she comes too close or somethin'?"

Walter turned and glanced at the younger girl. "Nah. She's a little shy and quiet is all. Probably don't wanna intrude on our spot."

Walter lay down his pole, waded back to the beach, and walked over to Cora Lee. "You ain't gonna ketch much over here. Why not come on out to the sandbar with us? Lots of blue catfish swimmin' around, and lucky-bugs is sittin' on Ruby's cork."

Cora Lee, happy to be invited closer, tucked up her skirt and joined Ruby and Walter on the sandbar where she found better luck. Almost immediately, the cork bobber on her line was jerked beneath the water. Cora Lee gasped and yanked hard on the pole to set the hook. Walter dropped his pole and reached for Cora Lee's. Together, they managed to land a large walleye up onto the shore of the sandbar.

"That's a good one!" Walter congratulated her. "That'll make fine eatin'."

"Not bad," Ruby added.

Cora Lee grinned proudly as Walter removed her hook from the fish's mouth and picked up a leafless branch lying nearby. He threaded one of the offshoots of the branch through the walleye's mouth and out its gills and then placed the fish back in the water at the shoreline. The fish flapped briefly, splashing water into the air in a spray of crystal droplets as Walter skillfully embedded the stump of the stick into the dirt and secured it with rocks. The fish held fast.

By the end of the afternoon the three of them not only caught plenty of fish for supper, but they also discovered they enjoyed each other's company.

When the sun began to set, Walter gathered up the poles and his and Ruby's makeshift stringer of fish. "Bring that bucket, Ruby," he said and then headed into the woods toward Poke Holler for home.

Cora Lee wanted to call after him to request an escort back to her cabin but thought better of it. After all, she thought, he had gone out of his way to bring her down here. She didn't want to impose on him further. However, Ruby noticed her distress.

"What's the matter? Afraid to walk home all by yerself or somethin'?"

Cora Lee, embarrassed, blushed and stammered, "Just—well, I—there might be—um—."

"Oh, I'll walk you back—part way at least. Grab yer stringer. You can carry that by yerself, can't ya? Besides, Ma told me about you foolin' around with them boys in the woods. Afraid of seein' 'em again and not bein' able to control yerself?"

Cora Lee's mouth dropped opened in astonishment at the way Ruby characterized the attack.

"I never was 'fooling around' with those awful boys!" she shrieked. "What a terrible thing to say! Why, those boys chased and attacked me. If your ma hadn't come along when she did—why, I don't know if they'd have let me go at all. I'd probably be just a haint in these here woods by now—my body moldering away under some pile of leaves down in your holler!"

Ruby, caught by surprise by the heat of Cora Lee's response, blinked a few times and broke out in a gale of laughter. "Them boys is well known around here to be troublemakers and wanna-be toughs," she said when she caught her breath. "I believe, fer sure, they probably attacked ya. Well, Ma was sure wrong about that little episode, weren't she?"

Cora Lee stamped her foot at her companion's response. "It was horrible," she sputtered. "I didn't think I was gonna live, and I sure don't wanna meet up with them boys again!"

"Oh, you know how to handle bullies, don't ya?" Ruby asked. She bent to pick up the bait bucket and took Cora Lee by the elbow. Starting to walk away from the riverbank toward the path to home, she continued, "Meet up with them fellers again, ya just square yer shoulders, look 'em right in the eye, and then spit. Spit on the ground right in front of 'em."

"Spit?! But they'll attack me again!"

"Yup. They probably will, but at least they won't think yer afraid of 'em. They'll keep on a'whompin' on you 'til they get tired of it or figure out it won't make ya back down.

"Either way," she continued, "it won't last ferever, and you'll get along better if you ain't scared all the time. Once ya see ya can take a punch or two and live, you'll find out it ain't so bad to be beat on."

"That's crazy! I don't wanna be beat on!"

"Have it yer way," Ruby laughed. "But Walter and me ain't gonna be yer personal protection service fer the rest of yer life, so you better figure somethin' out."

Cora Lee thought about Ruby's advice as they walked up the river path together. "Well, aren't you afraid of those boys at all?"

Ruby stopped and turned to her companion. "Them boys ever try anythin' with me, I'll knock their hats off with their heads still in 'em. 'Sides, if they ever mess with me—or you again, most likely— Walter'll set 'em straight, and that's fer certain."

Cora Lee shivered at the thought of ever having to see any of her tormentors again. "I wish I could be brave like you," she said.

A bitter expression twisted Ruby's face. "You don't ever wanna be anythin' like me."

She turned off the river path and disappeared into the woods toward the holler leaving Cora Lee to walk the rest of the way home alone.

CHAPTER 6

L ush forest greens and fields baked brown by the stifling summer heat at last gave way to cooler temperatures and autumn's palette of reds and golds. Over-large pumpkins and gourds strained against their vines eager to be harvested, and ripe apples in Otis McDaniel's orchard began dropping like juicy bombs on the ground. A slight breeze cleared away a low-lying fog and brought the promise of clear weather for Amanda's and Silas' much-anticipated, long-delayed wedding.

Mae's peach trees once again provided an abundant yield so that she and Cora Lee were able to trade bushels of fruit to Peddler Man Dan for new winter coats and shoes. Cora Lee bartered for a mid-calf length navy blue serge coat with matching piped trim and a pair of tan lace-up boots. Both the coat and boots were a little too big for her, but at the age of eleven and a half, she still had "plenty of growin' to do," as her grandmother said.

Mae traded for a more serviceable heavily-padded black cotton coat and a pair of black, thick-soled work boots. The coats and shoes were "used," but they were newer styles and still in serviceable condition.

"Miz Clarey, you always get the best of me in a trade," Peddler Man Dan complained. But all three parties in the exchange secretly believed they got the better of the other so were satisfied with the outcome. "And I ain't forgot you, gal." Dan reached into the pocket of his vest, produced a stick of peppermint candy, and handed it to Cora Lee. "So, don't be fergettin' ol' Dan, either."

"Thank you," she giggled as she accepted the treat. "You'd be kind of hard to forget, I think."

Dan's wagon pulled away, and Mae returned to the cabin with Cora Lee in tow.

"Thank you, Granny! I love my new things! I'm so happy you decided to replace that old blanket you called a coat, too. You needed a new one a lot worse than I did."

"Oh, I feel a bit foolish fer wastin' good trade on somethin' so fancified. But I did need the new boots."

"Now we'll both have somethin' fine to wear to the wedding," Cora Lee said.

"Well, I reckon I won't be goin'. Not feelin' up to it. It's about time they's married, though. And it looks like it'll be a fair day fer it. 'Happy the bride the sun shines on,' as the old sayin' goes. Full moon, too, and that's best fer a happy life."

"Coraaaa Leeee!"

Alice stood by the gate waiting to be acknowledged, then shouted again, "Coraaaa Leeee!"

Cora Lee hurried out onto the porch. A smile brightened her face as she greeted her friend.

"Come on up to the house. Granny will be so pleased to see you. She's been feelin' kind of poorly the last day or so, and company might be just what she needs to perk her up some."

Alice skipped up to the cabin as Cora Lee turned and called to her grandmother. "Look who's stopped in to say hello, Granny."

"Well," said Alice as she came through the door, "I've only come by to steal Cora Lee away to help us get ready. We, that is Amanda and Ma and me, is hopin' you might can spare her 'til after the weddin' tomorrow to help out. I've about wore myself smooth out with cleanin' and such.

"Ma and Amanda have been stitchin' a new dress fer the weddin'—it's blue, of course. 'Marry in blue, your man'll be true'—and there's still flowers to put together and all kinds of cookin' left to do. Amanda can't help with the cookin' her own bride's day feast 'cause that's bad luck. Ma won't even let her come in the kitchen in case she touches a pan or picks up a spoon, so's it's all up to me—and Ma."

Alice paused to take a breath, and Mae laughed.

"Oh, land, child," Mae wheezed. "Of course, Cora Lee can go. Do her some good to get out fer a bit. I suspect you girls will have some games to play of yer own, too, won't ya?"

Alice giggled. "Well, we might try to put on a dumb supper at midnight. They say if you do it right, it might tell you who you's gonna marry. It's just kinda eerie and spooky, is all. You ever heard of that? Where you only walk backwards and set the table at midnight and no talkin' or laughin' and wait fer the face of your intended to appear in the plate? Oh—I can show her what to do and all. Thank you, Miz Clarey! Cora Lee, you gather up what you need and come home with me."

Cora Lee turned to her grandmother. "Granny, you sure you'll make do without me here?"

"Oh, honey. I'll be as fine as snake feathers. Go on. Just be home 'fore dark tomorrow."

"Alice," Cora Lee said turning back to her friend. "You go on ahead, and I'll come along in a bit. I have a few more little things need doin' 'fore I can come."

Alice left after encouraging Cora Lee "not to linger" and still talking a steady stream as she walked through the gate to the road and away.

Mae shook her head and commented, "That gal makes more racket than a bawlin' redbone hound chasin' a three-legged coon."

A short time later, Cora Lee with her overnight bundle rolled up under her arm headed out the door and down the lane on her way to the Campbell farm.

The afternoon remained clear and sunny, the air crisp and sweet. The canopy of oak branches arching above her head dropped bright yellow leaves like golden rain all around her.

She stopped, awed by her surroundings. Tilting her head back, she lifted her face to the sunlight filtering through the branches above her head. She whispered a little prayer of thanksgiving to God for the gift of autumn beauty and for being able to be part of it all.

With a slight smile, she dropped her gaze, and her breath escaped her lungs in shock. A bolt of fear shot through her gut.

Lucas stood in the road about twenty feet from Cora Lee. She locked eyes with him, and a vicious grin slowly spread over his face. He smacked his fist into the palm of his hand with a loud "thwack" that shot through Cora Lee as if he had punched her.

"Well, I got you at last, didn't I ya little snitch. Thought you could hide from me ferever, didn't ya?"

Cora Lee said nothing. Trying not to panic, she looked around and tensed her body ready to flee, but she knew in the same heartbeat that escape was impossible. He was too close. He was too fast. And the expression on his face showed that he was determined to get his hands on her.

With a laugh, Lucas moved toward her. "Run if ya think you can get away. Ain't nobody around to save you this time," he taunted. His handsome face was twisted in an ugly, evil sneer as he came closer.

Cora Lee remembered that Ruby told her to "look 'em in the eye and spit." She managed to square her shoulders and look Lucas in his cold, blue eyes, but her mouth was dry. Her throat felt like she had swallowed a big wad of corn silk.

Lucas closed the gap between them and grabbed Cora Lee by her arms making her drop her bundle. "Don't even think of tryin' to run away," he growled and shook her. "I'm gonna teach you not to spy on folks and go blabbin' what ya seen."

Cora Lee froze, her mind locked in horror. Then an unexpected rush of anger and indignation suddenly flooded her and blotted out the fear and desperation that swamped her. She jerked her arms out of Lucas' grasp and stepped back, her face a mask of fury as she jutted her chin at him.

"Listen, you dumb whiffle-bird!" she yelled. "Your brain's got the dry wilts if you think I'm gonna tat tales about what you boys were doin'. I don't care anything about it. I'm not gonna tell anybody, and if I *was* gonna tell, I'd already have done it. And if you booger-headed suggins don't stop botherin' me about it, I *will* tell. I'll tell every single person on this ridge. So, you better decide you're gonna let me be in peace!"

Lucas blinked, and his mouth dropped open. Without another word, Cora Lee picked up her bundle and dusted it off before giving him a final rebellious glare. Rolling her eyes and expelling a loud

"Humph," she stomped around him and continued on her way without a backward look.

Lucas scowled at Cora Lee's retreating back, furious at having been spoken to like he was a nothin'—a nobody. He bent and picked up a good-sized rock. Taking aim, he cocked his arm, but something made him hesitate. His arm, oddly frozen, refused to move as the girl marched out of range. Shrugging off the temporary paralysis, he chucked the rock at a witch hazel tree, gouging a wound in its bark, and disappeared back into the woods.

***

The flurry of pre-wedding activity at the Campbell farm left little opportunity for Cora Lee to reflect on her encounter with Lucas, but she experienced an odd sense of having something heavy roll off of her, something that had had a grip on her for too long. She put the incident out of her mind and was able to enjoy the rest of the day.

Luther and Roy Dale cleared the front room of some of the furniture to make room for family and guests who were expected for the ceremony the next day. Ada put Alice and Cora Lee to work sweeping the floors and knocking down cobwebs while she and Amanda finished some last-minute stitching on the wedding dress.

At last, all preparations were completed, supper was over and dishes were done. Luther came in with an armload of firewood. Ada spread a thick cushion of blankets and quilts on the floor in the front room to make a pallet for Alice and Cora Lee.

"Amanda needs her bedroom to herself on her bride eve," Ada said as she dropped two pillows onto the blankets. "You two girls'll be fine out here."

Luther built up the fire in the fireplace, and Roy Dale settled down on the bed in the corner near an oil lamp with a book of Shakespear's sonnets from the family's sparse library. The two young girls wrapped up together in a quilt and giggled with excitement over the novelty of the sleeping arrangements and anticipation of the coming wedding festivities.

"Time to settle down, both of you," Ada said. "Lie down and go to sleep." She picked up Phineas and disappeared with the toddler into her bedroom.

"Here, now," Luther turned from the fireplace and dusted off his hands. "Settle down, and I'll tell you girls a bedtime story."

"A ghost story, Pa!" Alice and Cora Lee flopped over on their stomachs. "Make it a ghost story!"

"Well, now, I can't say if it's a ghost story or a true tale, but many know the tale of a lady who appears from the mists that hug the shores near Conner Falls when the moon is full. It's a story that's told often, so you may have already heard it?"

The girls shivered in anticipation as Luther sat down on a stool by the fire. Leaning his elbows on his knees, he fluffed his enormous beard and squinted his eyes at them. "Her voice, so I'm told as I've never seen or heard her myself, echoes like the hoot of a screech owl through the shadows cast by the trees in the light of the midnight moon.

"Some say the story is only a myth—just a yarn spun to frighten children and fill the empty hours between supper and bed. Others say they've heard the lady sing, or they claim to have seen her walkin' among the reeds at the water's edge. Nobody knows fer certain where she comes from or where she goes to, but whatever she's searchin' fer, she never finds."

"Oooh, Pa! Who is she?" The girls lifted wide eyes to Luther and edged closer together under their quilt.

Luther leaned against the wall, took a clay pipe and a pouch of tobacco from his shirt pocket and filled the bowl. Taking a burning stick from the fire, he lit the pipe and blew a cloud of smoke into the air. The fire threw eerie shadows over his face, and he continued his tale in a low voice.

"In early days 'fore Old Ezra Conner built his cabin up near the falls, a young couple reached the river's edge with their oxen and cart and their few worldly goods. They determined to homestead a claim there. After a few seasons, the husband ventured away and left his bride to manage alone while he went in search of somethin' better. I've heard tell he was after gold that was supposed to be hidden by thieves up in some of them caves up there, but I don't know if that part's true or not.

"Anyway, he left fer whatever reason. When the man didn't never return, the young wife struggled on through the hard, frozen winter months. She had almost no food and was nearly starved as all she had to eat was some old dry beans, the snow, and tree bark.

"With the spring, came the rain and a tremendous flood. The water carried away the woman and ended her long, lonely sufferin'. Perhaps the lady who comes out of the mists of the falls is that bride, searching fer her husband. Nobody knows fer sure, but they do say the lady's been seen and heard a'singin' a sad tune."

"That's so sad!" Cora Lee yawned. "Whyever would a bride put up with such bad treatment as that? It doesn't make any sense."

"Oh, a girl'll do 'most anythin' fer the man she loves," Alice said dreamily. "I 'spect she must have loved him somethin' awful, and he would have come back to her any day."

Cora Lee and Alice rolled to their sides and curled up facing each other. Alice toyed with Cora Lee's hair and yawned. "A great love story, but not too scary a'one, Pa."

"Well, a too scary tale might've kept you girls awake. Now, mind yer ma and close yer eyes. No more chatterin' out of you two."

The girls complied and were soon asleep.

The next morning dawned bright and cloudless as Mae had predicted. Cora Lee and Alice helped Ada set out sandwiches and cakes for the reception party. Alice picked up Phineas, and the two girls took him out on the porch to play to keep him from under foot.

Roy Dale swept the yard clear of autumn leaves and fed the goat, pigs and chickens. Luther carried in a fresh bucket of water from the well and lit a fresh fire. By the time the groom and the rest of the Bennett family arrived, all was in order.

The bride, dressed in her blue wedding frock, waited in her bedroom to make her entrance. The narrow, ankle length bottom skirt was embroidered around the hem with a few scattered sprays of white roses. The blue overskirt, trimmed in a matching row of decorative roses, was slightly flounced and floated softly to her knees. The overdress was a long, white voile blouse that fell softly to her hips and was banded at her waist by a wide, blue-satin ribbon.

Her blonde hair fell in loose curls to her waist and was tied back with a thin, dark-blue satin ribbon. The bouquet of rose verbena and blue coneflowers she clutched nervously in her hands was tied with a ribbon that matched the one in her hair and at her waist.

"Ain't no reason to be nervous, honey," Ada assured her quaking daughter as she pinned a broach to Amanda's collar. "Just trust in the Good Lord that things is gonna go as things is intended to go, and enjoy yer bride day. Silas is a decent man. You don't worry none about what's gonna happen after."

Amanda nodded, smiled, and allowed her mother to lead her out of the bedroom to meet her groom. Silas stood calmly in polished work boots and a clean, white shirt under new overalls. His hair was slicked down with pomade, his beard trimmed, and his face and hands were scrubbed clean.

Amanda smiled at him. The couple joined hands in front of family and a few of their neighbors. Silas placed a thin, gold ring on Amanda's finger as each promised to commit to each other for the rest of their lives together.

The ceremony was simple and short. The bride was careful to take her first step following the "I do's" on her right foot for good luck. The main event of the day, the celebration and good food that came after the ceremony, lasted until late afternoon.

The men drifted out to the yard to share yarns and moonshine. The women gathered in the kitchen to gossip and counsel Amanda on wifely duties and household tips.

"Now, honey, be sure that Silas wears his weddin' clothes now and then. It's bad luck if he puts 'em away and never wears 'em again," Varna Bennett advised.

"Yes! You can wear yer pretty dress or pack it away. That won't matter. But the groom must wear his clothes or the marriage won't last," added Laura Cole.

Varna presented Amanda with a set of two silver candlesticks. "These here ain't fancy, but they was give to me by Adam's mother when we was married. I been savin' 'em to give to my first married son and his wife."

Amanda took the gift and gave her new mother-in-law a hug. "Thank you! These will surely be treasured on our table always, Mother Bennett."

"Now, just call me 'Ma.' Yer my daughter now, ain't ya?"

Amanda nodded and smiled. "That's the best gift of all, Ma. Thank you."

Clyde Cole hollered from the yard for his wife, and Laura responded. "Be right there!" Turning to the rest of the women, she said her goodbyes. "Guess that means we need to be headin' back. It was a beautiful day, Amanda. Me and Mr. Cole wish you and Silas the very best of the day and the rest of yer lives together."

As the rest of the guests began to depart, Alice and Cora Lee were once again pressed into service as the cleanup crew. "I need to be goin' back home right after we're done," Cora Lee said as she dried a plate. The sinking sun reminded her of her promise to Granny Mae to be home by nightfall.

"That's fine, honey," Ada said. "Go on. I'll help Alice finish the washin' up."

Cora Lee gathered her things and prepared to leave while Ada packed up some items for Amanda to carry to her new home.

"Take this old coffee pot. I've been savin' it fer ya. It's bad luck fer newlyweds to start off with a new one, ya know. After you've used it fer a few months, you can get a good one, and we'll give this old one to Alice when her bride day comes.

"I 'spect you and Silas will be havin' visitors later tonight, too," Ada said as she covered some remaining sandwiches with a cloth and handed the plate to her daughter. "I hope the revelers won't get too overly drunk and rowdy."

"I don't think Silas will allow 'em to, Ma. You know, he ain't real tolerant of much of that kind of foolishness. He ain't real tolerant of any kind of foolishness, for that matter."

"Well, better to have a serious and good man like Silas than a silly and mean one like some have had!"

Amanda laughed at that. "That's so true, Ma!"

Cora Lee said her goodbyes and promised Alice to call in again soon.

"Well, maybe next time you spend the night, we can have some of the other girls over and have that dumb supper I was talkin' about," Alice suggested.

"Thank you fer all your help, Cora Lee," Ada said as she and Alice walked Cora Lee to the door.

"I'll come 'round to see ya soon," Alice said. "I'm glad you could be here fer the weddin'."

"I'm happy I could be part of the day. Thank you for letting me be here!" Cora Lee hugged her friend and skipped down the road back home.

***

The shivaree, which came as expected around midnight, was fairly tame by most standards on the ridge. The group of men that appeared at the newlyweds' cabin in the light of the rising full moon, aware that Silas was not the kind of man to allow himself to be kidnapped or manhandled, simply banged on pots and pans until the couple opened the door and offered them the leftover wedding food.

Three cheers were offered into the quiet of the night. The men clapped Silas on the back, congratulated him for winning 'our fair schoolmarm' at long last, and stepped up to give Amanda a kiss on the cheek. They offered Silas a drink. He took a small sip of the alcohol for good luck and to be neighborly, but declined to imbibe any further.

The rowdy group passed the jug around and drank to the pair's good health and long life with a moderate sampling of the Oakleys' moonshine. Otis McDaniel produced his fiddle and began to play as the men sang a chorus of "Let Me Call You Sweetheart."

After toasting the couple once more, they departed in high spirits. Their continued serenade, a rendition of "By the Light of the Silvery Moon," drifted back to the cabin through the trees as they went on their way.

"Well, now that's over, Mrs. Bennett, it's time we get to bed," Silas said. He shut the door, took his wife in his arms and kissed her. She trembled, and he tightened his hold on her.

"No need fer all that," he said softly. "I'll not hurt ya. Yer my wife. Yer my woman. I love you, Mrs. Bennett, and you'll always be the part of me that means more to me than my own self."

Amanda nodded and sighed. She relaxed against his chest, feeling safe and loved, and happy the day's festivities were finally over.

CHAPTER 7

"Y ou can't catch me!" Cora Lee's challenge rang out into the woods and echoed back from the bluffs around them. She ran a short distance ahead into the warmth of a shaft of sunlight breaking through the canopy of trees that arched overhead. "It was so cold in there! The sun feels so good!"

Ruby shook her head at her friend's enthusiastic antics and turned to Walter. "You go on ahead," she told him. "I gotta stop in at the McDaniels' farm and finish some chores up there 'fore I get home."

Walter glanced at Cora Lee who, arms out and face lifted to the sky, was spinning in slow circles beneath a shaft of summer sunshine streaming between the branches overhead. He responded to his sister without taking his eyes off of the girl in the sunbeam.

"That's fine. I'll see her home."

"You alright? You look like a sick dog with a bone stuck in its throat. Why you got that stupid expression on yer face?" Ruby glanced from her brother to the girl twirling in the sun. "She's just a kid, Walter, and so are you. Best wait 'til you both grow up a bit 'fore gettin' sweet on her."

Walter's face flushed red. "Why, phooey! I ain't gettin' sweet on nobody no how! She's just a kid! And if we're talkin' about somebody gettin' sweet on somebody, why you spendin' so much time up at Old Man McDaniel's? I ain't exactly seen ya bringin' home wages to match the time yer spendin' up there."

"That ain't none of yer concern, brother." Ruby stared hard at him. "And he ain't that old, ya know."

"Well, Ma ain't gonna like it."

"Just worry about yerself, and stay outta my business. And don't go carryin' tales to Ma that's gonna upset her, neither. She's got enough to worry about without you addin' to it by carryin' tales that's none of yer bee's wax."

Ruby spun around and walked away.

He watched his sister leave, shook his head, and then turned to his other companion. Cora Lee dropped her arms to her sides and met his gaze. With a broad smile, she ran back to his side, linked arms with him, and they continued on their way.

The three of them had just come from an afternoon of exploring one of the many caves carved into the hills around their homes. Walter could hardly wait to share the discovery he'd made when chasing honey bees in search of their hive.

The cave was a large one with a small entry hidden behind brambles and brush. A chill breeze wafting from the cave had attracted his attention. He pushed the vegetation aside and was thrilled by the find.

He immediately ran to find Ruby and Cora Lee, his companions in adventure over the summer. The three of them had been enthusiastic in their many explorations among the woods, fields, and hollows around their homes. They couldn't wait to explore this exciting find.

Entering the cave, they ducked under a low-hanging entry that opened up into a good-sized chamber with a vaulted, domed roof. Milky water dripped from stalactites into a chalky pond at the back of the cavern creating strange, eerie music as the droplets hit the pool. Cool air breezed by on its way out of the cave, and Cora Lee shivered.

Little sunlight illuminated the space. Walter took a small box of matches from his pocket and lit a torch he had brought along. The flickering flame danced across an uneven floor and bounced against white limestone walls and columns. The fire glittered in the crystallized formations around them.

"This is like a magic palace," Cora Lee said as she walked slowly forward. "I wonder if there's any secret passageways that lead to treasure in here."

Ruby snorted. "The only 'treasure' we're likely to find in here is bugs and bats."

"You never know, Ruby," Walter said. "Could have been a hideaway for the Bottoms Gang—maybe the Wild Bunch buried their gold in here."

"Sure. Billy Randolph could've left the money from that bank robbery in here 'fore they hanged him," Ruby laughed. "You got a wild imagination, brother."

The three walked along the walls of the cave and marveled at the irregularities, crevices, and textures in the rock. Walter stopped and, looking up, handed the torch to his sister.

"I wanna see if I can break off one of these icicle things up here."

He took hold of one of the smaller stalactites with both hands. He jerked it back and forth, but the 'icicle' refused to budge.

"Nope. I reckon it's stuck up there fer good," he shrugged, brushing off his hands.

The trio moved on together through the increasing gloom toward the back of the cave. The floor became even more rocky and uneven, and the three of them slowed their pace to take care not to trip and fall. They came to a strangely-shaped, half pillar, and stopped to examine it.

"Well, I think it looks like a curled-up dog on a fence post," Cora Lee said.

"It could be," Walter said, "but it looks more like a man's face with a beard, to me. See the nose and the eyes?" He pointed at the formation.

"It's only a big rock," Ruby contributed dryly. "I don't see no dog or no face."

Just then, bats flew down from the ceiling behind them. The swarm rushed about in a chaotic cloud of high-pitched squeals and flapping wings. Ruby ducked under the onslaught of the creatures using the torch to protect her head.

Cora Lee shrieked and pitched forward waving her hands wildly. She slammed into Walter. He grabbed her and held her tightly against his chest while bats circled the ceiling above them and began to settle. She cowered in his arms while he tried to soothe her.

"It's just a bunch of bats, gal. They ain't gonna hurt us none. Calm down, now."

It took a moment for her heart to slow and her breath to return to normal, but the reassurance of Walter's arms slowly brought Cora Lee back to sanity. She looked up into his face, half hidden in the gloom as he bent his head over her. Embarrassed by her silly reaction, yet reluctant to leave the strangely comforting shelter of his embrace, she stood still.

"I'm calm," she assured him shakily.

The torch that Ruby had managed to hold onto during the bat attack began to flicker and dim.

"I think the air's gettin' thin in here. We best be gettin' on out, I reckon." Walter released Cora Lee, took her by the elbow and turned back to the cave opening. "Come on, Ruby. Let's go."

The three of them emerged from the chilly grotto, shivering and rubbing their arms. Walter took the torch from Ruby and stubbed the flame out on the ground. He tossed the torch back inside the opening to be used the next time they came to explore the cave.

"That was really somethin' to see!" Cora Lee's nose was red from the cold, and her hair was coming loose from its braid in a messy tangle. Her eyes were alight and cheeks glowed with both excitement over their spelunking expedition and her unexpected reaction to her close encounter with Walter.

"That was fun, even if we did almost get killed by bats and didn't find any treasure!" She threw a side-long glance at Walter from beneath her lashes. How had she never noticed how tall and handsome he was?

The three of them walked along in silence until they reached the point where Ruby left them. Once Ruby went off to work for Otis McDaniel, Cora Lee and Walter walked on together toward home. Cora Lee took his arm and smiled up at her friend. Her cheery mood quickly dispelled Walter's dark one, and he smiled back at her.

"Thanks for takin' me to see the cave. It was fun. Sorry I was such a goose about those awful bats."

"That's alright. You couldn't help it, bein' just a little girl and all," he teased.

Cora Lee jerked away from his arm and stopped dead in her tracks, indignant at being called a 'little girl' by her friend. "Little girl! Why, I'm not so little, you know. And you're not so big, yourself!"

"Well, I'm big enough to not squeal about a few little ol' bats," he jabbed. "And big enough to do this!"

Walter reached around and jerked on Cora Lee's braid. He turned and ran, satisfied to hear the outraged shriek coming from the 'little girl' in hot pursuit.

They ran over rocks and tree roots, jumped over logs and rivulets of water, swatted limbs and bushes out of their path, and came into an open field at the edge of the meadow. Walter spun around and jogged backward as Cora Lee narrowed the distance between them. She was still fuming.

"I give up," he shouted and threw his hands up in surrender. He broke into laughter as she caught up to him. "Take yer revenge, and let's be friends again!"

She balled up her fist ready to strike. "Oh! You're awful sometimes," she huffed at him. "I don't know why I want to be friends with a mean boy like you."

"Aw! Yes, ya do. Me and you and Ruby have fun together is why. Who else is gonna take you fishin' and show ya a 'magic palace' cave?"

Cora Lee remained stubbornly silent.

"Come on, Cora Lee. Don't be all mad. I got somethin' else to show ya, maybe." He waited for her to respond. When she didn't, he entice her further with, "It's a secret I ain't showed nobody else."

Despite her best efforts, her interest piqued over the invitation to see something as delicious as a *secret*. She couldn't help but be curious. *Curiosity killed the cat.* Granny Mae's voice echoed in her head. Her resistance destroyed, she ignored Granny's warning and let herself be led into the trap.

"What is it?" she asked as she edged closer.

Walter reached into his pocket and pulled out his fist. "Look here," he said and waited until Cora Lee stepped up to him. She bent over to see what he had in his hand.

"It's this!" He opened his hand and quickly tweaked her nose. "That's what it is!" He laughed and ran off toward home leaving Cora Lee outraged over the dirty, rotten trick.

"I'll never be your friend again, Walter Douglas!" she stomped her foot and yelled at his retreating back. She'd never been so furious in her whole life! Fuming, she marched off toward her cabin as she continued yelling at him. "Just wait 'til I tell Granny about this! What a mean, low scoundrel you are!"

Still irritated, but not finding Mae in the cabin, Cora Lee walked around to the back garden and went into the outhouse. She lifted her skirt and pulled down her pantalettes only to gasp in shock at the sight of blood staining the fabric of her underdrawers.

Stunned, she sat in silence, not knowing what to do.

Did I get so mad that it busted somethin' up inside? Did I make myself sick? Am I dying?

That last thought horrified her. Terrified that she might die and leave her poor grandmother alone—the sweet grandmother who had already lost so many of her folks—her parents—her husband—all of her children. It would be unthinkable!

"I can't die! I can't do that to Granny Mae!"

Cora Lee burst into a loud wail as she looked around for something to stop the flow from her body. She tore off a handful of moss from the mound kept on the wooden toilet bench and stuffed it into her pantalettes.

With tears running down her face, she stepped out of the privy, careful not to dislodge her make-shift bandage, and walked back to the cabin. *Maybe the bleeding will stop soon since I've calmed down.* She glanced to the heavens and prayed, *Dear God, don't let me die from getting mad at Walter. I'm sorry. Please make the bleeding stop!*

Entering the cabin, relieved that Granny Mae was still out, her first thought was to hide. *I can't face her,* she thought in a panic. Scanning the small room, though, she realized there was no place that would keep her concealed. She looked around to find something to calm her mind and spied the supply of dried beans in the bag near the stove.

She scooped a cup of the beans from the sack and, shaking, carried them to the table. *I'll not think about it—keep myself busy, and it'll stop.* Her hands trembled as she sorted the beans from rocks and those that were worm-eaten or pitted with rot. *It's gonna stop. It's got to!* But a blooming ache in her lower belly told her that something must be seriously, terribly wrong, and fresh tears erupted from her eyes.

Mae entered the cabin to find her granddaughter, pale faced and awash in grief, crying over a pile of dried beans at the table.

"What's happened? What is it, child?"

Mae went to the girl, and Cora Lee buried her face in her grandmother's comforting waist. She threw her arms around her grandmother as Mae stroked her hair.

"I'm so sorry, Granny," she sobbed. "I'm dying from gettin' mad at Walter."

"Oh, now. What would make you say such a silly and foolish thing?"

"I must have broke somethin' in me, because I'm bleeding and aching, and it won't stop."

Mae's hand stopped stroking her granddaughter's head. She tucked her fingers under Cora Lee's chin and lifted the tear-stained face to meet hers.

"You ain't dyin'. You just got yer monthlies, is all. It means ya reached the age where God gifts women with bein' able to have babies. It happens to ever girl, but we don't talk about it. It's our own, special secret to keep to ourselves. Now, dry yer eyes. I'll fix you up some rags and show ya how to use 'em."

Overcome with stunned relief, Cora Lee sucked in her breath. "You said *monthlies*? You mean this'll happen again?" She wasn't sure if she was happy she wasn't dying or unhappy that she would have to go through this as a routine event.

"Ever month, unless yer carryin' a child or nursin' one, until you get old like me. While it's yer 'time,' don't be washin' yer hair or goin' in the water, even to wade in the creek. Don't be doin' any heavy liftin' or workin' too hard so's ya get tired out."

Cora Lee considered all of this new information, then she had a thought. "Well, do boys have to do this every month, too?"

Mae shook her head. "No, child. This is a blessin' just for women."

Cora Lee pondered this new knowledge and, once again, decided that God did, indeed, work in mysterious, if sometimes rather disagreeable, ways.

CHAPTER 8

Months rolled themselves up into years with little changing on Bennett's Ridge beyond the seasons. However, beyond the quiet isolation of the mountain, 1917 was ushering in an era of dynamic and, in some cases, frightening world events. A revolution was going on in Russia, and the Czar and his whole family were murdered. There were race and labor riots happening in Texas, Kentucky, and Illinois, and the United States had entered into the war on Germany.

News of those happenings in the wider world seeped through the blanket of isolation that wrapped Bennett's Ridge in its reclusive cocoon. Residents worried trouble would intrude on their mountain community. Little else was the topic of conversation as summer waned.

The month of August had been brutal, and little rain had fallen through the season. The heavy scent of dried fescue and the sound of cicadas sawing their incessant mating calls filled the hot, dry late-summer air. Cora Lee stood with Ruby and Walter in the shade of an ancient oak, resting after completing a long week of cutting hay. The work of raking it each day into windrows and getting it loaded into Old Mr. Bennett's wagon to be taken to his barn had all but exhausted the three of them.

They had readily hired out for the job. The five dollars they each earned was welcomed, even though the pay didn't quite seem enough compensation for the hours of back-breaking labor and the exacting demands of their boss. In spite of wearing wide-brimmed hats, they all had noses burnt red and peeling from the sun.

With the field shorn of its product, the dried grass forked into Mr. Bennett's wagons and hoisted into the loft of his barn, the three eagerly found refuge from the sun. The shade they enjoyed was welcome, but they found little relief from the shimmering heat as not even a puff of breeze stirred the oppressive air.

Walter leaned against the trunk of the tree and, taking a rag from his back pocket, removed his hat and wiped the sweat from his face and neck. He fanned his blistered and reddened face with his hat for a moment then dropped it on the ground at his feet.

"It's hotter than a fire in a pepper mill," he said as he reached into his shirt pocket and casually removed a pipe and a small bag of tobacco.

"When did you take up smokin'?" Ruby asked him. "It's such a grown-up, manly thing to do—ain't hardly like you at all," she teased.

Walter scowled at his sister's jibe and began to load a bit of tobacco into the bowl.

"Here." Ruby took the crudely-made corncob pipe and expertly packed the tobacco in its bowl. "It'll burn a bit slower if it's tamped down some." She handed the pipe back to him. "I had plenty of practice fixin' Otis'—uh, Mr. McDaniel's pipes fer him."

Smoke curled around their heads as Walter lit his pipe. Nodding, he acknowledged the improvement but ignored his sister's blunder in calling Mr. McDaniel by his first name. Blowing out a stream of smoke, he cleared his throat.

"Me and a few of the boys up here decided to go help fight the Kaiser," he announced. "Roy Dale's been drafted and is headed to Endurance tomorrow. I'm goin' with him and Lucas and Jacob in the morning to see the recruitment officer. Robert Dobson is coming later in the week. We'll meet up and stay down there 'til the train leaves fer Camp Pike down in Little Rock. I won't be back 'til we get leave after boot camp."

Cora Lee's eyes widened and, stunned, she blurted, "But, Walter, they aren't drafting men until they're twenty-one, and you're too young to volunteer before you turn eighteen on your birthday. Why, your beard hasn't hardly grown in yet!"

"They'll take me," Walter answered calmly, stroking the sparse hairs on his face. "My birthday's soon enough, and I'll just lie and say I'm already eighteen. They ain't gonna say any different—beard or no beard."

Ruby stepped away from her brother and shook her head. "What would make ya wanna go fight in a war that's so far away—a war that ain't got nothin' to do with us?" Ruby argued.

"The pay's $25 a month plus room and board, and they supply the uniforms, too. Seems like a fair deal to me, and marchin' around with a bunch of other fellers all day has to be easier than cuttin' hay. Besides, it's the patriotic thing to do."

"Patriotic!" Ruby snapped. "Idiotic more like!"

"Listen," Walter continued. "There's a whole wide world out there, and I wanna see some of it. Imagine me bein' someplace like France! Imagine me sailin' on a ship or even goin' fer a ride on a train! Why, I ain't ever even been down to Endurance. There's a lot more to life than fishin' and farmin', and I'm gonna do some of it 'fore I settle down—'fore I die."

"Well, it's a chance that yer gonna die sooner than later bein' shot at! What if you don't come back? What'll Ma and me do without you?"

Walter ignored his sister and stepped closer to Cora Lee. He reached up and removed a stalk of hay from the tangle of her hair making her shiver at his touch. Taking her hand, he held it against his heart and bent his head to hers. "What about you, Cora Lee?" His voice was low, and it rumbled up from his chest in a way that was new to her. "What'll you do without me? Will you miss me?"

Cora Lee opened her mouth but no sound came. Her heartbeat sounded like a drum in her ears. *Say something! Say anything*, her mind reeled. *Don't just stand here mute as a fence post. Yes—No—Anything!*

She pulled away from him abruptly, shaking her head to clear it. "Don't be a goose," she managed and cleared her throat. "Of course, Granny and I'll miss you. And—and we'll get along just fine, too. I guess the last thing you need to worry about, if you're truly going to join up, is how Granny and I'll be getting along. We'll all keep an eye on your Ma for you, too, won't we, Ruby?"

Ruby didn't answer but spun on her heel and marched away from her brother. Walter watched her go and then turned back to Cora Lee.

"I'll be gone awhile fer some trainin', then I'll have some leave and be home fer a bit 'fore we're moved fer combat trainin'. After that, we'll ship out fer more trainin' in France. Then they'll send us to the front. You can write me. Will ya write me sometime and let me hear how yer—how everone's getting' along?"

Cora Lee nodded. "Of course, I will—we all will. And we'll all be praying for you—for all you boys to be safe and come home in one piece."

"Well—I reckon that's it, then." Walter retrieved his hat and, as he started for home, Cora Lee spun around and turned her back to him.

"Why you turnin' yer back to me?" he asked. "Are ya mad?"

"Oh, no!" she answered without facing him. "But to watch a friend depart means we might never meet again." She blushed, glad that he could not see her face. "I wouldn't want that," she almost whispered.

Walter grinned, tipped his hat to her back, and laughed. "Good day, then—friend."

And with a low whistle, he walked out of the shade of the oak to the road and away.

***

Summer passed into fall, and the boys from the ridge returned on leave from training at Camp Pike. On this October morning the wind was still, and the early dawn mists lay so thick on the ground it seemed that Bennett's Ridge rose above Heaven itself. The autumn air carried the light, crisp scent of coming winter. The hills were painted in dark greens, russet golds, and bright yellows. Here and there, a burst of maroon sumac and brilliant red maple splashed against outcroppings of ancient, volcanic rock.

Mae stood on the porch near the doorway of her cabin watching the rising sun paint the tops of the highest peaks with pinkish-silver light as they emerged from the clouds. She held a large crockery bowl in one arm while her other hand whipped the contents in a clockwise direction. Her hands moved in a mechanical and practiced way, whipping the batter so that the flavor of dawn would infuse her corn cake and keep it moist.

"Would you like me to help, Granny Mae?" Cora Lee reached to take the bowl from her grandmother's hands.

"Oh, no!" Mae said, her voice soft and raspy. "Child, don't ya know it's bad luck if whoever starts the stir don't finish the stir? Otherwise, the cake'll be spoilt. Might as well throw it to the hogs. Go break us some eggs fer breakfast; I'll put this cake in the oven."

Bad luck to throw water out a window, rock an empty rocking chair, set two lights on a shelf, tell a dream at the table, cut cornbread with a knife. *Granny has more ways to keep bad luck at bay than a corncob has kernels,* Cora Lee thought. She knocked on the door frame three times and laughed. "Now we'll only have good luck today," she teased. "You making that sweet cake for the party, or is somebody coming to visit?"

The old woman's now toothless mouth turned up in a smile, and she stopped stirring to brush the hair out of her granddaughter's eyes. *How the child has grown,* Mae thought, feeling ancient. *How the last few years have rushed by!* "No, little 'un. I ain't had no signs of a visitor. It be fer the send-off party," Mae replied.

The boys had come home from training camp on a two-week leave of absence before they were to ship out for Europe. The community decided to send them off with a dance and pot-luck supper at the school house the evening they needed to catch the midnight train from Endurance back to camp.

"Make sure you don't sit in a corner with that guitar all night. Make sure and dance with those fellas, ya hear?" Granny ordered. "Yer goin' on sixteen now and gettin' to be about marryin' age soon. You don't want folks to start thinkin' yer an old maid, do ya?"

Cora Lee blushed at the comment. She looked forward to the table full of food that would be provided as well as the opportunity to play music with the more seasoned musikers on the ridge. She also had to admit that the chance to enjoy a dance or two would be welcome, as well.

The old woman turned her back on the cool morning air. She and her granddaughter went back into the cabin where a fire already heated the iron stove. Mae poured the batter into the iron skillet and slid the pan into the oven. A wave of dizziness and nausea washed over her as she straightened—not the first she'd experienced, but certainly the worst so far.

"Yes, I reckon you be a'needin' to be marryin' soon," Mae wheezed and sank into a chair at the table. "Need someone to take care of you when I'm gone."

"I don't think you'll be going anywhere anytime soon! Besides, all the boys are goin' off to war. Even when they come back, I don't know who on mountain or in holler will have me," Cora Lee laughed as she brought two plates of scrambled eggs to the table. "I'm not exactly any man's idea of a prize catch. Alice has turned down suitors a'plenty, but I haven't ever had one around to say 'boo' to."

"Pretty Alice may have her looks, and that she does, but pretty Alice Campbell can't string a bean or darn a sock to save her life. Flirty ways and idle chatter won't feed a man or keep a mended shirt on his back. Yer plenty enough to look at, and you can keep a house and help around the farm, too, which is more important.

"Besides, Alice is too free with her affections. She's after one boy or another like a pig on a pumpkin! Any boy gives her a compliment and she starts battin' her eyes at him like a frog eatin' fire!" Mae shook her head in disapproval. "Don't need to ever try to be like that! Remember this," Mae continued, pushing her breakfast aside untouched. "A man will take and gladly use what's easily given, but he keeps and treasures what he has to work fer to win."

Cora Lee laughed. "You're so wise, Granny. How'd you get to be so?" she teased.

"By listenin' to my grandmother and not bein' a smarty-mouth!" Mae answered in mock irritation.

"Now clear the table and run on out of here so's I can finish all my doin's!"

Cora Lee scampered outside and went to work on her morning chores. After lunch with her grandmother, she washed the dishes and cleaned the cabin in order to give her grandmother a chance to rest a little. Mae protested at being made to sit in her rocker while her granddaughter busied herself with housework, but Cora Lee insisted.

"You haven't been feeling the best, Granny. You ought not be getting up so early every day. Why don't you have a sleep-in tomorrow?"

"Why, ain't been a day in my whole seventy-two years of life I didn't wake up with the chickens!" Mae answered, outraged at the thought. "Don't intend to start now! Bad enough fer me to sit here doin' nothin' while yer flutterin' around like ya are. Hand me my sewin' basket, and get on outta here fer a while. Yer aggervexin' me with all yer fussin' about."

Cora Lee gave up trying to make her grandmother take things easier, grabbed the guitar and headed to her favorite spot on the small rise behind the cabin. She sat in the shade of a grove of witch hazel, black walnut and oak trees and picked at the guitar strings as she hummed a tune. A short time later, Walter found her there, surprised that she could play a guitar.

"I didn't know you could play that thing," Walter said, startling her.

"Only middlin' so," she answered, her annoyance at being disturbed quickly replaced by pleasure at seeing her friend. "I like to pick at it sometimes. Granny's pa, my great-grandpa, was a musiker. She told me this is all she has left of him after the war, and she's taught me to play some."

She lay the instrument aside and patted the ground next to her. "Sit with me and tell me how you been. We haven't seen much of you since you come home."

The six weeks that the boys had been away at army training camp had wrought a great change in all of them. Clean shaven, hair trimmed, and standing straighter, it seemed they had all grown taller and more mature.

Walter, in particular, had filled out with plenty of good food, exercise and hard work while away. He had left home a scrawny youth and had returned a muscular young man. Cora Lee, looking up into his handsome face, became a little unsettled by the change in him. He grinned at her as he flopped down on the ground, and her heart skipped a beat.

"Well, play somethin,' then. I wanna hear how it sounds. Sing me a song." He picked up the guitar and handed it to her. "Sing me a song. Please."

"Oh, no! You'll laugh at me. I'm not very good."

"I won't laugh. Why would I? I just wanna know how it sounds is all."

Cora Lee reluctantly took the guitar from Walter's hands and ran her thumb over the strings. Adjusting a few of the strings that were a bit out of tune, she pressed the fingers of her left hand onto the neck and strummed a quiet chord.

"See?" she said and lay the instrument aside. "That's how it sounds."

"No!" Walter pushed the guitar back at her. "Sing a song while ya play! I already said 'please' and all."

Coral Lee pressed her lips together. "Oh, alright!" she huffed. "Since you said 'please and all.'"

Cradling the guitar in her lap, she leaned back against a red oak tree while Walter lay back on his elbows in anticipation. "Don't watch me, though."

Walter pulled his hat down over his eyes and stretched out on his back. "I ain't lookin. Go ahead."

Strumming the strings softly, Cora Lee began a slow waltz she had been learning. She sang a ballad of a girl betrayed by her lover; her voice was sweet, uncluttered by trills or tremolo. It sounded as clear and pure as a rosewood flute, and Walter soon became lost in it. Mesmerized, he held his breath as the song flowed around and over him.

And when at last, the lass was found,
They lay her in the cold, cold ground,
Ne'er more her love to see,
Ne'er would she marry.
For she believed a thieving heart
Who promised ne'er to depart,
He left to sail the deep blue sea;
He left her in pain and misery.

The last sad, minor note hung in the air like a melancholy mist, dispelling the playful mood of a few moments earlier.

"Well, gosh darn it!" Walter sat up angrily. "Why'd ya go and sing somethin' so sad fer?"

Cramming his hat back onto his head, he jumped up and began to stomp off, leaving Cora Lee sitting with her mouth open.

"Well, don't ask me to sing again!" she yelled at his retreating back, all remnant of shyness banished from her mind. "I got lots of sadder ones than that I can sing for you if you do!"

Then, thinking better of her response, she shook her head and called after her friend. "Come on back, Walter. I'll sing us something happy, I promise."

Walter stopped and turned. He stood for a brief moment before returning to the arbor.

"All right." Walter flopped down once more beside her. "Go ahead."

The pair spent a pleasant hour with each other, and Walter even joined in singing a raspy baritone harmony to Cora Lee's soprano on some of the tunes that he knew. When the sun began to set, Cora Lee set the guitar aside, disappointed that the day was ending.

"Come have supper with us." Cora Lee stood and brushed a few leaves from her skirt. "Granny cooked a squirrel stew, so there's plenty to share."

"I'll come pay respects to Miz Clarey, but I can't stay. I need to go on home and finish takin' care of some things fer Ma 'fore we leave again. She still has a few things that need tendin' and mendin'. I promised to help set up fer the dance, too. Roy Dale asked me to come help him dig a pit fer a fire, and the only time I have to do that is this evenin,' I reckon."

"Well, if you're sure. We're just happy you're— all you boys is back. I—we just wish you didn't have to leave again so soon."

"Me and the boys all have to leave the party a bit early tomorrow to head back down to the station in Endurance. We're gonna ketch the train at midnight. It gets in at ten in the mornin,' and we're supposed to check in at the army base by noon."

Cora Lee's face fell in disappointment, but she recovered quickly. She picked up the guitar and strapped it on her back. Taking Walter's arm, the two of them walked slowly back to the cabin in silence through the gathering twilight.

Mae watched the two young people as they came across the yard and stepped out to greet the couple as they came up on the porch. "Walter! Wonderful to see you, boy. Stayin' fer dinner, ain't ya?" Mae invited.

"Can't, but thank you."

"Well, we'd love to have you stay and visit, but maybe another time." Mae started to return inside but stopped and turned back to Walter. She put her arms around him and gave him a hug, then patted his arm gently. "You take care of yerself over there, boy," she said. "We don't wanna lose you or any of the boys from up here. We'll be prayin' fer you all to come back safe and whole."

Walter smiled. "Thank ya, Granny. I know me and all the boys'll be fine."

With a quiet nod, Mae returned inside so that the couple could say good night to each other.

"Yer goin' to the dance tomorrow evenin,' ain't ya?" Walter asked.

"Of course," Cora Lee answered. "I helped organize it, and I'll be helpin' to play some of the music along with the others."

"Well, don't just play the guitar the whole night. Save a dance fer me, or I'll be stuck havin' to escort Ruby all night by myself."

"Well, we can't have Ruby bein' forced to drag her big brother around for the entire party," Cora Lee teased. "I'll be happy to rescue her from your attentions for a dance!"

Walter moved closer to Cora Lee and took her gently by the shoulders. The unexpected change from light-hearted banter to this sudden seriousness surprised Cora Lee, and she looked up at him with wide eyes. Standing so close together, she imagined that she could almost hear his heart beat as the heat between them became more tangible than the cloying, fragrant autumn air. Shyly, she looked away.

"Will you wait fer me?" he asked in a low voice.

Flustered, Cora Lee stammered, "I think I'll still be here when you come back. I—" she lifted her face to his and gazed into his golden-brown eyes—"I'll be happy to see you come home safe."

Cora Lee blushed and stepped back as Walter bent toward her, a kiss left wanting on his lips.

CHAPTER 9

The community spent the following day in a flurry of preparation for the anticipated send-off party at the schoolhouse. Cora Lee helped Mae prepare a pot of beans to carry over with the sweet corn cake baked the day before. Mae, exhausted by the work it took to prepare the food, decided to stay home rather than attend the dance with her granddaughter.

Cora Lee at first insisted on passing up the party to stay with her granny, but, after much argument, agreed to leave her grandmother at home.

"You go on and enjoy yerself," Mae said.

"But you'd have a good time, too. And everybody would be so glad to see you, Granny."

"I can't see the need in me a'goin'," Mae wheezed. "I reckon I got about as much use fer a party as a frog has fer a sidesaddle."

"I'll stay here with you, then!" Cora Lee declared stubbornly.

"Yer supposed to help with playin' the music. Not to mention you needin' to carry this food over and help the women set up fer the dance. Don't go tryin' to shirk work and use me as an excuse not to go."

Defeated, Cora Lee reluctantly gave in. "Very well, Granny Mae. Of course, I'm not trying to get out of work. I'll go along, but I'll leave early when the boys head out for Endurance and come right home."

"Don't worry about comin' home tonight. Stay and have fun. Be rude to do otherwise. And you don't need to be walkin' home after dark fer the haints to get ya, either. Go home with Alice after the party and stay with the Campbells. I reckon I'll still be here when you come home in the mornin'."

Cora Lee, at last, relented and gave in to her grandmother's wishes. Strapping the guitar on her back, she loaded the wicker basket with her grandmother's victuals and walked to the schoolhouse. The menfolk had already emptied the schoolhouse of benches and set them up in the yard around a recently dug firepit.

After helping some of the women set up a long trestle table for the food, she deposited the beans and cornbread and stored the wicker basket under the table. Assuring herself that the paper decorations were hung to her satisfaction, Cora Lee called in at the Campbell farm to collect Alice.

The girls planned to gather pine cones, evergreen branches, and fall leaves to make a centerpiece for the food table. Alice immediately took possession of her friend's arm and pulled the two of them toward the woods behind her cabin.

"I'm right glad you'll be comin' home with us tonight. Sarah Jean Dobson and Dora Oakley are comin' home with us, too. I have all kinds of plans! You remember when we played a game to tell who you's gonna marry? What fun! Papa says it's silly, but Ma says you never can tell, so we should try again. Maybe we'll have better luck this time."

Cora Lee shrugged. Her worry about Granny Mae's health rather than whom she might or might not marry occupied her mind. She let her friend prattle on.

"Here!" Alice stooped and picked a cockle burr from the ground. Holding it gingerly, she handed the burr to Cora Lee. "I'm gonna think of a fella, and you throw this at my skirt," she instructed. "If it sticks, then that's the fella I'm gonna marry."

Cora Lee took the sticker while Alice squeezed her eyes shut in concentration. Alice opened her eyes and nodded. Cora Lee tossed the cockle burr, but it did not stick and bounced to the ground at their feet.

"Oh, well," Alice tossed her golden curls as she shrugged. "I didn't like him best, anyways."

"How do you know a fella's gonna like you back?"

"Well, fer goodness sakes! I can be anythin' I need to be to get a fella to like me. They just need to be what I want 'em to be fer me to like *them*, is all. 'Sides, they's ways to make a fella fall in love."

Alice put her finger to her lips and lifted her skirt to reveal an empty wasp's nest pinned to her petticoat.

"See? I've made a few charms, but I ain't decided who I wanna marry yet, so I don't know who to work 'em on. I probably'll marry Jacob Bennett since his folks is richest. That'd make me and Amanda double-sisters and our kids double-cousins.

"But Joshua Oakley, Dora's brother, would do, too —'cept he's kinda young, and his folks cook corn whiskey. Pa don't like that about them. 'Course, Lucas McDaniel is the handsomest, but he's as mean as a man's hide'll hold. I'd as soon marry a mangey old pole cat as him!

"Dora says she has a shine on fer Sarah Jean's brother," Alice continued. "Robert's a good worker, but he ain't too smart. He's so dumb he can't tell a cat from molasses, and he looks like the back end of bad luck. Don't tell her I said that about him, though."

"How 'bout you? You and Roy Dale can marry, then we'll be sisters. You got a fella yet? Probably not. I don't reckon you've picked one out yet. Don't go pickin' one that I want, though, is all I'm sayin'."

Cora Lee shook her head, but she immediately thought of Walter. She had known him since she came to live with Granny Mae, and she had always thought of him as a playmate and friend. They had spent so many days roaming the woods and exploring together with Ruby. She had grown to care for both of them, and she thought of both of them as family.

Now, out of nowhere, she found herself thinking of him as more than a childhood friend. Something in the way he had looked at her with those eyes of his, the way he had spoken to her in that deep voice he now had.

He had changed since being gone. He was not the boy who left her that day under the oak in the hayfield. He had come home a man. It was unsettling, and she could not help but wonder if she seemed different to him, too.

"Oh, golly!" Alice exclaimed pointing to Cora Lee's skirt. "That old cockle burr is stuck to the hem of your dress. Ain't that funny?"

***

Having arranged their fall decorations on the food table, Alice and Cora Lee returned to the Campbell's farm to freshen up. Sarah Jean and Dora soon arrived, and the girls got ready for the party.

"We need to get there a little late so's we can make an entrance," Alice instructed the girls. "Won't do to have us standin' around waitin' on the boys to show up like we's desperate fer a dance or anythin'. Better they's waitin' on us."

Cora Lee, caring nothing for "making an entrance" and anxious to be with the other musikers, gritted her teeth in frustration and waited for her three friends to finish their primping.

Alice was the prettiest of the four girls, but Sarah Jean, with her waist-length black hair and violet-blue eyes, rivaled Alice in beauty. The two of them wore new dresses, Alice in pink and Sara Jean in sunny yellow, with matching ribbons in their hair. Dora, plainer in looks, wore a faded, homespun dress that failed to complement her spindly figure. The ill-cut dress gave her a rumpled, unkempt appearance.

"Here now, Dora," Alice said. "You should put a little flour on your face to hide some of your freckles. Ain't nobody gonna say nothin' about you wearin' a little bit of face whitenin'."

Alice went to the kitchen and pulled a packet of white flour from its spot under the rafters. Taking a palmful of powder from the packet she returned to her friend and applied the cosmetic. Licking her finger, she moistened the paper rose pinned to Dora's bodice and reddened her friend's cheeks and pale lips with the dye.

"Now! Much better," she declared with a satisfied nod. "Don't you think so, Sarah Jean?"

Not waiting for an answer, Alice turned to Cora Lee. "It wouldn't hurt none fer you to trigger up a little, too. Couldn't you have at least worn a different dress or curled your hair?"

Cora Lee was dressed in her everyday outfit of a simple brown skirt and homespun blouse cut down to fit her from something in her grandmother's

111

wardrobe. Her hair, brushed and clean, was pulled back from her face and fixed in her usual plain, single braid.

She shrugged and said, "This'll do fine for me. Don't need nor want triggering up, thank you." She bent to pick up her guitar and turned toward the door.

Alice picked up her shawl and went to the door. "Well, let's go then." She hastily took charge of the group and walked out in front of Cora Lee.

The party was in full swing when the four girls arrived. A few children chased each other through the yard, laughing and squealing loudly. Older men stood in groups here and there, some smoking and others drinking Charles Oakley's moonshine. Each was trying to outdo the others telling jokes and riddles or spinning tall tales of who had the smartest dog or had the best cook for a wife in a game of friendly one-upmanship.

"I tell ya, my dog's so smart, he's learnin' to sing and play the mouth harp," John Dobson boasted to the men standing around him.

"Oh, that so? Well, I'll have to tell my dog to put down his knittin' and write him a song, then!" Charles Oakley answered, lifting a crockery jug of corn liquor to his lips as the other men guffawed at his joke.

"What's big at the bottom and smaller on top, and somethin' inside goes flippity-flop?" Clyde Cole asked.

"Ah, that's an old one!" Adam Bennett scoffed. "My grampa laughed at that one in his crib. Everbody knows it's a butter churn!"

The five young men in their uniforms hovered around the food table that was laden with an abundance of food. Enormous platters of ham and sausages delivered by the Bennett family filled the air with the tantalizing smell of roasted meat. Piles of fried potatoes and stacks of buttered corn on the cob from the Dobson's farm sat alongside Mae's beans, cornbread and a big bowl of her famous peaches. Ada Campbell donated sweet cakes and blackberry cobbler, and apples from Otis McDaniel's orchard spilled out of two burlap bags into the forest-themed centerpiece provided by Alice and Cora Lee.

The setting sun lingered above the horizon sending fingers of orange-gold light through the trees around the schoolyard. As darkness began to fall, the evening air remained clear and still with just enough autumn chill to make the outdoor fire pleasant and keep the school room cool for the dancers. Pitch torches burned around the edge of the yard giving the party a festive air.

Cora Lee entered the schoolhouse and found an unobtrusive spot in a chair with her guitar behind Otis McDaniel with his fiddle and Ellen Oakley with her washboard. Joshua Oakley, too young to pass as old enough to join the army, sat at the piano. "I figure I'll join the fight if it's still on next year," he had grumbled. "I can shoot a gun better than most of them fellas they's allowin' to join up!"

Otis McDaniel drew his bow across the strings of his fiddle with a loud, dissonant screech grabbing the attention of the people in the room and calling to those who might want to dance. His fingers found their place on the neck of his instrument, and a tune emerged from the noise of the strings. Cora Lee recognized the song and joined in, the washboard keeping time and the piano animating the air with its robust tones.

Ada Campbell and the other women who stood along the edge of the dance floor began to stomp their feet and clap their hands making the schoolhouse rumble in time to the lively tune being played. The floor soon became filled with couples whirling their way through a polka.

The two-step that came next, slower in tempo, enticed older couples onto the floor. Luther and Ada Campbell, John and Rachel Dobson, and Adam and Varna Bennett danced near the warmth of the potbellied stove, while other couples danced near cooler air from the open windows. Silas and Amanda stood with Roy Dale near a table that had been set up in a corner to provide pitchers of water and lemonade for the party.

Alice and Sarah Jean came into the room and hooked arms with Dora. The three of them began to take a turn around the room pretending to pay no attention to the uniformed soldiers who had followed them in.

Jacob and Robert stood near the door watching the three girls as they promenaded around the room and waiting for a chance to ask one of them for a dance. Lucas stood with them, and when Cora Lee looked up from her instrument, she was unnerved to see that his attention was focused on her.

Lucas stared at her with an unsettling intensity. A cold chill went through her, and she quickly looked down at the strings of her guitar refusing to glance up again until the song ended. When she did, she was relieved to see that Lucas had joined Jacob and Robert, and the three of them were talking to her friends.

Otis began to play a waltz, and many of the couples on the floor changed partners. The three soldiers bowed to the three girls, and the six of them moved onto the floor. While Sara Jean danced in Lucas' arms, though, his eyes were drawn time and again to Cora Lee.

Several more songs followed before Cora Lee took a break. She was relieved to see that Lucas was still occupied with Sara Jean. Alice and Dora were dancing with Jacob and Robert, so she went out into the schoolyard. Seeing Ruby and Walter at the food table, Cora Lee walked over to greet them.

"Yer doin' a right fine job with the music, Cora Lee!" Walter commented. "You should take to the road and make a livin' with that guitar."

Ruby slapped her brother's arm. "Don't tease her like that, Walter! Cora Lee, nobody ain't hardly paid no mind at all when ya messed up. Don't you worry none 'bout that."

Cora Lee grinned and ducked her head. "Oh, I know I'm terrible. I'd rather be playing than dancing is all."

"Speakin' of which," Walter offered his arm, "you promised me a dance, remember?"

Cora Lee smiled and took his arm. The three of them walked back to the schoolhouse. Walter paused and allowed Cora Lee, followed by Ruby, to proceed him up the steps and through the door.

As she entered the building, Lucas, who was standing by the door, grabbed Cora Lee by the arm.

"Dance with me," he said as he pulled her to him.

Cora Lee jumped as he pounced on her and pulled away as Walter came up behind her.

"Sorry, Lucas," Walter intervened. "She's already promised this one to me."

The band began playing a slow ballad, and Lucas released Cora Lee. He stepped back with a cold smile, gave a slight bow, and extended his open hand toward the dance floor. "Sorry. Didn't know she was taken."

Walter calmly took Cora Lee by the elbow and led her onto the floor. He took her in his arms and pulled her against his chest, his arms a gentle vise as he held her close and began to two-step to the music.

A thrill went up her spine as she looked up into his face. She lay her head against the hollow of his broad shoulders and breathed in the scent of his woolen uniform. They didn't speak, and Cora Lee was glad that no words, no teasing banter between them, intruded on this moment. The world faded away, and only the music and she and Walter existed in this brief, sweet interlude.

Closing her eyes, she wished the music could go on forever. *But, of course, all good things come to an end,* she thought as she tripped.

"I'm sorry," Cora Lee apologized after she stumbled and stepped on Walter's toes as the song ended. "I guess I wasn't paying attention to my feet."

Walter laughed and led her off the dance floor as the band began another song. "It's alright. I reckon me and the boys is gonna have to be goin' soon. Silas said he'd carry us down to the train station in his wagon."

Walter escorted her out of the door. A full moon had risen that cast a patchwork of shadows across the ground. Islands of light flickered under each of the torches around the deserted yard. The band began another slow ballad that spilled out of the building and filled the night air with the haunting strains of a muted love song.

Walter guided her to the gloom at the edge of the woods. "We'll be gettin' our orders on where they's shippin' us out to once we finish the rest of our trainin'. I'm gonna send word to you and Ruby soon's I can. Be sure you write to me, ya hear?"

"Of course! We'll all be hoping to hear from you and the rest of the boys," she replied.

"No, Cora Lee. I ain't talkin' 'bout nobody else up here. I mean you." He moved closer to her and she raised her face to his. "You write to me—wait fer me. I want you to be my girl."

Cora Lee's stammered, "W—Walter, I…"

Walter's mouth came down on hers and cut off any further discussion. His kiss was surprising, intense, urgent but tender.

Cora Lee closed her eyes, and something like thunder rolled through her body. She swayed against him. Her mouth opened under the heat of his lips as his arms tightened around her, pressing her body into his. She raised her arms and encircled his neck, floating in the moment, melting into his embrace.

Then, he released her and was gone.

An icy emptiness suddenly filled the place where the heat of Walter's body had just been. She opened her eyes to see him walking toward the wagon where the other boys waited. Quickly, she turned her back to his departing figure. A screech owl's lonely call echoed in the woods, and she shuddered with a mixture of longing, loneliness and premonition.

"Yes, Walter. I'll wait for you. I'll be your girl," she whispered and put a trembling hand to her lips to hold his kiss there a little longer.

***

Mae lay awake in her bed and the cry of a screech owl, the harbinger of bad tidings, came from the woods. "Someone's gonna die soon," she thought. Her mind began to wander, bits of memory weaving through the fabric of the night. Her body felt different as she lay there, strange and foreign. She tried to sort out the odd sensations pulsing in her chest, but her thoughts strayed again and again to pictures of her past.

There was a time when she cast shadows as mysterious as any star. There was a time when a toss of her golden hair threw a net of rainbows that gathered all the fish in the sea—when a look from her green eyes flashed like lightening, and her smile thundered in young men's hearts. Those were the days when her skin tasted of summer melons, and she danced barefoot across the gypsy days of her youth.

"Come midnight, we're all stripped down to unbidden desires and unnamed fears," she thought. "Come midnight, ain't nothin' between us and the dark but our own feeble heartbeat and a few ragged breaths."

And she lay there feeling the beat of her heart ticking away the moments of the night.

Memories crowded in—scenes from her girlhood she had long since buried away. The bounce of guitar strings playing against her nimble fingers while an ancient mountain ballad flowed through her silken throat. Her girlhood friend, Bessie McFearon, convulsed with lilting laughter and running through the green grass of a meadow under a warm April sun. Nelson in shadowed relief against her heart bending on one knee with a tiny ring and murmuring a promise of love everlasting.

From a distance of an age, the thin strains of a fiddle floated, once again, through the thick air of an August night in the piney woods of the Missouri Ozarks.

She remembered the excitement of weaving ribbons through the ringlets of her hair and stepping into the voluminous, swelling skirts of her ball gown.

She could smell the heady scent of fresh-cut lumber in a newly-built meeting hall, hear the laughter of friends and family weaving through the buzz of cicadas and mosquitoes as she entered the room.

Her soul began to sway to a soft waltz playing in the ether, and the same joy of that fresh, young girl attending her first adult party so many decades ago consumed her—before the War Between the States tore her life apart—before tragedy and grief etched their way into the lines of her face.

The music, the soft strains of an ancient fiddle, came as a gentle whisper in the night. A breeze began to ruffle the trees in the dense forest that surrounded the memory of that old meeting hall sending up waves of sharply sweet, pine-scented air to the heavens.

The light from the meeting hall grew brighter as Mae became part of the wind, the light and the music.

And she danced away from the weight of her life and the sorrows that once bound her on earth, waltzing her way, at last, to her beloved Nelson and her long-ago lost children.

CHAPTER 10

The morning after the party, Joshua Oakley and Luther Campbell met at the schoolhouse to move furniture back inside. Cora Lee joined Alice, Ada, and Laura Cole there, as well, to clean up after the party. Ada set six-year-old Phineas to work picking up pine cones in the schoolyard to keep him from underfoot, then she set the two girls to work sweeping the dance floor.

After finishing most of the chores, Joshua and Alice walked Cora Lee home. The day had turned colder, and low-hanging clouds scuttled across a grey sky that threatened snow. The three of them hurried along, turning their coat collars up against the gusty winds that blew at their backs.

"I 'spect Granny will have some coffee on for us when we get back. I like mine with plenty of milk," Cora Lee said through her chattering teeth.

"Oh, I don't drink coffee," Alice said. "It stains the teeth somethin' awful.'"

"Coffee sounds good to me," Joshua said. "I'll take mine black and hot as a body'll stand!"

The three of them shivered and jostled each other as they clamored up onto the porch and burst through the door of the cabin.

They found Granny Mae lying peacefully in her bed with one hand folded beneath her chin, her half-opened eyes seeming to gaze at some distant, beautiful vision.

The shock of the discovery went through Cora Lee like a flood of icy water. She collapsed to the floor, stunned and trembling as a rush of air escaped her lungs in a moan. Alice gasped and ran toward the door.

"I'm goin' to go fetch Ma," Alice yelled. "You stay with Cora Lee, Joshua!"

Joshua turned to the grief-stricken Cora Lee and did his awkward best to console her. "There, now. Don't carry on so," he tried. Cora Lee burst into a torrent of tears, unable to hear him, unwilling to fight against the tide of pain that overwhelmed her.

Alice finally arrived with her mother and Laura Cole, and the two women took charge. Ada gently ushered the three young people out to the porch, then the two older women went to work to prepare Mae's body. They washed her with care and put Mae in a fresh dress. They removed the charm string of buttons from her neck and lay it aside—small mementos of Mae's life from the clothing of friends and loved ones.

Ada stripped the bed of its sheet, quilt, and pillow cases and carried them with Mae's nightgown to Cora Lee on the porch. "Here, honey. Go hang these things on the clothes line to air out. They'll be a sign to the neighbors and passersby that yer granny has passed. It's what we do."

Cora Lee numbly took the items and did as she was told, tears still falling unchecked down her face as the first few snowflakes began to fall.

"Joshua, go out and fetch us some bark off'n one of them wahoo bushes," Ada said and pointed to a group of shrubs growing across the road. "I need to make a tea to soak Mae's face cloth in. It'll keep her fresh lookin' fer her funeral."

Laura Cole came to the door and drew a deep breath. "It's about done," she said quietly. "I'll take the first watch, if you like, but I need to get back to the house and the kids shortly."

Ada nodded. "I'll send Alice down to the Dobson place to ask if Rachel and Sarah Jean can sit with her overnight. I'm sure that Ellen and Dora Oakley can come and spell them at sunrise. I'll be here 'til nightfall."

Joshua walked up and handed Ada the requested wahoo bark. "I'll go tell Pa to fix up a box fer Granny Mae," he said. He passed Cora Lee at the clothes line and stopped to give her a quick hug. "I'm miserable sorry 'bout yer granny," he said before walking out of the yard and turning toward his farm.

Cora Lee finished hanging the bedclothes and returned to the porch. Ada drew her close in a hug. "We're about done," Ada said gently. "You should go in and sit with yer granny until it's time fer the buryin'. You won't be alone."

Cora Lee nodded. Head down, she entered the cabin. She took up her place by her grandmother's side, a watchman against any evil thing that might disturb the woman's body or soul until she could be laid to rest.

***

Cora Lee spent the following weeks caught in an undertow of sorrow, swimming upstream in a river of grief. Those weeks had gradually become months, and those months had spun out the seasons.

Gradually, the fog in her mind cleared, and Cora Lee's world began to come back into view. While she didn't remember much about the days immediately following the loss of her grandmother, some of the events surrounding Mae's passing were stuck in her heart like photographs pasted in the pages of an old album.

Cora Lee carried a clear picture in her mind of her grandmother washed and laid out in a clean dress on the bed. She remembered walking behind Silas' wagon on the way to the Beautiful Gate Cemetery and standing at the gravesite. Snow fell in fat, feathery flakes that muffled the eulogy given by Old Mr. Bennett as the coffin was lowered into the ground.

All other events of the days surrounding that terrible event were a blur. While it seemed impossible that almost a year had now passed since Mae's death, Cora Lee still grieved as deeply as she had on that terrible day.

She had spent several months of the past year moving around from one cabin to another being supported by neighbors. For a short time, she tried living at her farm, but she found the place a sad, empty and lonely shell without her grandmother in it.

Alice insisted that Cora Lee come and stay with her family, and Cora Lee moved in at the end of the summer. She stayed into the fall months and helped with candle making and canning vegetables. Ada's motherly care and concern was healing, although grief is not always eager to be healed. Cora Lee still had many days she struggled to get through. On those days, Ada consoled her with stories of bygone days.

"I was yer ma's best friend in those days, ya know. We grew up together. Mary would've been so proud of you, of how you've grown into such a sweet young woman. You've changed so much since you came here as that timid little child I first met.

"Change is just a way of life, Cora Lee. Nothin' and nobody stays the same ferever. And we'll see yer ma and granny again on that happy day when we get to go home to be with the Lord."

Alice's relentless good cheer and constant talk of falling in love, first with one boy and then another, began to wear thin with Cora Lee.

"I'm sorry, Alice. I just don't feel up to playin' another 'who're we gonna marry' game with you right now. Nothing is farther from my mind after losing Granny than worryin' about something so silly as that."

Alice, in no mood for Cora Lee's continued grief and gloom, snapped back, "Well, yer about as fun to be around as a can of paint. Why don't you stop mopin' and moanin' and bringin' the whole world down in the dumps with you? Golly gee! It's been ferever since your granny passed. Why can't you just get over it?"

Cora Lee dissolved into tears, and Ada stepped out onto the porch to see what the commotion was about.

Seeing Alice upset and Cora Lee in tears, she shook her head. "You girls is gettin' along about as well as two cats in a sack! Some folks is better off bein' friends from far off!"

Cora Lee had to agree. With fall ending and another winter coming on, she decided to move on. She accepted Amanda's offer to move in with her and Silas.

Silas largely ignored their young ward although he made it clear that he resented the intrusion of their houseguest on his marriage and young family. "She can stay," he said. "Nothin' else a Christian man can do. She can't stay ferever, though. We'll move Junior out of our room and into the storeroom to make room fer the new baby that's comin'. She can sleep in there with Silas Junior 'til she's ready to move back to her own farm."

"You don't worry about Silas, Cora Lee," Amanda said, blushing at her husband's mention of her "delicate condition" and smoothing her hand over her swelling belly. "He'll get used to having you here, and I know you're going to be a great help to me with Junior and this new baby.

"There is so much work to do managing a farm like this—not only cleaning and sewing and cooking, but things like planting vegetables and canning and milking and quilting—things you might not yet have experience with. You're going to learn to make some man a wonderful wife, you wait and see."

Cora Lee said nothing, uncomfortable with the idea that her benefactors thought her a burden regardless of how hard she tried to be helpful. She determined to do her best to be even more useful—and to stay out of Silas' way as much as possible.

Amanda enthusiastically took on the responsibility of teaching Cora Lee the finer points of social graces. "You don't want to be so mannerless that polite society won't have you, do you?"

Amanda was six years older, and in Cora Lee's estimation, quite a lady. She could read and write, and, before becoming a teacher, Amanda had worked during a summer on one of the farms in the valley and experienced the "outside" world.

Amanda could sew beautifully, and she altered one of her old dresses for Cora Lee, remaking it as much as possible into an updated style. The narrower skirt and shorter hemline suited her shape, and Cora Lee was thrilled as she held it up to admire it.

"I'll save this to wear for something special," she vowed as she lay the garment on the bed and smoothed its skirt with a careful hand. "I'd hate for it to get stained or torn by wearin' it for an every-day dress!"

"Here," Amanda said giving Cora Lee a small packet. "I want you to have this, too."

Wide-eyed, Cora Lee pulled a sage-green, silk scarf with daisies in gold thread embroidered along the edges from its paper wrapping and draped it around her shoulders. "I've never seen anything so beautiful," Cora Lee gasped.

Dancing to the mirror that hung over the wash basin in Amanda's bedroom, Cora Lee twisted left and right and craned her neck to see the material that adorned her. The color matched her pale-green eyes, and she blushed prettily which only enhanced the effect of the scarf.

"Are you sure you want me to have it?" Cora Lee turned hesitantly, a surge of dread that the offer might be taken back ran through her as she waited for the answer.

"Of course! You make that old thing look perfectly stunning." Amanda laughed and walked up behind Cora Lee and leaned in to give the younger girl a quick kiss on the cheek. "I haven't worn that scarf in years, but I thought it would go perfectly with your new dress. You can wear it to the prayer meeting Sunday, if you like."

"Truly? Oh, that's so wonderful of you! I don't know how to thank you." Cora Lee turned and gave Amanda a quick hug, then she began to twirl around the small room humming a tune as she danced.

"Well, you're almost seventeen, after all. It's time you found a husband and made a family of your own, isn't it? Alice will be getting engaged to Jacob when he comes back from France, I expect, but you still haven't heard anything from—"

Amanda bit her lip as Cora Lee stopped her dance in mid-twirl, her happy expression crestfallen.

"I'm so sorry," Amanda said, quickly regretting bringing up Cora Lee's friend. "I'm sure Walter will be coming home soon, too. Robert Dobson got medically discharged and came home yesterday, and Jacob writes that he thinks the war will be over soon. You mustn't give up hope yet because you haven't received any word from Walter."

"There's work to be done, so git to it, gal." Silas' deep voice came from the doorway. "Wood box is near empty, and Junior's wakin' up in there. He'll be wantin' his lunch."

Cora Lee nodded and moved toward the door, but Silas didn't move. She hesitated, head down, and waited until he moved back a step so she could squeeze past him. A heavy hand on her shoulder stopped her.

"Take off that scarf so ya don't ruin it. That's too fine a thing to wear doin' chores."

She would have to squeeze back by Silas to return the scarf to Amanda, so she simply nodded, removed the ornament from her shoulders, folded it neatly, and tucked it into the pocket of her apron. Thankfully, Silas turned his attention back to his wife, so Cora Lee made her way down the short hallway to the kitchen and out the back door.

"Silas," Amanda said to her husband. "Why do you have to be so harsh with Cora Lee?" She moved closer and laid a hand on his arm. Looking up into his face, she pleaded with him to be more tolerant of their ward. "She's got nobody to take care of her. She does try to stay out of your way as much as she can, and she helps me around here."

Silas frowned, then his face softened. "I don't know why she rubs me so sideways," he said. "Just make sure she's earnin' her keep, is all. As long as she's not makin' more work fer ya, I reckon it's got some upside to havin' her here. But yer right to say it's about time she finds a man and makes a place of her own. We can't keep supportin' her ferever. Besides," he smiled, "she's takin' up more of yer time than she needs to—and I miss havin' all yer attention fer me and Junior."

Silas leaned down and placed a quick kiss on his wife's forehead. "Now how 'bout you put some lunch on the table. I got to be gettin' back out there. Fields won't plow theyself, and I'm burnin' daylight.'"

Amanda hurried to the kitchen stove and began to ladle out some chicken stew while Silas pumped water at the kitchen basin and washed the dust off of his hands and face. He lowered himself onto a chair at the table as Amanda put a bowl of stew in front of him. She went to the breadboard to cut him a thick chunk of bread and set that in front of him with a slab of butter.

"Cora Lee and I plan to go to the prayer meeting on Sunday up at the school house. Will you be going with us? Otis McDaniel will be there with his fiddle, so there'll be gospel singing, and your father will be doing the preaching."

"I reckon," he mumbled around a mouthful. "I'll hitch up the wagon so you gals don't get yer feet muddy by walkin'. You make sure ya don't carry Junior around—let Cora Lee tote him. That boy's near big enough to carry you." Silas laughed and swallowed another mouthful. "I 'spect the Dobsons'll be there, won't they? I need to talk to John about that calf he's been wantin' to buy off me, so I reckon I can take care of a bit of business, too."

Amanda nodded. "I'm sure they will. Rachael and her daughter, Sarah Jean, said they're going, and she always makes sure John goes with her."

Amanda brought her husband a glass of water and set it on the table. "Did you hear that John brought Robert home from the train station yesterday? Rachael

131

said poor Robert got gassed! He spent ten days in the Army hospital over in France. He was actually blind for a time and his face all blistered up and scarred. Sure am thankful Jacob's still safe!"

Silas nodded. "Jacob'll be a big help 'round here when he comes back. I think the Army's turnin' him off the bad path he was headed down. He'll make a good man, after all, I reckon. Ma and Pa's gettin' older. Boy'll need to find him a wife and take over the homeplace from 'em."

"Well, I think he's sweet on Alice."

"Yer sister don't have the foggiest idea who she's sweet on. She changes her mind more often than a cat licks its paws."

Amanda laughed. "You're right about that! He'll find him a wife soon enough, though."

Cora Lee fumbled with the door, her arms loaded with wood. She managed to open the door without dropping anything, grateful not to make too much noise and annoy Silas while he ate. She carefully delivered her load to the wood box by the stove and hurried to the storeroom to take Junior from his crib before he started crying and disturbed Silas' meal.

She lay the boy on her cot and removed his wet diaper and shirt. After she had powdered him, she put him in a fresh diaper, socks and a long-sleeve gown, then picked him up and settled him on her hip. Cora Lee gave him a quick kiss on his cheek. She carried Junior into the kitchen and handed him to Amanda, glad to see that Silas had finished his lunch and was gone.

"Can you dip up some carrots and potatoes for the baby?" Amanda settled Junior on her lap at the table. "And put a little broth into a cup to cool for him, too."

"I'm sure looking forward to Sunday," Cora Lee said as she took a plate from the shelf and fished a few of the vegetables out of the pot on the stove. "This last year has been a fair-sized test of faith for me," she said, "and I can use a fair-sized dose of God's blessings about now!"

"I think we can all do with a little bit of that," Amanda agreed.

CHAPTER 11

"Why don't you want to go? Mr. Bennett is going to be giving the sermon."

Cora Lee and Ruby sat at the table in Ruby's cabin. Pearl was out of the house, and the two young women were shelling a sack of purple hull peas harvested from the garden.

"I don't have a single, solitary use in this world to go hear that ol' hypocrite preach at me about doin' unto others," Ruby grumbled as she slid her thumb down the slick inside of another pod. The peas rattled into a large bowl in front of her, and she tossed the shell onto a growing pile at her feet. "I ain't particularly impressed with how him and the rest of the folks on this ridge has treated Ma and me. They's been friendly with Walter, mostly, but that's 'cause Walter works hard. He's a good hand, but, aside from yer granny, the rest of 'em treat us like dirt."

"But, you went to the dance when the fellas left for the war, and you were treated just fine!" Cora Lee snapped the ends off a pod, pulled the string down the middle and ran her thumb down the seam spilling peas into her bowl.

"I weren't treated no way at all, Cora Lee. I went to that shindig fer Walter—and because they was food there. Ya might a'noticed I didn't talk to nobody else."

"I saw you dancing with Roy Dale."

"Sure. I bumped into him, and he sort of felt like he had to ask me, I reckon. Then, he made some sorry excuse to escort me off the floor halfway through the song. He just walked out the door to get in the wagon to leave. Ya call that bein' particularly neighborly?"

Cora Lee couldn't say that Ruby was wrong. Most of the people on the ridge had never extended a hand of friendship to the Douglas family.

"Miss Amanda and Granny Mae and me have always been happy to spend time with you."

"Yer granny's gone. Miss Amanda has her hands full with her new family and don't have time for nothin' else but keepin' her husband happy. Livin' with Silas Bennett is full-time work in itself, ain't it? I don't know how you tolerate livin' with him."

"Silas may go around with his stinger half out, but he doesn't mean anything by it. He does spend a lot of energy on being sour, for sure." Cora Lee laughed. "He doesn't talk much, and he laughs less. That's just how he is. He treats Miss Amanda like she's made out of gold nuggets, though, so I reckon he's not all bad. But, anyway, please think about going tomorrow? You can't let other folks keep you from coming to the prayer meeting if you want to be there."

"I already said I don't wanna be there. I got no use for preachin' and singin' and such. I doubt yer friend, Alice, will appreciate you havin' me around, either."

"Well, Alice can like it or not. She'll be there with Dora and Sarah Jean, so she'll have plenty of company without me. And the preaching will do us good. Besides, Otis McDaniel is gonna be there with his fiddle, so there'll be lots of good gospel singing, too."

Ruby's face flushed red. She dropped the pod she was working on, almost knocking her bowl over. Her hands flew to her waist and twisted together in her lap.

"Why should I care if Otis—Mr. McDaniel is there or not?" she said hotly. "I work fer him, is all!"

"I didn't say you should care. I was just saying that he's gonna be there to play for us to do some gospel singing. I didn't mean anything else. Why?"

"Never mind. It ain't nothin'. Ruby stood. She took her bowl and dumped its contents into Cora Lee's bowl. "That's all the shellin' I can stand fer now. You go on home. I got other things I need to get done fer Ma."

"I didn't mean to get you upset, Ruby." Cora Lee stood and grabbed her friend's hand. "Please think about coming to the meeting with me tomorrow."

Ruby pulled her hand away. "I said I ain't goin,'" so stop wartin' me about it. I'll see you some other time."

Cora Lee nodded and left. Walking home, she pondered Ruby's strange behavior and, worried that something important might be troubling her friend, said a prayer for her.

"Dear Lord, I know you know what's on Ruby's mind, and I know whatever's troubling my friend is in your hands. I'm just praying that you'll let her know that, whatever's wrong, you're there for her if she'll just reach out and ask for your help."

The prayer meeting on Sunday was uplifting, and Cora Lee felt renewed by the message Adam Bennett had shared in his sermon. He had reminded everyone of God's love and forgiveness. He had also delivered a powerful prayer for protection of the soldiers in harm's way in Europe and asked God to deliver them back to the ridge safely and quickly. The message had reached Cora Lee's heart, and she had added her own plea for Walter's safety. Otis McDaniel's fiddle had led the singing of many of her favorite hymns, as well.

In spite of his wounds, which were still healing, Robert Dobson had attended. His right hand and face were wrapped in bandages, and everyone in attendance had shaken his good hand or hugged his neck to welcome him back home.

Halfway through the service, though, Robert began to feel weak and ill. His father had carried him to their wagon and taken him home. Adam Bennett said a closing prayer, and sent everyone home after that.

Cora Lee was sorry that the prayer meeting had ended so soon, but was glad to have been able to attend. "I guess a little bit of a service was better than no service at all," she said.

Amanda agreed. "I'm happy that we all got to see poor Robert. What a shame such a terrible thing happened to him. Hopefully, he'll recover soon."

***

Cora Lee lay shivering and delirious from fever in her old bed at her grandmother's cabin. The morning after the prayer meeting, she had walked back to her grandmother's farm to check on things. By the time she reached the gate, she already began to feel weak and the tickle at the back of her throat became a violent, suffocating cough. Suddenly exhausted, she only managed to climb the two steps to the porch and get through the door, when she staggered a few steps and collapsed on the floor.

A cool cloth now lay across her forehead, and she tossed fitfully under its weight. A cup of some noxious liquid was being pressed to her parched lips. "No," she weakly protested, unable to do more than draw enough breath to whisper the word.

"Shush, now. Lay easy." The rough voice was familiar, and Cora Lee struggled to open her eyes. It was an impossible feat, however, and, giving herself over to the relief of blessed darkness, she slipped back into the arms of unconsciousness.

Pearl Douglas, who had seen the door of Mae Campbell's cabin ajar and entered to see if anything was amiss, found Cora Lee prostrate on the floor. Shivering, coughing, and delirious with fever, Cora Lee was unaware of the aid the woman provided.

Pearl stripped the girl out of her sweat-soaked dress and moved her to the bed. After covering the patient with a quilt, Pearl left and returned to her cabin.

"I'll be gone a few days, likely," she informed Ruby as she gathered supplies—yarrow, blackberry root, and witch hazel leaf to help clear the lungs, honey to soothe the throat, and willow bark to make a tea for the fever. "You stay here, and don't you go near anyone on this ridge, ya hear. There's bad business about, and folks is dyin' left and right. Mae Clarey's granddaughter is in a bad way. I'll help her if I can. I'll bury her if I can't."

It took almost three days for Pearl's efforts to help Cora Lee struggle to wake, fighting against the wet cloth that cooled her brow and the herbal concoctions being forced between her lips.

"Shush, now. Lay easy."

Pearl had slept very little. Sitting in Mae's old pine rocker with her knees pressed against the edge of the bed, she kept close watch over her patient. She left the cabin only to relieve herself, fetch fresh water from the well, and restock the wood box.

"I wouldn't give two buttons to help if ya weren't Mae's kin and but fer yer friendship to Walter and Ruby," she muttered as she smoothed away the strands of light-brown hair plastered to the girl's sweating face. "The rest of these folks up here on this ridge can all go to the devil fer all I care. Yer granny was the only decent woman and true Christian around. I 'spect she's reapin' her rewards up in Heaven now. You go on and be with her if ya need to, but if not, you better come on back here and get well. Ain't o' no use in lingerin' halfway between this life and the next one."

Cora Lee's eyes fluttered for a moment as if in response, and then she fell into a deep sleep as her fever broke at last. She slept through most of the night until a strange wave of giddiness wafted through her mind. She giggled and woke as the sun rose, making the translucent oilcloth window glow rosy pink. Laughing, choking, gasping for air, she sat upright in the bed, aware only that the world seemed like some great joke.

"Here, now. Rest easy." Firm hands pressed against her shoulders forcing Cora Lee to lay back against the pillow. Through her bleary eyes, she made out the face hovering above her and shimmering in the candlelight.

"Walter?" Cora Lee giggled again.

"It's Miz Douglas. Walter ain't come home. I guess that's a good thing, too, with this sickness goin' 'round up here. Shush, now. You need to rest. I'll

140

come check in on you again later today. Sun's comin' up, and I need to go back to check on my Ruby."

Cora Lee sank into herself, falling into sleep that was like some great, dark pit. Satisfied that the girl had come through the worst of the fever and delirium and was now on the mend, Pearl left Cora Lee to rest. She placed a biscuit and a pitcher of water next to the bed, blew out the candle, tucked her patient snuggly beneath the quilt, and left the cabin.

The morning was cold, and mists were thick as Pearl made her way from Mae Clarey's cabin down a ravine and through the woods to her home in the holler. When she reached her cabin, she found Ruby sitting by an open fire, her few belongings tied in a bundle on the floor at her feet.

Pearl stared at the bundle, then studied Ruby.

"Leavin'?"

Ruby stood and stepped up to her mother. The desperate emotion flooding Ruby's face surprised Pearl.

"Can't stay—I—" Ruby choked. She spread her hand over the front of her skirt, flattening the fabric and revealing the slight swell of her belly.

"Oh. 'Tis that, then. Thought it might be that. Who's the sire?"

Ruby turned her face away. "Won't say."

"Won't say or can't?" Pearl sneered at her daughter.

"Won't. He's dead now, so what's the point in it?"

"What do ya plan on doin' now?"

141

"I'm goin' down to Endurance and ketch the train to Little Rock. I'll leave this wood colt at the orphan house there and get me a job. I'll be all right."

"What kinda job you think you'll be gettin'? How'll ya manage in a big place like that?"

Ruby gave a cynical snort of laughter. "What do ya think I'll do, Ma? I'll do whatever I have to do, and I'll get along fine. I'm gonna look fer information on Walter, too. They have an Army headquarters near there where I can ask after him."

Pearl turned away from her daughter. "Can't say I'm not disappointed in ya. No decent man'll have you now that yer ruined. Big cities ain't moral, and a young gal like you…"

"Moral!" The word exploded out of Ruby's mouth. "Do you think stayin' here's better? What's 'moral' about workin' yerself to death on a dried-up, rocky scratch of land like this, dressin' in rags, eating dirt, bein' shunned by neighbors? What's 'moral' about givin' yerself up like you did to a man who spent any nickel he ever got on liquor and beat the tar outta ya fer meanness. What 'decent man' runs off and leaves his family to scrape out some pitiful hell on earth fer a livin' on our own? Is that what ya want fer me, Ma? A 'decent man' like that?"

Pearl stared at her daughter as though she was seeing her for the first time. A pained expression crossed her face, but she said nothing.

Ruby shook her head and took a quaking breath. "Or maybe a man who promises to marry you, puts a

baby in yer belly, and then just—don't." Her
shoulders slumped, and she turned toward the door.
"It's time I left this mountain, anyway, Ma. There
ain't nothin' fer me here. Never was. Never will be."

Ruby stepped up to her mother and, reaching out,
touched Pearl's arm. "I'm gonna be fine, Ma. I'll send
word once I get settled in."

She drew her shawl up over her head and picked
up her bundle of clothes. Casting a final look around
the poor hovel that had been her home, she walked out
into the gray light of dawn, and disappeared into the
mists that shrouded the hills.

CHAPTER 12

Cora Lee woke a few hours later to the crowing of a rooster in the yard. Confused, weakened by her illness and disoriented at first, she lay still. *I've been ill*, was the first clear thought that passed through the fog in her mind.

Looking around at the room colored by light filtering through the oilcloth-covered window, the familiar surroundings began to come into focus. Her grandmother's rocking chair sat next to the rope bed in which she lay...the iron stove in the far corner...the low rafters overhead.

She took a deep breath, her lungs fully inflating for the first time in what seemed like a coon's age. She lay still, enjoying the simple act of breathing as she took stock of her condition. Her throat was dry and rough, but the awful scratchiness that had made her cough violently and uncontrollably was gone. She could tell that her fever had broken, and she was no longer exhausted to the point of delirium and utter collapse.

With shaking limbs, she pushed the quilt aside and, with effort, swung her bare legs over the side of the bed. Her body was feeble, and she wondered if her legs could support her weight. Pulling the quilt from the bed, she wrapped it around her shoulders and stood holding onto the rocking chair to steady herself.

With slow, shaking steps, she made her way outside and found a perch on the porch steps, grateful for the full-bodied sunshine that warmed the spot where she lowered herself. Leaning back against the porch post, she tilted her face upward with closed eyes and drew a breath of cool, fresh autumn air.

Although the air was crisp, the October afternoon sun was warm and soon baked through the quilt. She lowered the blanket from her naked shoulders to absorb its healing rays. Within a few moments, she drifted into a pleasant stupor.

"Hullo, Cora Lee."

Coming out of her semi-awake state, Cora Lee sat up and turned toward the voice. Joshua Oakley stood by the gate, a shovel in one hand and the lead rope of his mule in the other. "It looks like you pulled through. So many ain't." He shook his head. "Glad to see yer finally up and about a little."

Confused by his statements, Cora Lee pulled the quilt back up over her shoulders and stared. "Wha— what do you mean?" she stammered.

"Can I come up and sit a bit? They's a lot to tell 'bout since you been sick."

Cora Lee nodded, and Joshua tied his mule to the gatepost before walking up to the cabin. Leaning his shovel against the porch, he took off his wide-brimmed straw hat, sat down next to Cora Lee, and sighed.

"The sickness you've had, 'bout ever family's had some, too." The sun glinted on his white-blonde hair and illuminated the few white whiskers beginning to emerge on his chin. Turning his pale blue eyes to her, he studied her condition. "Looks like you come through alright, but lots of folks didn't make it."

"What are you sayin'?" Cora Lee shook her head in confusion. "Other folks been sick like me, too?"

Joshua nodded, and Cora Lee struggled to rise. "I've gotta go back to check on Amanda and Junior and make sure that they're alright!"

Joshua put out a hand and stopped her. "Ain't no need. She and the baby she was carryin' is gone. Miss Amanda's gone." He shook his head and cleared his throat. "Silas made it, barely, but he's in a bad way in the head about losin' her and that baby." His voice broke. He rubbed his eyes, then continued. "He's spendin' ever day, all day long, down at the cemetery, just broke up and cryin'. He won't talk to nobody."

"Oh, that's awful!" The thought of Silas, someone who she had always seen as so strong, so solid, so untouched by emotion, being so broken by tragedy

146

and sorrow was almost impossible to fathom. "And what about Junior? Surely the baby's safe?"

"Pa found Junior cryin' in his crib. It was only by some miracle that he got to the little boy when he did. Junior was so weak from no food or water that his cries sounded as weak as the mewl of a new-born kitten. Pa loaded up Miss Amanda and that stillborn, left Silas some water while he was recoverin,' and then took Junior to Adam and Varna Bennett. Junior's still stayin' with 'em, and they's all doin' good, now."

"But what is it that made us all so sick?"

"Robert Dobson brung it—some been callin' it the Purple Death or the Spanish Flu—when he come back from the war. He was processed back home through Camp Pike, and that disease is awful bad among the troops down there. He give it to folks at that thanksgivin' prayer meetin' where we all was celebratin' his return."

"Is he still sick? Is he getting better?"

"Robert got better, but his sister, Sarah Jean, is still fightin'. We don't know if she'll come through or not, but we're prayin' for her. They parents, Rachael and John, didn't do so good and died right quick. Poor Robert, he's still recoverin' from bein' gassed, too. He was so sick and weak, he could only manage to drag his parents out to the yard in hopes someone would come by and gather they bodies."

Cora Lee shuddered and tears welled in her eyes. "Oh, no, Joshua. That's awful. Please let Robert know, and Sarah Jean, too, if she's able to hear, that I'll come by and visit as soon as I can."

Joshua nodded. "They's no rush. Me and Dora are checkin' in ever day with all the folks that's still sick. I'm sure they'll be glad for you to visit when ya can, though, too."

Joshua was silent for a few minutes, then he continued. "There's more, if ya want me to go on."

No, I don't want you to go on. I don't want there to be more. She could only nod in shock.

"Pa found Otis McDaniel layin' up under his lilac bush. His face was turned a deep, reddish-purple. Laura Cole lost Clyde, too. She's a widow now, and her boys and baby girl is half-orphans."

Cora Lee could scarcely comprehend the magnitude of his tale. To lose so many so quickly? It seemed impossible. "What about your folks, Joshua?"

"Oh, my ma and pa and Dora didn't get sick. Pa says it's 'cause we all drink his moonshine, and that's what's kept Ol' Death from our door. Or, maybe it's just the way God planned it. Who knows?"

He grew quiet for a moment and turned his pale, blue eyes on Cora Lee's tear-streaked face. "Um, that ain't all they is to tell."

She wiped her face with her hand, clutched the quilt more closely to her, and nodded for him to continue.

"The Campbells was among the first to get sick. Luther and Miz Ada and their youngest child, Phineas, got better after a few days. But, Cora Lee—" Joshua's quiet voice trailed off.

Cora Lee's face puckered in sudden anguish and she grabbed the boy's arm. "Alice! Joshua, is Alice sick, too? Is she doin' alright?"

Joshua shook his head.

Cora Lee gasped, a tiny 'no' escaping between her pale lips as Joshua continued.

"Alice seemed to get the worst of it. When Pa and me took her, she was turned black to the very bottom of her feet. We reckon she drown in the water in her lungs, her face all covered with blood and foam from coughin' 'til she died. She weren't," he sobbed, "she weren't pretty no more. I'm so sorry."

Cora Lee wailed aloud. "Nooo! Not Alice!"

Wave after wave of grief had washed over Cora Lee as Joshua recounted the tragedies of the last several days. The things he said were so terrible that they were almost impossible to believe. Hearing how her dear teacher and mentor, Amanda, had suffered, that Sarah Jean was ill and might still die. That her and Robert's parents were gone. Old Man McDaniel's music would no longer come floating through the woods at twilight; Laura Cole left widowed with her three children.

But Alice! Sweet, Pretty Alice! It couldn't be true. The loss was too much to bear. Cora Lee was unable to speak. The shock, the devastation to their little community, the horror of it was too great, and she lowered her face to her lap, weeping uncontrollably.

It was a few moments before she realized that Joshua had stopped talking, and a few more before she regained her composure enough to speak. She wiped her eyes and nose on the corner of her quilt and sat up. She studied the pale, grim features of the young man beside her and realized that he and his family must have been carrying an awful burden over the last many days.

"We been gatherin' up the dead and diggin' graves," he said. "Pa couldn't make boxes fast enough, so some of the bodies was wrapped in quilts by Ma and Dora, and we buried 'em. We always had a little ceremony and said a prayer for 'em, though. We made sure to keep track of where they's put, and Pa's started workin' on makin' the markers for 'em."

"Oh, Joshua! It must have been terrible for you and your folks to take care of the dead like that! What can I do? How can I help?"

Joshua patted her knee. "Yer right. It's been some awful sad and sorry days. But all you need to be doin' right now is just to get well. Plenty of doin'll still need to be done when yer strong again." He stood and put on his hat.

"Folks'll be awful glad to learn ya made it. Ma'll come by later and bring some vittles. Let her know if ya need anythin'. Pa's been makin' sure folks that's been sick's had firewood and been feedin' the livestock—milkin' Silas' cow and deliverin' the milk 'round to them that needs it. I'll ask Ma to bring you some, too."

Picking up his shovel, he turned to leave. Cora Lee, still weeping, asked, "What about Ruby and her ma?"

Joshua stopped but didn't turn around. "Don't know 'bout them two," he said over his shoulder. "Nobody's said they's seen 'em."

Cora Lee watched him depart, stunned that none of her neighbors were looking in on the two women who lived by themselves in the holler. Horrified by the thought that they might be ill, or even worse, Cora Lee determined to visit as soon as her legs were able to take her there.

***

Several days of rest passed, and Cora Lee finally regained some of her strength so that she was able to pay a visit to the Douglas place. Although she had not fully recovered, she did not feel she could wait another day to check in on Pearl and Ruby.

The walk over the spongey ground through the thick woods to the holler brought back memories of the hours she had spent visiting the shack. She thought of the times she had helped skin and dress out the animals Miz Douglas hunted, had worked alongside her friends in their meager kitchen garden. She remembered the fun and adventure she had found while roaming the hills and exploring nearby caves with Ruby and Walter.

Making her way over the familiar ground to the remote cottage through the thick woods was made difficult only by foreboding and dread at what she might find when she arrived. Would Ruby and her mother be sick from this dreadful flu or even alive?

She slowed her steps as she neared her destination and lifted her nose toward the Douglas homestead. Relieved to find that the air was filled with the scent of woodsmoke, she lifted the hem of her skirt and hurried on through the woods.

A break in the trees ahead revealed the cabin. Pearl Douglas was sitting on a low, wooden bench outside the door. The woman's head was down, her chin resting on her chest, and her shoulders were slumped.

"Hello, Miz Douglas." Cora Lee approached the woman. "Are you doing alright? Is anything wrong? Is Ruby well?"

Pearl squinted her eyes at her visitor. "Ruby's gone away. She left a few days ago. I ain't got no word or nothin' from her."

"You haven't been sick, then?"

"No. We didn't go to that meetin' where everone passed it around. I wouldn't let Ruby leave the cabin while I was seein' to ya, so she didn't get that fever."

Cora Lee said nothing and sat down on the bench beside Pearl.

"My girl got herself in the family way, and she took off fer the train station. Said she's gonna leave the baby at an orphanage in Little Rock, not that anybody up on this ridge needs to hear about it." Pearl gave Cora Lee a warning glare.

"I don't go tattin' tales," Cora Lee assured her, trying to keep her shock at Ruby's condition from showing on her face. "Whatever you tell me, I'll keep to myself."

"Don't reckon she'll be a'comin' back, but I wish she would once that baby's been seen to. She's got no business in a big place like that, but I couldn't stop her goin'. She was fixed on it."

"I'm so sorry. I had no idea." It was all Cora Lee could say, but her thoughts were in a jumble.

"She had her mind set to go find a new life in the big city. Said she's gonna see if she can find somethin' out about Walter, too. I hope she'll send me word about that if she does." Pearl sounded defeated, and her shoulders slumped even more.

"Is there anything I can do?" Cora Lee, although powerless, was compelled to offer her help in any way she could. She had to do something for the woman who had tended her during her illness and delivered her back from the brink of death.

Pearl was silent for a long while, then she turned to Cora Lee with fire in her eyes. "You can go find my girl. She's a lamb in a den of lions, and she ain't got nobody to help her. Go find my Ruby."

The request took Cora Lee by surprise, and she didn't answer immediately. "The thought of leaving the mountain hasn't ever entered my mind." The request was an absurd, almost impossible suggestion.

After another period of silence, Pearl continued. "What's up here fer ya, anyway? Yer granny's gone, and you ain't got no other family up here. You should get off this mountain. Like my boy always says, they's a whole wide world out there if yer not too scared to find it. You could get a job and make yer own way like my Ruby's doin'. Why stay up here on yer own? Ain't nothin' fer ya here."

"I'll—think on it," Cora Lee stammered. "It's nothing I've considered but—but I'll think on it."

Pearl looked as though she wasn't satisfied with the answer and was about to continue pushing her request. Cora Lee quickly cut her off.

"I understand you must be worried sick about both Ruby and Walter. But the Lord is watchin' over 'em—and, I'm sure they're safe in His care."

Pearl shook her head. "Well, I reckon that's all I can ask, fer now, is that you consider it."

She rose from the bench and went into her cabin. Cora Lee sat for a few minutes, stunned, her thoughts in a whirl over the news of Ruby's condition and the impossible suggestion that she leave home to go look for her.

Slowly, she stood and started to walk back to her cabin muttering to herself, "Could I? Could I go to

Little Rock all alone? How on earth would I find Ruby in a big city like that? Impossible!"

All things are possible with God.

Granny Mae's quiet voice drifted through the tumult in her mind and brought her up short. How many times had her grandmother said those words, a reminder to trust in God when one's mind is troubled? She could feel her grandmother's comforting presence all around her as she lifted her hand to the button necklace she wore tied around her neck.

She raised her face to Heaven and pressed her lips together. "I said I'd think on it, Granny!"

CHAPTER 13

The notice read "Clean, safe accommodations for ladies of good character. Reasonable Terms, Private Room. Irma Malone, Proprietress."

Ruby tore the advertisement off the bulletin board at the train station. Clutching her bundle of belongings, she entered the depot to ask the clerk behind the ticket window for directions to the address listed at the bottom of the paper.

"Third Street is up that hill," he pointed, "and that block is about three or four streets east, I think. Might be a long walk carrying a burden."

Ruby startled at his comment and then realized the man was speaking of her clothes bundle. Her pregnancy was not advanced enough to be observed unless one looked closely. She knew she would be able to disguise it for weeks, maybe even a few months. Then she would find her way to a rescue home where she would stay until the baby was born.

Rescue home. Home for Unwed Mothers. Ruby's face burned at the thought of what her near future held. Shaking her shame away, she determined to deal with that problem only when she absolutely had to, and not a minute before.

Now she found herself sitting on an upholstered chair in the small, tidy parlor of a boarding house. She sat on the chair's edge, her bundle of belongings balanced on her knees with her hands folded on top.

"Breakfast is served at six and is porridge or oatmeal and milk. Supper is at seven and it's either soup or stew, fish on Friday. Lunch, if you have it, is on your own."

The landlady handed Ruby a piece of paper with "House Rules" written across the top. No drinking, no gambling, no dancing, no tobacco, and no foul language were on the list.

"You can call me Irma," the woman said. "The room is $5.00 a month in advance. I furnish a set of sheets, a pillow, and a bath towel. Linens are washed first Monday of the month and runs another fifty cents. No guests are allowed above the first floor, and none in the house after eight o'clock in the evening. I lock the doors at ten during the week and eleven on Saturday.

"I understand," Ruby said.

"This parlor is available to entertain guests until eight at night. It's closed to boarders on Thursday afternoons as that's when I entertain the Ladies of Virtue League. If all that's agreeable, sign here." Irma spun an open ledger book sitting on her desk toward Ruby and handed her the stub of a pencil.

"I'd like to see the room first," Ruby said.

The woman paused, nodded, and removed a ring of keys from the desk's lap drawer. Standing, she jerked her head toward the door to the hallway. "This way."

Irma led Ruby up the first flight of stairs to a long hallway with doors on each side and one door at the end. "That door on the end is your shared washroom. Make sure you don't spend too much time in there. Too many of you sharing it to linger. Make sure you clean up when you finish. If the washroom ain't available, there's also an outhouse out back, although that's more for the servants' use."

They continued up the second flight of narrow stairs to a small garret landing. The odors of cabbage and onions cooking in the kitchen below filled the air, and Ruby had to fight off a wave a nausea that threatened to overwhelm her. "Cabbage stew fer dinner?" Ruby asked, trying not to choke on the words.

Irma looked at her but did not answer the question. "Here," she said and opened one of the two doors at the top of the landing. "Like I said, rent's five dollars a month per bed." Irma held out her hand expectantly.

"Per bed? The notice said that yer rentin' out a 'private room,' not shared space."

Sharing space with another woman would be difficult. She was only four months gone, and she hoped to keep her swelling belly hidden under layers of winter clothes through the coming months. The baby wasn't due until March, and with any luck, she could manage until the last month or two undetected. By then, she would be able to slip away to some home for unwed mothers, and no one would be the wiser. Sharing a space this size with another woman would make that plan almost impossible.

The room was scarcely large enough to accommodate the two beds and small dresser it contained. The single, bare window was too filthy to allow in much light, and the floor was strewn with trash, newspapers, and a woman's clothing.

"You receive ten dollars a month in rent fer this—rabbit hutch of a room?"

"You don't want it?" The woman withdrew her hand and turned to escort Ruby back down the stairs. "I can find other takers, and they'd be happy at twice the price. But, for now, you'll be the only gal in the room. The other tenant left recently."

Ruby dug in her pocket for the money and walked over to the window. Looking out at the street below she said, "I'll take the room." She turned and handed the money to the landlady. Ruby accepted the key and closed the door on the woman. "Fer now," she added as she scanned her dingy lodgings. "Fer now."

After she had unrolled her meager bundle containing her only other set of clothes, Ruby set about cleaning the debris from the floor. She wiped the window free of as much dirt and grime as she was able using some of the newspapers scattered on the floor.

She picked up one of the papers from the floor, and the 'Help Wanted' section headline caught her eye. She smoothed the paper out on the bed and noted that the paper was only a few days old. "Good," she said to herself. "I'll study on that and maybe I can find me a job right quick."

Once the room was set to her satisfaction, she descended the narrow garret stairs and walked down the long hallway on the floor below to the shared bathroom. Hoping to find a wash bowl and pitcher with enough water to at least clean her face, she was surprised to find that the facility had a pull-chain flush toilet and running water in the sink. There was also a claw-foot bathtub with its own set of faucets for both hot and cold water in the room.

"Well, if that ain't the berries!" she said aloud as she played with the sink faucets and flushed the toilet a few times. "I think I'm gonna like the city just fine!"

Once she finished in the washroom, she returned to her rented room and studied the help wanted ads in the newspaper she had picked up from the floor. Ads were listed for waitresses and cooks and charwomen. A few places were looking for women with experience or specialized training such as stenographers, clerks, and milliners. One ad asked for a washwoman to do laundry in the yard. "With winter comin' on? Don't think so!" Ruby snorted.

Ruby kept searching and found an ad for "all types of help" at the Hotel Marion. She applied the next day and secured a job as a scullery worker. The pay, though miserly, was enough to cover her expenses. She hoped that no one would pay attention to a girl scrubbing pots and pans or notice her swelling figure.

The weeks passed quickly. Ruby kept to herself at work and, as she hoped, was generally ignored by other kitchen staff. She ate in her room and paid her rent on time, slipping the money in an envelope with her name on it under Irma's office door to minimize any contact with the landlady.

Luckily, the room she occupied remained her own as no other tenant moved in, and she successfully continued to keep her condition hidden under layers of thick winter clothing. As the holidays approached and passed, Ruby was more and more hopeful about her plan to keep her pregnancy secret until her baby would be born sometime in the early spring.

She worked hard at her job at the hotel and, as she hoped, none of her co-workers paid attention to her. In November news came that the war in Europe had ended, and there was a national celebration. The hotel increased its business as people flooded into town seeking news of their fathers, husbands, and sons fighting in Europe. Like Ruby, they hoped to find information about when the troops would be returning.

A new girl was hired to help Ruby keep up with the increase in work in the hotel restaurant. Ruby was alarmed when she learned she would be sharing her workspace.

The scullery was a smallish room off the hotel's main kitchen, dedicated to the work of boiling water in large tubs for soaking and scrubbing large pots and pans and for washing and ironing table linens. There was also a slop sink where plates and cooking utensils were rinsed before placing them into steaming sinks of soapy water and then rinsing, drying, and storing them on shelves to be used again and again.

Because the room was small, there was nowhere that Ruby could go to keep her condition hidden. She began to panic, worried that she would have to quit her job or be exposed and fired. It was too soon to lodge at a maternity home.

But, the new girl immediately put Ruby at ease. "Don't worry. What's it to me? I ain't gonna squawk. I'm just here to get enough money to buy me some swanky clothes so I can get a job at a dancehall. This job's for deadbeats who ain't goin' nowhere. You should check into the dancin' life once you drop that kid. The swells all love a redhead, you know. You'd be a real-life Sheba at one of the dance emporiums in town. I'm already hired at the Something Wonderful Dance Emporium down off Rock Street, but I need to buy me a dancing frock and shoes. When you're ready, look me up there. My name's Edith."

***

He was born clutching his dark head with balled-up, red fists. Blue and shriveled and with a strong heart beating in his chest, he drew his first breath and wailed a challenge to the world as if ready to fight.

Ruby looked at the newborn lying in the muck from her body. His struggle for breath seemed a distant war, and she was strangely unaffected by the child's battle. The midwife, a stern woman who wore her judgement like armor, silently took the tiny mass away after severing the gelatinous cord still connecting him to his mother. The midwife's assistant went about the business of cleaning the bloody, wet mess in the bed and putting Ruby into a gown that was only somewhat less stained than the linens she replaced.

"You'll be wantin' to feed him soon. We'll bring the wee one back as soon as the nurse cleans him up for you." The assistant was a roundish, older woman who spoke with a soft, motherly voice that was meant to be soothing, but Ruby would not be comforted.

"He'll not be havin' more of me," Ruby snapped. "He's taken enough. Feed him yerself or give him a bottle if he's hungry."

"Oh, now, Miss, you'll feel differently once you hold him." She turned to go but stopped and went back to the bedside. "It isn't unusual to be a bit irritable right after, but you'll be up and about and feeling strong again in no time. You'll see."

163

She turned and left as the midwife came back into the room clutching a clipboard in boney, claw-like hands. "Baby's name?" she asked. Her voice was as sharp and unfeeling as a shard of arctic ice.

"Micah—just Micah, no middle."

"Father's name?"

Ruby didn't answer but turned her face to the wall in silence. The midwife knitted her brow and marked "bastard" on the form.

"You'll be needin' to sign this so we can file it with the clerk," she informed her coldly. "I'll leave it here next to you so's you can read it. If you can't sign, you can mark your 'x' and one of us'll witness it."

The midwife walked out of the room without looking back, but not without leaving behind her ill-concealed opinion. The bite of it washed over Ruby so strongly it was like a punch in her belly. She picked up the birth registry form. Without reading the information, she signed her name.

Later that morning, the assistant brought her son to her. He was wrapped in a coarse blue blanket.

"The little boy's hungry, Miss. He won't take the bottle. Stubborn little mite he is," she laughed. "He'll be having his mum or starve to death. You must take him and try," she added softly. "Here, take him now."

There was nothing Ruby could do at that point but to accept the bundle being gently forced into her arms. Her arms were clumsy, at first, but the assistant helped her to adjust the baby so that his weight rested more easily on her body.

She hesitantly pulled back the corner of the blanket that covered the baby's head. Ruby studied the face of the child and did not see, as she had so fearfully expected, the face of his father. Instead, the face of an angel lay cradled in her arms. An angry, stubborn, strong little angel with his mother's blood in his veins.

Reluctantly at first, then with some determination, she unbuttoned her gown and placed the baby to her breast, gasping as he latched on. And she wept— quiet, private tears that were for her and her son alone.

CHAPTER 14

Winter passed slowly to spring, and 1919 began boldly beautiful on Bennett's Ridge. Lush green grasses and fields of early wildflowers soon covered the hills in blankets of rustic charm, and as winter slipped into spring, Cora Lee turned seventeen.

Unwilling to return to the sadness that filled Silas' home after the illness that had cost so many so much, she had spent the long days of the past winter in her grandmother's cabin. The familiar objects of her home now comforted rather than grieved her, and she found she had been content to spend the last few months there. Only the request the previous fall from Pearl Douglas to leave the mountain and go in search of Ruby weighed on her otherwise easy mind, and the warming days of early May began to stir in her an unfamiliar restlessness.

She found her thoughts turning again and again to Walter, wondering where he was and if he was injured or ill. Did he think of her at all? Had he truly asked her to wait for him, or had that only been a dream?

So much had happened in the time that he had been away. He had sent no letter, and she didn't know if any of her short notes had reached him over the last many months. Would he still want to marry her when he returned?

News that the war had ended last November reached Bennett's Ridge over Christmas, but neither Pearl nor Cora Lee knew if or when Walter would return home. The worry that he may have died of the Spanish Flu or been killed on some battlefield across the ocean, as so many had, was too dark a thought to entertain. Cora Lee steadfastly refused to consider it.

One short note had been received from Ruby in December delivered to the postmaster in Endurance and brought by Charles Oakley on his return from town. Cora Lee had carried it to Pearl.

"Dear Ma, hope this note finds ya doin good. Found work and am rentin a room at a boardin house fer women on 3rd Street near the train station. News here is all about the war bein over and about how women votin is a good or bad thing and people makin how much licker a man drinks any of their business. I wrote Walter soon as I got here to let him know where I'm at but I aint got no word back yet so dont know where he is. Ruby"

Cora Lee could not help wondering how Ruby and Walter were doing and if she would see them again anytime soon. She sat on her grandmother's porch unraveling an old, crocheted scarf and wrapping the yarn into a ball to be reused later. The sun was out after several rainy days, and she was enjoying the warming spring weather.

Pearl's request that she go to Little Rock and find Ruby continued to trouble her. As Cora Lee weighed the pros and cons of going away from Bennett's Ridge, the arguments for going and staying continued to see-saw in her head, each overriding the other. The idea both frightened and excited her, but she could not find a way to imagine herself actually taking such a bold step.

Exasperated, Cora Lee shook her head to clear it. She wound the last strand of yarn and put the ball aside. A wagon rattled up the rutted road as she stood. Shielding her eyes, she looked eastward as Mr. Oakley's wagon approached her cabin.

"Hullo, missy," Charles cried.

Cora Lee lifted her hand in greeting, stepped down from the porch, and walked to the gate as Charles drew his wagon to a stop in front of the cabin.

"How do, Mr. Oakley," she said. "You been to town this mornin' already?"

"Just comin' back, and I brung another letter from that Ruby Douglas." Charles hopped down from his seat on the buckboard and, reaching into his shirt pocket, produced an envelope. "Reckon it might have some news of her brother?"

"That's the hope, Mr. Oakley!" Cora Lee took the letter and could scarcely contain her excitement. As Charles climbed back into his wagon, slapped the reigns and his wagon moved away, she turned to dash back to the cabin and cried over her shoulder, "Thanks awfully for bringing it! Gotta take it to Miz Douglas right away!"

Tucking the envelope into her apron pocket, she entered the cabin and threw her grandmother's old shawl over her shoulders. She could hardly wait to reach the Douglas cabin and deliver it to Pearl.

She found Pearl sitting at the table inside the cabin, cleaning her shotgun. Parts of the disassembled gun were spread out on the rough-hewn table, and Pearl rubbed a small piece she had in her hand with an oily rag. Raising her head as Cora Lee entered, Pearl said nothing as she waited for Cora Lee to speak.

"Mr. Oakley brought another letter from Ruby! I carried it right here as soon as I got it."

Pearl dropped the rag and gun piece on the table, started to rise, then sank back into her chair. "Well, go on and read it, then."

Cora Lee opened the envelope with trembling fingers and pulled out the letter. Opening the tri-folded paper, a dollar bill fell out onto the floor. Cora Lee picked up the bill and set it on the table before beginning to read.

Dear Ma hope ya is still well. I had the baby a solid boy and Im keepin him and named him Micah. I been checkin at the Army headquarters but all they tell me is they aint had a word about Walter bein killed or hurt or sick which is good news I reckon and they say its gonna take months fer all the troops to come home from over there. Sent him another letter but still no reply. This dollar is all I can send fer now but will try and send more when I can. Ruby

Pearl stood, her face crumpled in worry. "Now she's decided to keep that young'un, she's gonna need help." Pearl came around the table and picked up the dollar bill. "Take this here dollar note, and go down to Little Rock and find her." She gripped Cora Lee's wrist and pressed the bill into her hand. "I don't need this money. Use it to go find my girl."

"I don't know how on earth I can do that! Leave home and venture out on my own?" Although she had been thinking about it throughout the winter, the idea still frightened Cora Lee. It was an unreasonable, almost impossible thing to ask of her.

"Home!" Pearl snorted. Her grip on Cora Lee's wrist tightened. "Home is where and what ya make it."

Cora Lee shrugged and shook her head. "I—I've only ever wanted a home. Granny gave me a home and a family—I have a belongin' place here. I don't want to leave it."

"Well, you had that fer a time. That's luckier than lots of folks." Pearl paused, and her voice softened. Releasing her grasp on Cora Lee's wrist, she stepped back. "Home ain't so much a place as it is a feeling about where yer at and who yer with. It's friends and family. You ain't got no friends here anymore, and ya ain't got no family. Ruby and her baby, that's who's yer friends and family now, and they need you. Why stay up here on yer own?"

Cora Lee looked Pearl squarely in the face, and the challenge Pearl had issued grew in the silence between them. At last, Cora Lee nodded.

"I'll think on it some more," she said. "It's all I can promise you for now. I'll pray on it and ask the Good Lord what I should do."

Cora Lee spent a few days considering Pearl's request. She prayed for answers, but she received no sign or even any nudging from the angels on what she should do. There was only a rising disquiet in her soul. As warm-weather restlessness increased, so, too, did the idea of leaving the ridge continue to trouble her.

This night, like many others since she had carried Ruby's letter to Pearl, she stepped out onto the porch to try to clear her head and ask for guidance. She leaned against a corner post in the cooling night air as a bright, full moon rose above the ridge peaks. Fear of leaving home, mixed with images of Walter's face and worry over Ruby's situation, jumbled together in her thoughts.

She bowed her head and prayed, "Lord, show me what I should do."

A gentle breeze brushed across her cheeks like a whisper. She took a deep breath and lifted her face to the night sky. A comforting peace filled her, and the words "*trust and be strong*" drifted through her mind.

She squared her shoulders and lifted her chin. "You're going, and that's final!" The words came as a definitive answer along with a sudden sense of relief. The decision was made.

With a determined nod of her head toward the rising May moon, Cora Lee went into the cabin, packed a bag, and made plans to find a ride to the train station in Endurance. She took the dress that Amanda had remade for her off its peg and lovingly laid it over a chair. She smoothed the fabric and lay the green, silk scarf alongside it, ready to be worn the next day as she began her journey.

Cora Lee pulled the money she had saved through the years from its hiding place under the bed and counted it, adding the dollar Pearl had given her. Satisfied that there was enough to buy train fare and lodging until she could find work, she made ready for bed.

She banked the fire in the stove, changed into one of Mae's old nightgowns, re-braided her hair, and climbed into bed, snuggling deeply under the quilt. Lying there, she remembered the first time she had slept in this bed that long-ago wintery night, snuggled close to her grandmother so safe and warm and loved.

She closed her eyes and said a prayer asking for traveling grace.

"Please God, my Father, watch over me. And keep Walter and Ruby safe—and baby Micah safe, too. And please bring Walter home soon."

The next morning broke warm and bright. Cora Lee, with no loss of her previous night's determination, experienced a dawning excitement about her trip as she began to tidy the cabin. She wanted to leave everything secure, clean, and in order when she departed.

Who knows when or if I'll ever be back.

As she moved through the cabin, she rubbed the buttons on the string tied at her neck, touching each disk as if the necklace were a rosary. Each of the charms was a memory, and, although not all of them were her memories, they were each a part of her family history. One button came from her mother's wedding dress, one from Grampa Nel's work shirt, one from Granny Mae's nightgown, and another from her grandmother's girlhood friend, Bessie McFearon, who drowned in the Yazoo so long ago.

Cora Lee had added two buttons of her own, too. The grey button was from the collar of one of Walter's old shirts, and the button made from shells was the one she had traded with Alice at a pie-supper prayer meeting when they were children.

The charm string around her neck comforted her. Wearing the necklace reminded her that she was loved—and, yes, lucky, too. As long as the string remained unbroken, she believed nothing would break the history and friendship she shared with the giver no matter how long ago they had lived or how far away they might be.

With one last look around the cabin, she assured herself the place was secure. She gathered her bag and set out for the Oakley's farm with a plan to ask Joshua to carry her to the station in Endurance where she would catch the midnight train to Little Rock.

And begin what she hoped would be a grand new adventure.

CHAPTER 15

Walter walked along the sidewalks in the market area of Brest, looking in shop windows and watching the residents of the bayside town going about their daily affairs. The day started off sunny but was now clouding up as he set off from his barracks. The early May air held the slight scent of a coming storm but, even if it rained, Walter was determined to enjoy his day off in the city despite his ever-growing desire to leave Europe and the horrors of war behind him.

The French town was beautiful, and it had many interesting places to explore—a medieval tower and castle, the wide and glassy Penfeld river, and the ocean shore where numerous quaint cafes offered delicious food and wine and gorgeous sunset views on the western horizon.

How excited I was to travel, he thought. *It was all I thought I wanted, but all I want now is just to get back stateside and go home.*

Although the war had ended five months ago, the military was slow to demobilize the one-and-a-half million men and women it had sent to fight the "War to End All Wars." Debarkation had been underway for over three months, and ancillary personnel were being given first priority.

Walter knew he was fortunate to be among the troops in France being debarked first, and not among the troops from the Western Front who would be the last to return home. Either way, there were few ships to accommodate the number of defense forces waiting for a ride, and he and his fellow soldiers were impatient for space on one to open up for them.

The French set up training classes in skills and trades to keep anxious service personnel busy and out of bars and barfights. The upsurge of violence and drinking in the port city where men and women were waiting for a seat on a ship home was getting out of hand. American and English doughboys were wearing out their welcome. Walter sighed and pushed against his frustration at having to wait longer to return home.

He stopped in front of the window of a small shop to peruse the items on display. *Boutique de Souvenirs* was painted on the window, and his attention was drawn to a hunting knife lying on a table next to its leather sheath. The blade seemed well turned, the handle sturdy, and it had a gut hook on its tip.

Ma would like that, he thought. An unexpected melancholy washed over him, an ache to return to the simplicity and familiarity of home. *I'll get it fer her if I can afford it.*

He couldn't see a price on the knife, so he entered the shop to inquire. A brass bell hanging over the door rang to announce his presence and, within a few seconds, a young woman emerged from behind a blue curtain at the back of the shop.

She was petite and blonde and very beautiful. She wore a short, chemise-style dress with a squared neckline trimmed with a draped collar, and her waist was loosely tied with a sash. Her curly blonde hair was bobbed, and she had fashioned a finger wave on each cheekbone. Little enameled earrings dangled from her earlobes. They caught the light as she walked toward Walter drawing his attention to the curve of her neck.

Walter, embarrassed to find himself staring at her with his mouth agape, cleared his throat and stammered "*Bonjour. Combien coûte…?*"

The young clerk twittered a laugh and, looking him up and down, noticed his uniform of an olive tunic, loose tapered breeches tucked into canvas leggings and boots, and a khaki-brown Montana-peak styled hat. "*Bonjour.* You are American—a 'doughboy,' yes?" Her English was very good, and her accent, though heavy, was charming.

Relieved that he would not have to struggle with his French, Walter pointed at the knife and asked "How much for this?"

The girl picked up the knife from the table and, turning it over, read the price from a small sticker on the back of the blade. "Only twenty francs."

Walter calculated the price. "It looks like a good little frog sticker."

He took the knife from her hands, noticing her delicately shaped fingers. He ran his thumb across the blade's edge testing its sharpness and the quality of the steel. "That's about three and a half dollars. Pretty expensive fer me." He moved to return the piece to its place on the display table.

"Here," she lay her hand on his arm and stopped him. "I let you have it for only twelve francs, yes? And the sheath, too. See how well the leather is tooled." She slid a glance at him coyly and smiled.

"Good. Yes, fer that price, I'll take it."

"*C'est pour offrir*? It is a gift? Perhaps—for your girl back home?"

Walter shook his head. "Not fer a girl, no. It's fer my ma. She hunts."

"Wonderful! I will wrap it nicely for your mother." She took the knife and its sheath toward the back of the shop and disappeared behind the curtain.

Walter could not keep his eyes from following her, from appreciating the sway of her hips and the way her blonde curls bounced as she walked. He shook his head and thought of Cora Lee.

He pictured her as he'd seen her so many times, barefoot and muddy from working in the garden or sweaty and disheveled from chopping wood or cooking over the iron stove. Was she waiting for him as he asked her to, or had she forgotten him and taken up with someone else?

The idea that she might be with another fella was like a stab in his gut, and he pushed the thought from his mind. If she was still his, as he hoped, he would take a gift for her as well. He began to look around the shop for something affordable and easy to pack.

The store was small and cluttered with trinkets and souvenirs. Shelves were lined with delicate porcelain figurines, carved wooden boxes, dainty tea sets, and embroidered linen handkerchiefs. Artistic paintings in the newly-popular art deco style hung on the walls alongside vintage photographs of well-known landmarks and tourist sites around Europe.

Walter walked down a row of shelves and tables filled with colorful glass vials with beautiful crystal stoppers, lace bags filled with potpourri, vases of silk flowers, snow globes, and various seashells. He picked up a small, silver-backed mirror and studied it.

"Here you are. It is all wrapped up well. It will make the trip back to your mother safely. Your mother will like it, I am sure."

"I'd also like this," Walter said as he handed her the little mirror.

"Also, for your mother?"

If Cora Lee had not waited for him, then yes, he would give it to his mother. "Perhaps."

"Very good." She smiled as if pleased.

The sales clerk returned to her curtained alcove to wrap the mirror, and Walter waited patiently for her return. He wouldn't normally spend money on trinkets, but he didn't want to return empty handed from such a long time away. He imagined how thrilled those two important women in his life would be to receive something from him coming all the way from France.

Besides, he reasoned, he'd been able to save just about every dollar of his pay. It was his hope that he and Cora Lee would use the money to open up a machinery and automobile repair shop in Endurance. He believed he could make a good living at that occupation. A good enough living to keep them both comfortable and raise a family.

After Walter had completed the purchases, he thanked the clerk. As he turned toward the door, a clap of thunder shook the walls, and the sky opened up in a torrent of pounding rain. Sheets of water cascaded down the shop window, and another bolt of lightning split the clouds.

"Seems like I'll be stuck here fer a time. That's an awful goose drowner out there."

The girl looked puzzled at his description of the storm and then broke into a cheerful laugh as his meaning became clear. "Not to worry," she giggled. "This little cloud burst will pass soon, I think. I will make us some *chocolat chaud*—hot chocolate while you wait, no? Come with me."

She motioned with her hand for Walter to follow her into the back room where a kettle was on a small electric hot plate. She flipped a switch to turn on the burner, removed two pink cups and saucers from a shelf, and opened a decorative tin of cocoa.

Examining the cozy room, Walter noted a chair and a desk with a crook-necked lamp leaning over a pile of receipts and files. A stack of boxes leaned in one corner full, he supposed, of additional merchandise. A chest of drawers topped with a colorful scarf, some books, a velvet pillow bristling with hatpins, and two brass candlesticks took up much of the remaining space. He sat down on a stool next to the desk and removed his hat, hanging it on one knee.

"What's yer name, miss?" Was it disloyal to Cora Lee to ask? He wondered if he might be flirting.

"Gabrielle Garnier. Friends call me Gigi, and so may you if you like. And you?"

"Walter. Walter Douglas."

"Well, *Monsieur* Douglas…"

"Just Walter."

"Well, Walter, this is a *tres agréable* way to spend an afternoon, no? Perhaps the rain will continue, and we will be trapped in this comfortable salon all day." She smiled and cocked her head coquettishly.

Walter shifted in his chair and cleared his throat as his hostess handed him a cup and saucer and took her seat at the desk. "What shall we discuss to pass the time?" she asked and smiled at him.

Walter tried to think of something to say and finally managed to ask, "This is a swell little store you got here. Do you own it?"

"My father's. I work here to help him with the sales. My father does the buying of the merchandise and keeps the books and does the banking."

"That sounds nice. Do you like it—workin' in sales, I mean?"

She sighed. "It gives me something to do, I suppose. And what of you? How do you spend your time while waiting to return home?"

"We—I mean me and some of the boys is takin' classes, so I mostly do that. Ain't much else to do except to go out drinkin' and carryin' on in town. I don't do much of that. Don't see no sense in it."

"What classes do you take?"

"I'm studyin' about workin' on gasoline engines. I'm learnin' a little French, too, but, as I demonstrated earlier, the lessons ain't sinkin' in too good, I think."

Gabrielle laughed. "No! Don't say so. I could almost understand all the words you said, *mon ami.*"

Walter briefly joined in her amusement. As their laughter died away, an awkward silence filled the room. Walter blew a cooling breath over the top of the cup in his hand and took a sip of the cocoa. The liquid was thick and rich, and he found he liked the sweet, hot liquid. He took another swallow and put his cup back on the saucer. He awkwardly held the drink over his lap for a few seconds then carefully slid it onto the corner of the desk.

The room was warm, and he pulled at the high collar of his wool tunic, uncomfortable with the need to make additional small talk. He could hear that the rain was no longer pounding on the roof; it sounded like it was slacking off and stopping. Rising, he flicked the curtain aside and looked out at the view of the street through the large front window.

"The sun's comin' out. I reckon I need to be goin'." He nodded at the cup on the desk and put on his hat. "Thank ya fer the chocolate."

Picking up his two packages, he walked out of the office toward the door at the front of the shop. Gabrielle followed closely in his wake. He started to exit the store, then stopped and turned back to Gigi. "Is there a place to have lunch near here?"

"Very near is a *très bon café*. It is my lunch hour. Come. I will show you."

Before he knew what was happening, Gabrielle pinned on a wide-brimmed hat, locked up her shop, and took Walter by the arm. She walked with him the two blocks to the café, pressing warmly against his side. He could smell the lingering rain in the air mixed with the delicate scent of her perfume and feel the soft swells of her body against him.

His head swam with desire. Desire to forget the awful gruesomeness of war and death and carnage, of rats and lice and mud, suffocating plumes of sulfuric smoke, and the screams of missiles, horses and men.

Desire for tenderness, and normalcy, and for the gentle touch of a woman. To be with Cora Lee back among the hills and valleys of home.

They found the café largely deserted. A few men in suits occupied a table in the corner, and two elderly women in hats elaborately trimmed with ostrich feathers and lace sat near the door. The *maître d* led Walter and Gabrielle to a table by an over-sized picture window overlooking the street freshly washed and glistening from the rain. Within moments, a waiter appeared and handed them each a menu. Walter scanned the list and ordered two glasses of chilled white wine.

The waiter brought their drinks and stood waiting to take their orders. Walter ordered a sausage dish made with the bold flavors of tarragon and sage; she preferred a delicate dish of sole seasoned with lemon and thyme. He ordered for her, remembering that his mother once told him that "ladies never speak to wait staff."

The girl across from him was a delicate, porcelain-skinned doll who blushed and tossed her head coquettishly when she laughed—the tinkling twitter of a music box escaping through her perfect Cupid's bow mouth. He studied her surprised that such a girl would have lunch with him. He felt awkward in his shabby, badly mended army uniform and embarrassed by his calloused, beefy hands, sure that every rough edge of his life was on display.

The waiter delivered their dishes, and Walter was thankful for the interruption. He had exhausted the questions he had asked to keep the conversation light—carefully appropriate questions about her work and life and home. He was saving conversations about the weather for a chat over their coffee, and perhaps an observation about the latest moving picture shows for the walk back to her shop after lunch, guiltily thinking their conversation might lead to another engagement.

"Would—would ya care to have lunch with me again sometime?" he stammered. And he was thunderstruck when she blushed the most gorgeous pink and said, "Yes."

He immediately regretted his impulsive invitation, and he wondered why he would have asked for another lunch date with this girl. Yes, she was pretty and seemed sweet. But she wasn't his Cora Lee.

They sat together over a meal he could ill afford in one of the nicer cafés in Brest. He suddenly could hardly imagine being able to swallow the food that the waiter had put in front of him. He sat and watched her as she ate and attempted to make conversation as he toyed with the sausages on his plate.

"This is a fancy place. You come here often?"

"*Oui.* It is very good here the food. I am happy you like it." Gabrielle glanced at him. "Tell me about your family," she said as she forked the tiniest bite of fish into her pretty mouth.

Walter sucked in his breath, surprised and unprepared for her question. He looked down at his plate for a moment as heat bloomed in his face. What could he tell this perfect, petite, cultured girl that wouldn't shock and disgust her?

Should he confess that his mother was a slattern who lived in the meanest cabin in a poor, backwoods mountain holler? That he was uneducated and could barely read and write? That he and his sister had two different drunkards for fathers?

Should he tell her that his sister was the mother of a bastard and working in some boozy dancehall making her living as a ten-cents-a-grab-and-grind dancer? The letter he had received from Ruby informing him of her situation had almost sickened him. He could not wait to get back to the States to find her, make her see sense, and talk her out of the kind of life she was living.

"Ma's just a woman," he mumbled. He stuffed a bite of his lunch into his mouth, almost choking on the sausage and suddenly eager for the date to be over. Now, he wished desperately that he had not asked her for another lunch.

"Go on," Gabrielle prodded and leaned forward, eager to hear more. The low, square neckline of her dress revealed the tops of her breasts as she pressed against the table's edge. Her perfume drifted across the table mixed with the odor of her fish and his spicy sausage, and his stomach lurched. He swallowed hard before he answered.

186

"She's what some folks call a 'hillbilly,' and she lives in the Missouri Ozark mountains. She raised me the best she could. I don't know a lot about her." Walter shifted uneasily in his chair, beginning to get annoyed that the topic had been raised. "She's just a mother. I never asked her much about her life. Maybe I should do that when I go back home."

Embarrassed and afraid that he might disgust this perfect girl with more information, Walter pushed his plate away and raised his hand to call for the check. He'd shared too much.

"I don't like to talk about all that," he said, irritated now and wanting the date to end.

She finished her meal in silence as they waited for the check to arrive. Walter observed her as she ate, and she fluttered her eyelashes at him playfully. *Her eyes are the most unremarkable, dull shade of brown,* he thought, remembering how Cora Lee's eyes changed from green to blue to gray depending on her mood—how they had shone in the moonlight the night he had kissed her goodbye in what seemed an age ago.

"I'll walk ya back to yer shop," he said.

Walter paid the bill, and the pair of them stepped out of the restaurant onto the sidewalk leading back to the curio shop. Although the rain had stopped, the clouds remained. The air had taken on a heavy, damp feel. Gabrielle again took Walter's arm and began to fill the silence between them with empty chatter.

"Thank you so much for the lunch, *mon ami*. I enjoyed my dish of fish very much. Do you think you would like to try there again? If no, I know of another place—a bit more *romantique* where we can dine together next time."

Walter stammered, "Um, yes—well, I'll have to see what my schedule is. I'm not sure when I'll have another day off…"

The two were approaching the gift shop when Gabrielle stopped and turned to Walter. Reaching up on her toes, she put her gloved hand behind his neck and pulled his face toward her lips giving him a loud kiss on his cheek.

"You are a dear man! I look very much forward to seeing you again," she trilled.

"Hey! Ho, there!" a male voice rang out from across the lane. "I swear, if it ain't Walter Douglas, I don't know who else it could be!"

Walter, stunned by Gabrielle's bold move, spun away from her toward the shouted greeting. Lucas McDaniel was crossing the street toward them. Surprised, and happy to see a familiar face, Walter grinned and hastily detached himself from Gabrielle's grip on his arm.

"Lucas! Don't this take the rag off the bush!" Walter stepped forward and enthusiastically shook Lucas' hand. Although he wasn't who Walter had considered a friend, he was still happy to see a familiar face from home. "What're ya doin' here?"

"Shippin' home! Got me a seat on the ship leavin' out tomorrow. Thought I'd spend my last day seein' the town one more time, though truth be told, I've had about enough of these here Frenchies to last me a lifetime—present company excepted, Miss." Lucas turned toward Gabrielle, removed his Montana-style hat, and extended his hand. "I'm Lucas McDaniel. I know Walter from back home."

Gabrielle blushed pink and twittered a small laugh. *"Bonjour."* She fleetingly allowed Lucas to take the tips of her gloved fingers in his grasp.

"How 'bout you, Walter? You got a date yet?" Lucas spoke without taking his eyes away from Walter's pretty little companion.

Walter shifted his feet uneasily and swallowed hard. "Date? Well, me and Gigi here talked about maybe goin' to lunch again, but we ain't got nothin' set up."

A look of surprise crossed Lucas' face and, turning his attention back to Walter, he laughed. "No! I meant do ya have a date fer shippin' back home? Do ya have a seat assignment, yet?"

"Oh! No, not yet. I'm checkin' the ship lists ever day, but my number ain't come up."

"Well, I'm sure yer time'll come sooner or later. They can't keep ya here ferever."

"That's the hope!" Walter jumped a little as Gabrielle again took his arm and hugged herself close to his side. "Plannin' on goin' back to work yer farm?" he asked.

"Nah! I had plenty enough of farmin' life. I'll either sell or rent out the old home place. I've saved up my pay, and I think I'll move to the big city. I met a buddy here that's offered me a job sellin' Woodsmen of the World insurance down in Little Rock. I'm gonna give that a whirl and see how it works out."

"Well, it seems like you have it all laid out fer yerself. Maybe I'll run into ya sometime again. Have a smooth trip back, and say 'hullo' to the folks back home, if ya happen to run into any of 'em," Walter said as Gabrielle began to pull him away.

Lucas watched the couple walk away as a sly grin spread over his face. Walter didn't hear Lucas mumble, "Guess ol' Walter got himself a new gal."

CHAPTER 16

C ora Lee stepped off the train and onto the station's platform gripping her suitcase in one hand, the scarf that Amanda had given her clutched tightly at her neck in the other. The noise and bustle of travelers coming and going disoriented her. She squeezed through the milieu to take up a position against the safety of the brick wall of the station house until the crowd began to clear. After a few minutes, the train pulled away from the depot bathing the platform in a suffocating cloud of steam.

A group of soldiers gathered around a table where three women wearing sashes across their chests that read "Ladies Relief League" were handing out coffee, oranges, and cigarettes. She searched the soldiers' faces, but she did not find Walter among them.

"That would have been an almost impossible turn of events," she mumbled as she turned toward the door that led into the station's large waiting room.

Making her way inside, she approached one of the ticket clerks at one end of the room. "Could you tell me how to find a boarding house on Third Street near here? I'm hoping to find a friend who wrote that she has a room there, but she didn't give the address."

The clerk, a pudgy, middle-aged man wearing a black visor on his balding head, looked up from the ledger book he was reading and smiled. "New in town I suppose, miss? Third Street is up at the top of that hill." The clerk pointed the way with a stubby, ink-stained finger. "As to any boarding house up there, you'll have to inquire from door to door."

Cora Lee thanked him, and he went back to working on his ledger. She walked out of the station office, squared her shoulders, and began the trek up the hill.

The two blocks from the train station to Third Street made for an easy walk. The morning was sunny and warm, and Cora Lee experienced a quick surge of excitement at the thought of seeing her friend again. She reached the corner and looked at the homes on both sides of the pretty, tree-lined street. The houses were clean and neatly kept, though not grand or stately. She decided to start by knocking on the door of the houses on each of the four corners, hopeful she would not have to search much farther to find information on Ruby.

"If she doesn't live in one of them, perhaps the residents may be able to point the way to any boarding houses on the street that they know of," she reasoned.

The first two houses proved unsuccessful, but the woman who answered the door of the third house gave Cora Lee addresses of two boarding houses closer to Main Street to the east. Cora Lee thanked the woman and made her way down the street.

The first address led her to a white clapboard three-story home set well back from the street. She walked up a long concrete path to three wide steps leading up to a covered porch. The front door was painted bright blue, and a sign that read "Irma Malone's Boarding House" hung above it. Cora Lee rapped on the door and took a step back to wait.

A short, middle-aged woman with iron gray hair soon answered. Wiping her hands on the front of her apron, the woman eyed Cora Lee up and down, then barked a clipped "Yes?"

"I'm searching for a friend who may be a resident here. Her name is Ruby Douglas—a redhaired girl about my age. Might she be renting a room here?"

The woman narrowed her eyes. "Was. Ran her off when I discovered she was expecting a baby. I run a decent place here, and I don't allow no unmarried women of loose morals to board in my home. Sent her packing. If you're a friend of the likes of her, you can get off my porch and be on your way, too!"

The door slammed in Cora Lee's face before she could ask the woman where Ruby went. She raised her fist and knocked again, but the woman did not answer. Disappointed, she turned away from the door and descended the steps to the sidewalk below the porch. "What do I do now?" she said aloud.

"Psst! Miss!"

A young girl in a maid's uniform peered around the side of the house and gestured to her. Curious, Cora Lee walked over to the girl. The maid grabbed Cora Lee's hand and pulled her around the corner away from the prying eyes of anyone who might be watching them from inside the house.

"I think I can tell you where your friend is or, at least, where she probably went to from here." Glancing over her shoulder, the girl continued. "When Miz Irma found out Ruby was in the family way, she kicked her out without so much as a howdy-doo. Ruby was so mad! She had no place else to go.

"I told her about the Florence Crittenton Home here, but they were going to make her stay up to a year and study nursing and read the Bible. She didn't want to do that. So, I think she decided to go to the city-run Rescue Home for Unwed Mothers. It's across the river in Argenta—North Little Rock is what they call it today.

"I had a cousin who went there last year, and they treated her good. Don't know if Miz Ruby would still be there or not, but you can ask about her and maybe find out something."

"Oh! Thank you, so much!" A great rush of relief to have found a direction for her search washed over her. "Can you tell me where the home is and how do I get there?"

"There's a trolley that you can catch by the big clock in front of the Armstrong Shoe Company on Main Street that will take you across the river. You'll have to change lines and take a trolley up to Levy. That car will stop right in front of the home. It's a pretty easy route, and it runs a few times a day during the week."

Thanking the maid, Cora Lee set off to find the clock on Main Street and waited until the electric trolly to Levy stopped. She boarded and put a nickel in the tin dish next to the driver, then found a seat on one of the wooden benches near the door.

The speed of the electric trolley was unnerving at first, but she was soon able to relax and enjoy the experience. As the maid at Irma's boarding house had predicted, finding the Home for Unwed Mothers was a simple task. The transfer on the other side of the river was easily done, as well.

The slower speed of the mule-drawn streetcar she took from North Little Rock over the unpaved, dirt roads in Levy was less exciting, but the scenery moving past the open-air window next to her seat was interesting.

The town of Levy, though small, was bustling with activity. Through the busy business district, they passed stores and buildings with signs that read Dr. Pairet's Drug Store, Stanley's Hardware, Stanley's Mercantile, and a few other establishments.

Once outside the downtown area, they passed homes surrounded by heavy woods, then entered an area near the military base, Camp Pike. Here the streets were paved, and the small shops and houses built, she assumed, to serve military personnel were crowded together in a disorganized jumble.

At last, the streetcar stopped in front of a four-story, red-brick building surrounded by a wrought iron fence. A painted sign near the road let Cora Lee know she was in the right place.

She stepped down onto a sidewalk and made her way through an ornate gate that stood open and allowed access to the paved pathway leading to the front door. The door was locked, so she pushed a black button that rang a bell inside. Within a few moments, an older woman in a white bibbed apron and wearing a white linen cap came to open the door.

"Yes? May we help you, dear?"

The woman's demeanor was gentle, and her soft voice kind. Cora Lee was instantly put at ease. "I've come to inquire after a friend who I believe may have had her baby boy here. My friend's name is Ruby Douglas. She named her baby Micah."

The woman's face lit up in a toothy smile. "Yes! We know Ruby. She remained with us for a few weeks after Micah was born. She has left him in our care until she can get established in a permanent home of her own. Would you like to see the baby? He's such a charmer. We all just love him!"

"Yes! Please! I would love to meet Micah. I've been praying for him every night, and it's such a relief to see that he is well and being taken care of."

The woman stepped back to allow Cora Lee into the foyer. The air was much cooler inside than out. The day had warmed quickly, and Cora Lee was happy to be out of the late-morning heat. She set her valise down on the marble floor. "Is it alright if I leave this here?"

"Yes, of course, dear. Come this way."

Glass-paneled doors on either side of the long hallway were lettered with the names of the offices — "Administration," "Personnel," "Accounting," "Records," "Maintenance." They came to an open archway leading to a small room comfortably furnished with two wing-back chairs and a sofa.

A carved-oak table sat in front of a picture window framed by heavy, green-velvet curtains that provided a pleasant view of a well-kept lawn and garden. A bookcase filled with photographs in frames sat against one wall with a doorway leading to an interior room next to it.

"If you'll wait here," the woman indicated one of the chairs with her hand, "I'll go and fetch the baby."

She disappeared through the doorway leading to the interior room, and Cora Lee took the chair. She fidgeted in excitement and looked around the waiting room.

Numerous framed photographs of babies and mothers with babies hung on the walls. One young woman held twins in her arms and grinned into the camera. She stood beside an automobile waiting, Cora Lee supposed, to whisk the new family away to some perfect home, a perfect father, and a perfect future. The picture made her sad as she wondered what the future held for Ruby and Micah. Would their future be perfect, or even bearable?

Within a few minutes, the door next to the bookcase opened, and the nurse entered carrying a bundle swaddled tightly in a blue blanket. She walked over to Cora Lee and placed the bundle into her arms.

"He's just over two months old now," the nurse said. "He's had a bit of the colic, and he cries a lot. The tight wrapper soothes him."

As if on cue, the sleeping infant opened his eyes and looked Cora Lee in the face. His mouth opened in a wail, and his little face turned red. Cora Lee jiggled him, bounced him, and rocked him to no avail. She put him on her shoulder and patted his back. He immediately emptied his stomach onto her blouse in a sour eruption of curdled milk.

At that, the nurse took the baby and offered a cloth to wipe away the mess. The smell, however, lingered, and Cora Lee turned her face away from the odor, fanning the wet spot with the soiled rag.

"Babies do that, I'm afraid, miss."

"Well, I'm sure I'll have to get accustomed to it since I've come to help Ruby with him. Her mother is so worried about her, and she's anxious to hear about Micah, too."

She dabbed at the wet patch on her blouse. "Can you tell me where Ruby is staying? Could you give me her address?"

"Yes, miss. I'll go and write it down for you. She doesn't live far, just over the river in Little Rock. I believe she is working at a hotel of some sort."

The nurse walked to the oak table in front of the window. She shifted the baby onto one arm and took a notepad and pencil from a drawer. After she scribbled the information, she gave the paper to her visitor.

Cora Lee stood and thanked the nurse. Taking her leave, she walked back to the entrance where she collected her suitcase. She kept the address in her hand and returned to the street to wait for the trolley to take her back over the river.

CHAPTER 17

The address on the piece of paper that the nurse at the orphanage had given Cora Lee led to a building in a rundown part of town near the banks of the Arkansas River. The odor of fish and wet riverbank permeated the damp air, and the sound of a river barge blowing its horn signaled its approach to the docks on the water below.

She walked through a hodge podge of three-story, ramshackle tenements strung together by numerous pulley lines overhead hung with laundry. The tenements were clustered along a maze of narrow lanes and sunless back alleys and had a worn, grimy air about them. A large rat scavenged in the gutter. The wail of a baby pierced the dank air, and a dog began to bark.

Cora Lee checked the address once more, unsure that she was walking in the right direction. A group of rough-looking men stood on the street corner ahead of her, but she hesitated to ask them for help. Instead, she crossed the street and approached a woman who was sweeping the front stoop of one of the buildings.

"Excuse me, ma'am. I am looking for this address. Can you tell me if it's close by?"

The woman stared at Cora Lee, then slowly accepted the paper. Reading the address, she curled her lip. "Sure. 'Bout two more blocks that away, and turn left at the little corner store on Rock Street. Hard to miss it."

Cora Lee thanked the woman and continued on her way. The woman's directions led her to a three-story establishment near the river, its construction only a little less forlorn and dreary than the buildings around it. A sign with red letters that read "Something Wonderful Dance Emporium, Abel Ray Dickson, Proprietor" hung above the door.

She hesitated, surprised that this was the place that she would find her friend. Noting that the afternoon was wearing thin, however, she entered the building hopeful that she could locate Ruby without delay and find a place to stay the night.

She walked into the foyer. A woman behind the barred window of an enclosed booth was counting money laid out in neat piles of coins and paper bills on a table. Wheels of paper tickets were stacked next to the money. Cora Lee approached the woman, set her valise on the floor, and cleared her throat to get the woman's attention. The woman looked up, and Cora Lee greeted her. "How do?"

The woman replied, "If you're wanting Abel, he's upstairs. Go on up."

Cora Lee opened her mouth to ask if the woman knew where Ruby was to be found, but the money-counter had already turned her back to the window. Cora Lee picked up her valise and headed up the stairs.

The landing at the top of the stairs was small, and an open doorway let her into a large, windowless room with high ceilings and a hardwood floor. A raised bandstand was in the corner to her immediate left, and three electric chandeliers gave out feeble light above what appeared to be a well-worn dance floor.

A waist-high wood railing ran along a portion of the right side of the room near the entry door, and two rows of straight-backed chairs were aligned inside the pen. Next to that, a similar area appeared to be meant for taking refreshments as tables and chairs were organized inside. At the back of the room along the wall opposite the landing, an ornate mirror hung above a long counter outfitted with high stools. Brass spittoons sat on the floor beneath the chairs. Large containers of lemonade and ice water were lined up next to a few coffee urns. Glasses and mugs were arranged in pyramids alongside stacks of coffee cups near the cash register.

A man who Cora Lee assumed was Abel stood beside the counter, his sleeves rolled up above his elbows and his pants tucked into his boots. A clay pipe jutted from his thick, black beard. He looked up as Cora Lee's footsteps echoed across the cavernous room at her approach.

"How do," she said. "I'm looking for…"

"A job!" he cut in, jerking the pipe from his mouth. "Yeh. Ain't you all." He looked her up and down, and she opened her mouth to protest. "You'll do," Abel grunted and shouted, "Mavis!"

"No, I'm looking for Ruby Douglas," Cora Lee finally managed to say. *Although, a job wouldn't be a bad idea*, she thought and added, "What kind of job?"

"Friend of Ruby's, huh? Well, if Ruby says you're good, I reckon you're good. Mavis!" he shouted again. "Job ain't hard. Just be nice. The men that come in here are payin' for a friendly face, a warm reminder of the gal they left back home, or someone to make them forget their ball and chain. Someone to dance with—maybe get a little handsy with. That ain't gonna hurt ya none, is it?

"Ask 'em if they wanna buy you a lemonade, a cup of coffee or a glass of tea. Encourage 'em to spend a little of that easy pay they got burnin' a hole in their pockets. We have to be real careful about servin' anything else, ya know. Arkansas' Bone-Dry Law don't allow liquor sales, even if that Prohibition law ain't started up in the rest of the country, yet."

203

Cora Lee nodded although she hadn't quite taken in all that the man was saying. She frowned and pursed her lips in an effort to make sense of his words.

"We only sell lemonade, coffee, and tea here, now, 'cause that's all that's legal." Abel scanned the room uneasily. He leaned closer and continued in a low voice, "If they ask for anythin' else, make sure you tell 'em to speak easy so they ain't overheard. You never know who might be hangin' around and listenin'."

Cora Lee's face paled as it began to dawn on her that Ruby was living, not in a hotel as she expected, but in a dancehall—and one that sold illegal alcohol on the sly. She scarcely heard what this man was saying for a few moments while she struggled to regain her composure. She managed a nod, stunned at the idea of being asked to play such a deceptive, dishonest part in the business of dancing with men for money.

"You mean," she stammered, "you want me to push men to spend all their money in here?"

Abel grinned and relaxed. "You're startin' to catch on, doll. As much of their dough as they're willin' to part with. The more they spend, the more you make. You earn a penny for every drink they buy you. The music stops twice during each song. If you ain't drinkin' or at the 'talk tables,' it's your job to keep your dance partner on the floor with you. You get a ticket for every piece of a song you dance, and you get a nickel for every ticket you turn in at the end of the night.

"The girls in my establishment make good money—twice what they make at other jobs. Stay out of the pen and on the dance floor or at the talk-time tables as much as you can." Abel chucked Cora Lee under the chin and gave her a leering wink. "You'll do fine."

Cora Lee pulled away from the bartender's hand. The idea of staying and working here seemed wrong, but it would do until she could find something more respectable to do. And she needed to be where Ruby was if she was going to be able to help her friend.

"What about a place to stay and meals?"

"Meals are on you. Room runs you two dollars a week. You'll share Ruby's room. I expect you girls to keep up your looks. No shabby clothes; no busted-up shoes; and keep your face and hair done up. You go out in the streets, out to the mercantile, you'll be advertisin' this place. My girls need to look high-class—clean."

Abel put two fingers in his mouth and blew a piercing whistle. Cora Lee jumped, and Abel motioned for a heavy-set, buxom woman who had entered the hall to come over. She approached wearing a shockingly short dress that exposed half her lower legs—legs that appeared bare in tan-colored silk stockings. Her cheeks and lips were heavily rouged, and her eyes were lined with black kohl. Her blond hair was cut short in a bob.

"Mavis, this is a new gal. She needs a bit of trainin'. Show her 'round the place, then get her settled upstairs in Ruby's room."

"Oh, Abel!" Mavis complained in a voice that was something between a siren and a whine. "Why you gotta always stick me with the punks?"

"Come on, doll. You're my most experienced dancer. Show this new tomato the ropes."

Mavis led Cora Lee back out of the ballroom to the landing and up a second set of stairs to the third-floor rooms where some of the girls lived.

"The men that come in here buy their tickets downstairs. They don't come up to the dancehall if they ain't paid to dance. Abel don't allow 'em to loiter. It's gonna be your job to collect as many of those tickets from 'em as you can. That's how you get paid."

Cora Lee nodded. She was still shaken by the idea that women would dance with men for money. Curious, she asked, "So, what made you want to take up dancing for a living?"

"I tried workin' in service, but I don't have references. It don't pay, anyway. I don't know how to operate Singer sewin' machines, and I can't type or do stenography or work a phone board. My cookin' skills are good enough for fixin' up eggs and boilin' water, but not good enough to work as a cook in a diner. I got work as a waitress, but tips are hard to live on."

Having reached the third floor, Mavis led Cora Lee to a room on the left of a long hallway. "Here you go. Ruby has the bed on the right. I'll tell her you're here when she comes back." She leaned against the door frame and watch the new hire with a critical eye.

Cora Lee walked into the room, relieved that she had found Ruby and had a place to stay as night was coming on. She looked around and set her valise on the bed. Opening it, she began to unpack. "Is the work here hard? I'm not sure this is right for me—I mean—dancing?"

"And what's wrong with dancin'? Like it ain't respectable or somethin'?" Mavis immediately jumped to the defense of her profession. "There's been pay-to-dance halls like this out in California and up in Illinois for years. Abel opened this one about a year ago. 'Sides, ain't nothin' wrong with places like this. They're a place for men to com and enjoy some social time.

"People go to dances all the time, don't they? There's the annual Christmas dances at the Elks Lodge and Masonic Hall. The city puts on public dances down at the tennis courts, and they charge people to attend, too. People give parties in their homes and hire bands so their friends can dance. The only difference in what we do is we give men who love to dance but don't have a way of findin' a partner a chance to enjoy what other folks do."

Cora Lee considered this, and it made sense to her. "Well, that makes it seem alright, I reckon. I'm not sure I'll be good at it, though."

"Well, honey, you have looks, and that's about all that's needed to make it here." Mavis' voice tore through the room as she suddenly gave a loud laugh. "Don't expect to meet a sheik or some rich swell to sweep you off your feet, though. Most of the fish that come here can't get a woman because of their looks. Lots of 'em are scarred or maimed from the war, some are fat or bald or pock marked. But they all love to dance, and they don't get rejected here like they would at "respectable" dances. We're doin' 'em a service."

Cora Lee nodded and began to feel better about accepting this new job. *Besides, it's to help Ruby,* she reminded herself.

Mavis continued her lecture. "It's our job to say 'yes' to the fellows. Most of 'em are more than willin' to pay for extra attention, too, if you catch my drift," she added with a wink. "You wanna make decent money, you be extra friendly with the fish. Just don't try to pull anythin' over on Abel."

"I don't know what you mean…"

"Listen, fellas that come in here, they ain't wantin' to find no wife. A few of 'em already have a henpeckin' missus back home. Nope. The men that come in here are mostly too short, or too ugly, or plain too *strange* to get a woman without payin'. Some are business types from out of town. Most wouldn't be caught dead out in daylight with one of us. All of 'em wanna spend a little time with a girl that'll let 'em be a little touchy-feely and not squawk about it.

"They're just lonely. Play your cards right, keep your mouth shut about what you see and what you do, and you'll do alright. Smile, be friendly, and don't try to horn in on any of our regulars."

Cora Lee nodded. "I understand," she said.

Mavis continued to lean against the door jam and watched as Cora Lee unpacked. "Do you even know how to dance?"

"Well, I can two-step and waltz and polka. I don't know any of the newer dances, but I'd like to learn."

"Most of the fish like the fox trot, and you'll catch on to that fast enough. Just hold on and let 'em drag you around the floor. Hey, those all the clothes you have?" Mavis sauntered to the bed and plucked at the sleeve of Cora Lee's best dress, eyeing it critically. "This old-maid rag won't carry you very far. We're gonna to have to see what we can do to get you outfitted. We can shorten the hem of this one to start. It'll do for an ever-day dress if we add a sash—and these old cotton stockin's!" she hooted. "Don't you have any silk ones?"

Cora Lee blushed and held out the skirt of the dress Amanda had remade for her. "No. These are all the clothes I own. I don't have money to buy more." She pulled the sage-green, silk scarf from her shoulders and held it close to her heart.

"Oh, don't worry about money, honey. Wilson's Mercantile has some cute frocks on sale for about six dollars. You'll need dancin' shoes, too. Can't be clompin' around the dance floor in those clodhoppers."

Cora Lee looked down at her boots, embarrassed by their worn condition. Noticing Mavis' well-manicured hands, she compared them to her own hands, baked brown from the sun and calloused from years working on the farm. Her nails were broken and dirty. She hid her clenched fists in the folds of the scarf.

"We can go over to Wilson's and get you outfitted on Abel's account. You can pay him back with your earnin's." Mavis ran her eye up and down Cora Lee's form. "I don't reckon it'll take you long."

"I've never borrowed money. My granny would never approve…"

Mavis cut off the words with a loud bray. "Ahhh, doll! Don't even worry about what your sweet old granny would or wouldn't *approve* of. You're in a whole new world here! Just do as the other gals do, and you're gonna do fine!"

"I'll take over from here." Ruby stood in the doorway, surprise on her face as she discovered her young mountain friend in her room. "Beat it, Mavis."

"Gladly!" Mavis shrugged and left the room without another word.

"Ruby!" Cora Lee dropped the scarf on the bed and ran to her friend. She threw her arms around her, smothering Ruby in a bear hug. "I'm glad to see you!"

Ruby disengaged herself from her friend's embrace and eyed the suitcase on the bed. "What're you doin' here, and how did ya find me?"

Cora Lee pulled Ruby into the room, and the two girls sat down on the edges of their beds facing each other. Cora Lee took stock of the changes in her friend. Ruby's red hair, cut short in a curly bob, was held in place by a bright-yellow headband. She wore red lipstick, and her eyes, like Mavis,' were lined with black kohl. Her dress was a yellow and pink plaid sheath with a low waist and a short hem, and she had on skin-colored silk hose, and tan high-heeled pumps.

"You've changed a lot since you've been here."

Ruby said nothing, but raised an eyebrow and waited for an answer to her question.

Cora Lee recounted the events on Bennett's Ridge since Ruby left following the ravages of the Spanish Flu that had swept over the community.

Ruby looked at her, dry eyed. "None of that is nothin' to me. I wanna know what yer doin' here. Why ya come?"

Cora Lee paused for a breath. "Well, mostly I came because your ma begged me to find you. But, in truth, I wanted to be here to help you with Micah— and help you look for Walter, too. Hasn't there been any word from him?"

Ruby shook her head. "No, but that old Lucas McDaniel showed up, right as rain, not a scratch on him. Showed up like nothin' had happened, like his daddy weren't told he was missin' after that big battle.

He weren't at all broke up when I told him his pa had died from the flu, either."

"Lucas is here? Here in Little Rock? Did he have any information about Walter?"

Ruby nodded. "He's here. Said a fella he met over there got him a job sellin' insurance. He didn't have much news about my brother. Said he seen him the day 'fore he left to come home, but that Walter didn't have a return scheduled, yet. I ain't taken the time lately to go down to the Army place and ask about him again. We can stop in later this week, I reckon."

"That sounds like a good idea. Mavis said she was going to take me to buy new clothes tomorrow. Maybe I can go make an inquiry while we're out?"

"I'll take you shoppin'. You let Mavis carry ya to the store, and you'll never get out of debt from the things she'll make ya buy. Stick with me, Cora Lee. I'll see yer set up right, and set up where you won't spend yer last dime on foolishness ya don't need."

Cora Lee nodded, glad to have found a job, a place to stay, and the object of her rescue mission so very quickly.

CHAPTER 18

As promised, Ruby took Cora Lee to the downtown area where tall buildings on either side of the street housed shops, restaurants, banks, and other businesses. Some of the buildings had colorful awnings that stretched overhead. Broad sidewalks provided plenty of room for pedestrians. People flowed around the girls in clumps and streams, some stopping to look in shop windows, others rushing by in a hurry to get to their destinations.

The sky was laced with electrical lines strung between streetlights that were planted on every corner. Signs advertising street names and the names of businesses or promoting products that promised to cure all manner of ailments hung everywhere. Along the sidewalk, vendors put out samples of their merchandise arranged to attract the eye and entice shoppers to spend money in their stores.

A double set of tracks and overhead electrical cables ran down the middle of the street, and from time-to-time trolley cars stopped and clanged their bells at points up and down the road as passengers got on and off. Automobiles were parked here and there or drove by honking their horns and disgorging clouds of rank smoke from their tailpipes. The air was filled with the odor of gasoline mingled with the smell of horse dung from carriages that were mixed in among the road machines of this new, industrialized era.

Cora Lee was overwhelmed by the noise and confusion of the busy downtown area, but Ruby confidently took charge and ushered her into a department store. Quickly and expertly rifling through the sales and half-price racks, she pulled first one garment then another off its hanger and held it up to Cora Lee. She folded some over her arm to be tried on in a nearby dressing room and tossed others aside.

"This one. Not that one. This might work, but it's a little long on you. We could hem it. Nine inches off the floor is okay fer a street dress, but we can go a little shorter on yer dance frock. Ugh! This color is horrible. Nope, too expensive. Try this."

Once the approved dresses had been tried on, Ruby selected a simple dress with a round neck, short sleeves, a narrow silhouette, and a wide, fringed sash tied loosely at the waist for Cora Lee's street dress. "I have a hat that'll go with this, so ya won't have to buy one," she said. "And you'll need some new shoes, too, fer sure."

Cora Lee was thrilled with the soft cotton fabric and the deep navy color of the dress Ruby selected. She thought that the fringed sash was unnecessarily fancy, but the style was unexpectedly comfortable. She liked how she looked in it in the full-length mirror outside the dressing room.

"I haven't ever seen my whole self all at once. I never knew there was so much of me!" she joked.

The dance frock Ruby chose was another story. The flouncy pastel lavender taffeta had a row of pink silk roses sewn in a diagonal row across the sleeveless bodice. The hemline was too short for decency, too.

"This is much too fancy for me!" Cora Lee exclaimed. "And too much skin shows! I couldn't ever wear it!"

Ruby ignored Cora Lee's dramatic objections and said, "You can. You will. Yer gonna need a pair of dancin' slippers, too. Shoe department, next up."

By the time the girls finished shopping, Cora Lee was fully outfitted with two dresses, two new pairs of shoes, two pairs of silk stockings, and two linen chemises. "One to wash and one to wear," Ruby said as she paid for the items. "It's better to owe me than Abel," she said over Cora Lee's protest." I don't charge interest, and if things don't work out here fer ya, you won't have to worry about payin' me back in a hurry. It ain't so easy to leave if ya owe Abel any money. He'll be sure he's paid back, one way or another."

On their way out, Ruby stopped at the dry goods counter near the front of the store and looked at bolts of material stacked there. She turned to Cora Lee and said, "Edith, one of the girls, is a decent seamstress. I'll ask her if she can make you a skirt and a couple of blouses fer day wear. We'll have to do somethin' about yer hair, too. Girls is wearin' it short, not in long, messy braids like you."

Cora Lee put her hand up to her head. "Oh, no. I don't want to cut my hair!" Cora Lee turned her back to Ruby. "Let's go, please. I'm exhausted with all this shopping."

Ruby picked up a pair of large shears that were lying on the dry goods table. Grabbing Cora Lee's thin braid, she cut it off in one smooth motion. Cora Lee let out a loud shriek as Ruby tossed the braid onto a bolt of gingham. "No more arguments. Mavis can trim it up in a bob when we get back."

Ruby took Cora Lee by the elbow. She ushered her still-screaming friend out the door past the hostile glares of store clerks and customers. Cora Lee struggled against Ruby's hand as her protests escalated into an uncivilized commotion.

"Ruby! How could you! My hair!" Cora Lee gasped and yelled at Ruby.

"You'll find you'll love it once you wear it fer a bit. The shorter hair complements yer face, anyway. That farm-girl braid was plain jakey and a big, old 'NO' here in the city. You'll thank me fer freein' you up from it, you'll see."

Cora Lee caught her reflection in the store's picture window. Her hair, short in the back and longer on the sides, now hung in a loose jumble as the breeze blew whisps of it around her face. "You're horrible! How could you do such a terrible thing to me?"

"Enough. It's done." Ruby took off her own wide-brimmed hat and put it on Cora Lee, tucking the loose whisps of her hair back. "There. It looks perfectly fine, but it'll be even better once Mavis trims it up."

The two girls returned to their rented room in silence except for an occasional sob from Cora Lee. Mavis was summoned, and she immediately took charge of the hair cutting calamity while Ruby sat on her bed giving suggestions on which style she thought would be best.

"Actually, it ain't half bad as it is," the older woman consoled Cora Lee. "It needs a little here and there to even it up some. Now," she took Cora Lee's face in her hands and studied her from all sides, "your hair is straight, and that's an advantage. You won't have to be fussin' with rag curls and hair goop to try and make waves, and I don't think you'd look great with bangs."

Ruby chimed in with, "I think bangs would work fine on her."

Mavis ignored her. "I think a straight boyish bob will work better for you than a Dutch bob. It'll be great loose, or you can dress it up with a headband or a long scarf tied 'round it."

She continued talking as she worked, but Cora Lee was still fuming and said nothing. When she was finished, Mavis handed Cora Lee a mirror. "Here. All done. What do you think?"

Cora Lee took the mirror and, begrudgingly, had to admit, if only to herself, that the style was cute. Her hair, cut in a short, stacked bob in the back, swung on both sides of her face in a curve to her chin. It made her look older and more modern. She handed the mirror back to Mavis with a mumbled "thank you."

Ruby grinned and said, "I told ya you'd like it. We'll have one of the girls do yer fingernails, too. What say you and me go see Micah after that? I ain't been in a while, and I'm startin' to miss the little bug. You can have a quick wash off tonight in the tub and wear yer new street dress. With that new bob, you'll look like a modern, city-born-and-bred glamour girl."

"Fine," Cora Lee mumbled, not too sure she wanted to be a 'glamour girl.' "But we better remember to wear a rain slicker or at least take plenty of burp cloths."

***

The time with Micah passed too quickly. Ruby was reluctant to leave her baby and handed him over hesitantly at the end of their allowed hour-long visit.

"I'm savin' my money. I'll be ready real soon to get a good place fer us to live," she assured the woman who took Micah from her.

"You'll have to," the matron informed her. "Unfortunately, we aren't able to keep him. If you can't take him soon, we'll have to transfer him over to St. Joseph's Orphanage. They're much better equipped to house children than we are here."

"It won't be much longer 'til I can bring him home with me," Ruby assured the woman. "It's what I want most in the world."

The girls rode the streetcar back across the river and, having transferred to the electric trolley to downtown, got off in front of Stein Company Five and Ten. As they stepped off the trolley, Ruby said, "Are ya hungry? Let's go have a glass of tea before we walk back to the dance hall. We've got a long night ahead of us, and I think we could both use a bite to eat, too. There's a lunch counter in here. It's air conditioned, and I'm ready to get out of this heat fer a bit.

"We'll need to buy you one of them Lady Schick razors while we're in here. Can't be wearin' silk stockin's and sleeveless dancin' frocks with more hair than Aaron's beard on yer legs and under yer arms."

Cora Lee, surprised at the absurd idea of shaving like a man, could only stare at her friend in silence. She had already discovered that saying 'no' to Ruby was useless. And, she grudgingly admitted, Ruby had been right about the haircut and manicure.

She was anxious about her first night on the job and more than willing to delay their return to the dance hall in favor of a bite to eat. They entered the store, and Ruby led the way to a long counter lined with red-vinyl and chrome stools. A menu was posted on the wall, and the two girls studied it, then sat down at one of the booths that ran along one wall.

Once the waitress had taken their orders for egg salad sandwiches and iced tea, Cora Lee leaned forward and asked, "What do I do tonight? How do I make the fellas dance with me?"

The waitress put napkins and two glasses of tea on the table in front of the girls. Ruby took a long drink of her tea and set her glass down.

"We sit or stand in what we call 'the pen' 'til the guys come ask one of us to dance. The band plays from eight 'til about midnight—about sixty songs or so. They stop each song twice in the middle, so if a fish wants to dance fer a whole song, he'll give you three tickets. All ya have to do is smile and be flirty and try to stay on the floor or in the talk-time area as much as possible."

The waitress brought two sandwiches to the table. "Anything else I can bring you ladies?" Ruby waved her away. Cora Lee smiled at the girl and shook her head causing her new bob to swish across her face. The waitress walked away, and Cora Lee brushed her hair back as she pressed Ruby for more information.

"How much will I get paid every night?"

Ruby took a bite of her sandwich and swallowed. "Depends on the night. If you was to dance all three parts of sixty songs at a nickel each part—well, first off, you'd kill yerself havin' to stay in the arms of those losers that long without a break, but you'd make—" she closed her eyes and tried to calculate the number. "Well, you'd make a lot. It's fifteen cents a song times sixty. You work it out."

"So, how much do all the girls usually end up with? Counting dancing and drinks?"

"Most of us keep our business to ourselves, but Mavis makes plenty 'cause she's easy. She lets the men grope and pet, so they like to keep her on the dancefloor. They give her extra tickets to let 'em dance real close, if ya know what I mean."

Cora Lee winced at the idea of 'dancing real close' to a strange man. She took a bite of her sandwich and let Ruby continue uninterrupted.

"Some nights, I only make about four dollars. Most times I come out with six or so countin' the money Abel pays us fer the drinks the fish buy us. I'm 'thirsty' a lot." Ruby laughed and finished her tea.

"We ain't allowed to be out of the pen where we sit unless we're dancin' or drinkin' or one of the fish has paid fer 'talk time' with us. Can't move around loose on yer own, you have to have be talkin' or dancin' or drinkin' with a fella or sittin' in the pen."

"What's 'talk time'?"

"The tables and chairs that are set up are so a fella can take a dancer there just fer talkin' to her. Some of the regulars wanna get to know a girl better. They have to pay fer that time. They'll pay you a ticket fer ever two minutes, so most start out with five tickets fer ten minutes. Beats bein' on yer feet all night.

That's when you'll try to encourage 'em to buy ya a drink, too. That'll increase yer take. And, believe me, Abel keeps an eye on the clock when we're at the tables, too, so make sure you make yer fish pay."

"Well, I owe you a lot for the clothes and all the other things you paid for. I'll pay you back as soon as I can, but I don't think I want to let any men 'grope' me. That sounds awful." Cora Lee shuddered as she let herself imagine a stranger touching her like that.

"It ain't so bad. Think of it like we're providin' a service to all the sad and lonely men in society. The ones ya have to watch out fer are the 'slummers,' the rich boys out on the town, out of sight of their mammas, gettin' drunk and lookin' to make mischief. They come in like big shots doin' us all a favor. They talk big, spend big, and can be big trouble."

"If you can't socialize outside the pen, how do you make the men give you tickets? I mean, how many dancers are there?"

"There's about thirty of us in all, and different ones show up on a given night. You'll find ways to attract attention. Some of the girls are pushy. They coo and wink and lift their skirts to fix their stockin's when the boys are lookin' us over. You'll figure out yer own 'gimmick' that works fer ya."

Ruby lifted her hand to call the waitress over. The waitress refilled their tea glasses and put their ticket on the table. "I'll get the tab," Ruby said. "It's on me this time. You can pay fer the next one."

The two girls purchased the razor that Ruby insisted was necessary along with an inexpensive bottle of scented toilet water, tooth powder and a toothbrush, and some Everdry antiperspirant cream. They had just paid for their lunch and personal items when Lucas walked into the store and spotted them.

"Hey, Ruby! It's swell to run into you again so soon after our last meetin'." The girls turned as Lucas approached them. "And who's yer friend—"

Lucas turned to Cora Lee and surprise crossed his face as he recognized her. "Well, fry me brown! It's Cora Lee from back home. Why, I didn't even recognize ya!"

Cora Lee put a hand to her newly cut hair and shrank back from her old nemesis. She had not forgotten the ugly ways he had treated her, even if years had passed since he attacked her, and a great many months had passed since she had last seen him.

"Say! You gals wanna go to the movin' pictures with me tonight? That new Mary Pickford film, *Captain Kidd, Jr.*, is playin' over at the Gem Theater. Come on! My treat, what do ya say? We'll have a swell ol' time."

Cora Lee's stomach twisted at the thought of going anywhere with him. Ruby declined the invitation for them both. "Sorry, sport. We're workin' tonight. Maybe another time, but thanks, anyway. Cora Lee, let's go. Take care, Lucas."

Cora Lee was relieved to have been saved from having to answer. Lucas McDaniel still gave her the heebie-jeebies. As they walked away, though, she remembered that Ruby had said he'd seen Walter. She didn't want to get anywhere near him, but determined to brave a discussion with the man she loathed in order to get information on the man she loved, she squared her shoulders and stopped. "Give me a minute, Ruby. I'll be right back."

She returned to the store as Lucas was walking out the door. He stopped and smiled. "Forget somethin'?" he asked, surprised to see her approach him.

Cora Lee swallowed hard and managed to meet his eyes. She forced herself to smile back at him and, with a toss of her bobbed head, said, "Why don't you come to the dance hall tonight? Ruby and me are working at the Something Wonderful Dance Emporium. Do you know where that is?"

A slow smile spread across Lucas' face as he nodded. "Sure. I seen it. It's that place down by the river. Sounds like a 'somethin' wonderful' idea. I'll be there with bells on."

"We'll be working 'til midnight. We can catch up with each other." *It might be the only chance I get to ask him about Walter*, she thought, *if I can stand being close to Lucas long enough to find out what he knows.*

Cora Lee flashed him another smile. "That's fine! See you there, then."

Lucas' eyes narrowed as he watched Cora Lee hurry back to Ruby's side. He'd never gotten over how this little orphan had refused to dance with him and treated him like he was nothing.

"Sure. I'll be there, Miss Cora Lee McMillan. You and me still got some unsettled business between us."

CHAPTER 19

"Here, at least put a little petroleum jelly on yer eyelashes and lips," Ruby barked shoving a glass jar of the goo at Cora Lee. "I can't see why yer so against a little makeup. We all wear it, and there ain't a thing wrong with it."

Cora Lee relented and took the jar from her friend. "I still don't know why I need it." Looking in the mirror of the dressing table, she dabbed a little jelly on her lips but declined to enhance her eyelashes or brows. "I think I'm perfectly fine the way God made me," she added.

Ruby snorted but said no more about it. It had already been an exhausting back and forth making Cora Lee shave her legs and underarms before getting her into the lavender dance frock her friend now wore. And wore quite stunningly, Ruby had to admit.

"Do I look alright?" Cora Lee asked. The amount of leg showing below the shortened hem of her dress, and the sheer, tan-colored silk stockings made her feel almost indecent.

"You'll do. You'd look a sight better with a little makeup, but we can attack that next time. You will let me put some on you tomorrow, or else."

Cora Lee sighed. Perhaps it would be better to give in and not continue the fight. *If it means I can make more money to help Ruby, then I guess there's no harm in it. Besides, the dress is pretty, and it's a lot like what the other girls are wearing.*

Several girls had poked their heads in during the evening and introduced themselves. All of them had their hair bobbed and wore makeup. Many of them wore necklaces, bracelets, rings and earbobs. Cora Lee, whose only enhancement was the gloss on her lips and the string of buttons around her neck, was sure she would never remember all of their names.

Ruby pulled Cora Lee up from the dressing table in their room. She wore a pink taffeta dress with a low-cut square neckline trimmed in silver braid and with a black satin rose pinned at her waist. A long strand of silver beads hung from her neck, and more beads were twisted around her wrist in a bracelet.

Cora Lee reached out and took Ruby's necklace in her hand.

"Ruby, I'm not criticizing you, but, if you're trying to save up money for Micah, how come you to spend money on things you don't need like this?"

Ruby laughed. "These only cost a few pennies, and they's an investment. The better I look, the more tickets I get. These cheap things were paid fer the first time they caught the eye of someone lookin' me over and handin' me a big wad of tickets. You'll learn."

Music drifted up from the dancehall, and Ruby pulled Cora Lee toward the door.

"Come on, doll. Time to face the lions in the 'den of iniquity' we work in. I reckon yer as ready as yer gonna be," Ruby said. "Let's head down and join the others 'fore Abel finds out we're late."

The two of them walked down the stairs to the second-floor ballroom and took up their place behind the banister that separated the pen from the dance floor. A number of girls leaned against the waist-high railing wearing an array of eye-catching dresses in every color. A few of the dancers sat in chairs waiting for an invitation to dance, but most of "Abel's Stable" (as he called them) were out on the floor or sitting in the "talk-time" area with their drinks.

A lively girl in a red, shift-style dress came off the floor and stood next to Ruby. "Who's your friend, Ruby?"

"This is a friend from home. Cora Lee, this is my friend, Edith. We worked together before Micah was born, and she's who helped me get a job here."

Edith smiled. "You're new? Welcome. How do you like workin' here?"

Cora Lee eyed Edith and noticed she wore a bejeweled headband that wrapped around her forehead

228

and disappeared amid the curls of her jet-black, side-parted bob. "I'm not sure yet," Cora Lee laughed. "This is my first night, and I'm just figuring this all out. I like your headband."

Edith touched the rhinestones on the headband and laughed. "Kress had these on sale last weekend, and I couldn't resist. I love anything that's got sparkles and jewels on it. That's an interesting necklace you're wearin,' too. Is that made out of buttons? How fascinatin'! Ooop! This one's mine."

The girl jumped up and a tall, thin man with a prominent Adams apple and pockmarked skin handed Edith tickets. Tucking them into a pocket on her dress, she twiddled her fingers at Ruby and Cora Lee and let herself be led out of the pen and onto the floor.

The band stopped playing for a few seconds and then started up again in the middle of a jazzy tune. Dancers on the floor tucked additional tickets into their pockets during the brief intermission, and some returned to the pen. Ruby was led out onto the floor by a man in a grey blazer, leaving Cora Lee alone.

"Okay," Cora Lee mumbled to herself as she put her hand to her neck and rubbed her button necklace. "I see how it's done." She relaxed, content to watch as the band played another song, stopping and starting during it as dancers accepted more tickets to keep dancing or returned to the pen. Some of them were led, tickets in hand, to the "talk-time" area and ordered drinks by their partners. Many of the men pulled flasks from their hip pockets to pour something in their cups.

Ruby sat down next to Cora Lee after her two-song "date" with the grey-blazer man. "You ain't gonna get paid if ya don't dance," she said. "Stand up on yer feet, and take an interest in the fellas. Smile a little. Yer washed out in this dim lightin' without the makeup I told ya to put on. You look like a wet blanket, and no man wants a wet blanket fer a date."

Cora Lee nervously stood and smiled at a man who had entered the room. He was dressed in a brown, three-piece suit with notched wide lapels, a white high-collared shirt and a thin dark-brown tie. He hung his fashionable bowler hat on one of the pegs near the door and walked further into the room. From their distance, Cora Lee could see no obvious physical flaw in him; he appeared to be quite handsome—and young.

"Not him!" Ruby pulled Cora Lee back down into her chair. "That's one of Mavis' regulars. She'll snatch ya bald-headed if she sees ya dancin' with him. He's more than a regular, in fact. He's her favorite, and he does business with Abel." Leaning closer, Ruby added in a lower voice, "I think he brings in the liquor, but don't go blabbin' that around."

Two men approached the pen each clutching a streamer of about a dozen tickets. One of them was tall and thin and had a thick mustache; the other was shorter and had an enormous stomach. "Dance?" they both said in unison to none of the girls in particular.

"You bet!" Ruby accepted and grabbed Cora Lee's arm as she jumped up. "We'd love to."

"Well," the tall one with the thick black mustache said, "we're not sure how many tickets you need."

Ruby took both batches of tickets from their hands and handed one of them to Cora Lee. "Oh, these'll do fine. Come on boys, we're gonna have a swell time."

The night sped by, and Cora Lee found that dancing with the various men who paid her became easier with each "date." By the end of the evening, she was glad to be wearing the soft-soled "ballerina-style" dancing shoes that Ruby had insisted she needed, and was looking forward to the final song so she could go soak her feet.

The two girls had returned to the pen when Lucas walked in the door holding a string of tickets. The dancers in the pen began to twitter and coo, excited to see such a handsome customer come in the door.

"I'll bet he's married."

"Gotta be something wrong with him. Maybe he has terrible breath."

"Nobody like that ever comes in here."

"Over here, lover boy."

"Maybe he's a murderer or something."

"I wouldn't care if he was—I'd dance with him for free and be happy to die in his arms!"

"I'll bet Mavis takes him as one of her 'regulars,' so none of us'll have a chance."

"Yeah, she takes all the fish that look halfway better than a gargoyle."

Cora Lee's mouth went dry as Lucas spotted her and walked over to the pen. "There you girls are!" He grinned and held out his hand to Cora Lee. "You can have all my tickets, but I don't wanna dance just yet. Let's go sit and talk and have a drink."

Cora Lee nodded as Lucas took her by the elbow and led her to a table in the talk-time area. She stole a glance at him as she slid into the chair he held for her, noting the changes in his face from how he looked in her memory.

His jawline was more defined. His eyes were still the same cold blue, but were now housed atop cheeks that were leaner, hardened. His smile, although not the malicious grimace she recalled from their school days, still did not reach those emotionless, icy blue eyes.

Lucas took his seat across the table. "So," he said as he crossed his arms on the table between them and leaned closer. "What's brung you to the big city? I wouldn't a'thought ya could've been chased off'n that mountain with a mop and a bucket o' mud."

Cora Lee gave him a sad little smile. "Granny passed away the night you boys left for the war. The flu took so many more the next year. Then Ruby came here, and her ma asked me to come find her and help with—" she stopped before she revealed that Ruby had a son. It wasn't her secret to tell anyone, and certainly not this man. "—with getting' adjusted to life here. I found it wasn't so bad in the 'big city' and thought I'd stay here for a bit."

"Well, I reckon that calls fer a drink, don't you?"

Lucas got up and walked to the bar to order two cups of tea. When he returned to the table, he put the drinks down and moved his chair around to the side closer to Cora Lee. He sat back down and scooted his chair in so that his knees pressed against her thighs.

Cora Lee squirmed uncomfortably and twisted her legs away from him. "Thanks for the drink. I was a might dry."

"I'm sorry to hear about yer granny passin'. She was a fine woman, and that had to a'been hard fer ya."

Cora Lee nodded. "I expect losing your pa was hard on you, too."

Lucas shrugged. "He was a mean old buzzard. Used to beat the tar outta me—belt, tree limb, boot— anythin' he could find at hand. Maybe sometimes I even deserved it. Once, he cracked a wood plank over my head. I was out like a light for a while with that one." He took a swallow from his teacup. "I don't miss him."

"That sounds horrible, Lucas! I never knew Mr. McDaniel was like that!" She shook her head. No wonder Lucas had been so mean as a boy.

"I don't reckon many folks up there really knew him," Lucas said. "He had a special likin' for yer friend, Ruby, though, ya know? I reckon she got to know him pretty well."

Picking up her cup, Cora Lee shook her head and glanced toward the bar. Abel was watching them. *What did he mean by 'special liking?' Ruby worked for him, but she never indicated that she did any more*

233

*than that. She had never said that Otis McDaniel ever
took advantage of her like that, but she wouldn't say
who Micah's father was, either.*

Shaken, she took a small sip, gasped, and wrinkled
her nose. "That's more than tea!" She sputtered and
set her cup down.

Lucas laughed. "Yeah, I added a little of my
favorite flavorin' to it." He pulled a flask out of his
hip pocket and added more gin to his cup. "Didn't
think you'd mind a little of the 'good stuff' since you
grew up on moonshine! Yer quite a little actress, ya
know? You almost have me convinced that ya ain't
never tasted gin."

"Oh, of course, I've tasted alcohol! Granny Mae
kept a jar of moonshine for when we'd have a sore
throat or a fever. Was a good tonic, too—at least a
might better than turpentine and sugar!" She
shuddered at the memory of being dosed with the
concoction as a child. "I just wasn't expecting it in my
tea, is all."

Lucas took a swig of his drink and wiped his hand
across his mouth. Cora Lee took another sip from her
tea cup. Confused about his statements about his
father and Ruby, but desperate to hear any news about
Walter, she put her cup down.

Pushing it aside, and hoping to cut her interactions
with him short, she decided it was time to interrogate
Lucas. Clearing her throat, she turned to face him and
began, "Ruby said...," but she was interrupted when
Mavis approached.

Wearing a revealing, skin-toned dress, and in the company of her escort in the brown suit who had come in earlier, she eyed Cora Lee and gave Lucas a pouting, flirtatious look. "You can dance with me next, honey, when you're bored with this one. I'll make sure you have a real swell time." She winked and smiled.

Lucas eyed Mavis up and down and smiled back at her. "Thanks, doll. I'll keep yer invitation in mind. Save it fer another night, though." Turning his attention back to Cora Lee he added, "I already gave my tickets to 'this one' fer the night."

Mavis gave Cora Lee a hard stare, took her escort's arm, and ambled off. The band began to play the last song of the evening—a popular slow waltz called "I'm Sorry I Made You Cry." Lucas stood and held out his hand to Cora Lee. "One dance?"

Cora Lee nodded and allowed herself to be led out onto the floor. She hadn't had a chance to ask about Walter, and she wanted Lucas to tell her everything he knew about him. She opened her mouth to ask, but Lucas started talking and cut her off.

"There's a big street fair startin' up downtown tomorrow. Earlier today, they's puttin' up a carousel and one of them Ferris wheels. Say you'll let me take ya to the fair?"

Cora Lee looked down and shook her head. "No. I can't. I'm sorry."

"Aw! Come on, gal. We can ketch up on everthin'. I admit, I was a rotten kid to you. I'm sorry. Let me make it up to ya. I ain't the same, terrible kid I was back then. War changes a man, ya know."

Cora Lee raised her head and eyed him with suspicion as he swung her around in three-quarter time. Here was the person who had tormented her. A man who, as a boy, had tried to kill her. Had he truly changed? Would going out with him to "ketch up on everything" be disloyal to Walter—or safe?

"I'm sorry, Lucas. I already have plans to go with Ruby," she lied.

"Well, that's fine, too! Safety in numbers, right? Bring the old girl along!"

"Yes, but, you see," Cora Lee stammered, "I don't think that Walter would approve of me stepping out with you. I wouldn't want to do anything to disappoint him while he's still away."

Lucas seemed surprised by her answer. "Walter! Why, what's he got to do with anythin'?"

"He asked me to wait for him, and I have!"

"Well, I'm sorry to break it to ya, doll," he said in a tone that seemed more delighted than sorry. "Walter and me bumped into each other in France the day 'fore I shipped out to come home. He was with a very pretty girl—um, Gigi was her name, I think. They was lookin' very chummy—I mean, she was kissin' on him and all. She was quite a little tomato, and ol' Walter was quite taken with her."

Cora Lee sucked in her breath in shock. Of course, he'd met someone. Why would he not have? He'd been away a long time. She was foolish to believe that a brief, stolen kiss on the night of his departure would have meant anything to Walter. He had only been speaking in a moment of excitement over his new adventure, not out of any true sentiment for her.

Lucas, enjoying the opportunity to bring Cora Lee hurtful news, embellished his tale further. "They might even be thinkin' 'bout getting hitched. Lots of soldiers is bringin' back Frenchie wives from over there. Those gals was latchin' onto American men like we was made of molasses. Sure seems like Walter ain't been waitin' fer you, is what I'm sayin'!"

She put her fingertips to her lips, feeling again the warmth of Walter's body against her own, the rumble of thunder in the pit of her stomach as he had held her close and pressed his lips to hers. So briefly. What a fool she'd been to wait for him!

Tears sprang unwanted into her eyes. Stiffly, she jerked herself out of Lucas' arms and spun away so he wouldn't see them. She was angry with herself for having been so foolish.

"In that case, yes, Lucas," she choked and wiped at her face. "I'd love to walk out with you at the fair." She shook her head to clear away the pain that washed over her and turned back to face Lucas with a forced smile. "Ruby and I will meet you at eleven in the morning, and we'll have lunch if you like."

A sly grin spread across Lucas' face. "Sure, doll. I'll see you tomorrow. It'll be fun."

CHAPTER 20

The street fair was a cacophony of sound, sights and smells that neither Cora Lee nor Ruby had ever experienced. Booths offering all manner of arts, crafts, contests, and curiosities lined both sides of a street crowded with fair goers. Music from a Wurlitzer Band Organ played loudly near a carousel of sleighs, colorful benches, and beautifully painted wooden horses. The aroma of popcorn and a spun sugar confection called 'fairy floss' filled the air, and flags and banners fluttered above their heads. Barkers shouted at passersby, eager to attract their attention and, perhaps, coax some money from their pockets.

"Hear ye! Hear ye!" yelled one man in a loud tie and clownishly-large striped suit. "Guess this woman's weight, and win a prize!" He held a stuffed toy turtle above his head and waved it in the air. An overweight woman wearing a dress cascading with ruffles and, no doubt, hiding a great deal of padding, sat on a blue loveseat behind the man. "Only five cents a chance! Only a nickel! Just one thin nickel for a chance to win a wonderful prize!"

Across the street a booth sporting a sign that read "Cutest Kitten Contest" gave the public a chance to vote on their favorite feline. Several cages were lined up on tables surrounding the exhibit and held small cats of every color and type. Cora Lee and Ruby walked over to the exhibit and stuck their fingers through the wire cages to stroke some of the animals.

"I like the little white one with the green eyes," Cora Lee said. "He's the cutest!"

Ruby stuck her finger into the cage of a short-haired, tiger-striped kitten that crouched down with a low growl and struck at her finger with its claws.

"Oh!" Ruby jerked her hand back and checked the scratch for blood. "This one's my favorite." She laughed and put a penny in the glass container in front of its cage. It was the only coin in the jar as no one else had voted for the poor thing. "He might not be a winner, but he's a fighter. I like that."

The two girls next stopped at a booth manned by women wearing sashes across their chests that read "Ladies Relief League." One of the women called to Ruby, "We're raising money for the boys overseas. Won't you donate?"

The women were selling flavored soda water. "Have you ever tried cola?" Ruby asked. Cora Lee shook her head, and Ruby bought a glass. "Never hurts to support the troops," she said. "Here, try it." She handed the drink to Cora Lee.

Cora Lee tentatively took the glass, eyed it suspiciously, and took a tiny sip. "Oooh! The bubbles!" she yelped. She took another gulp of the drink and giggled as she tried to stifle a burp. "But, it's good. I like it!" She handed the rest of the drink back to Ruby who drained the glass. She set it back on the counter, and they continued on their way.

Cora Lee was still aching from the news Lucas had given her about Walter, but she was bravely trying to be cheerful. She didn't want Ruby to know how hurt she was, and how very disappointed she was in herself for having been so gullible in love. Cora Lee was certain that Ruby would have no sympathy for her, anyway.

They passed a table with an array of homemade cakes, pies and cookies on sale. On the other side of the street were an exotic-looking tent with a fortune teller inside and a booth selling flowers and hand-painted ceramics of all sorts. There was a stall bearing a sign that read "Swat the Kaiser – Three Balls for a Dime." Empty milk bottles were lined up on a shelf at the back of the stall sporting the cardboard likeness of the German leader, and stuffed-animal prizes hung from the booth's ceiling.

At the end of the street and apart from the rest of the exhibits, an over-sized tent was set up. A sign reading "Hoochie-Coochie Dancers – Hula Girls, Geisha Girls, Belly Dancers" in large letters with

"Adults Only" in smaller letters over the ticket booth drew their attention. Ruby and Cora Lee stopped and tried to peer inside the darkened tent.

"No looking without buying a ticket," the barker said raking Ruby's body with his eyes.

"Why not?" Ruby answered, looking back at him in the same manner. "You are."

Cora Lee stepped back, shocked at her friend's bold reply. "Ruby!" she gasped.

Ruby curled her lips in a seductive smile, stared pointedly at the man, and said, "Come on. There ain't nothin' to see here."

They started to walk on when Lucas called out to them from a few yards away. "Here you girls are!" He came toward them with a smile. "I thought ya might have given me the slip."

"No such luck," Ruby muttered under her breath.

"Come on. Let's go find some lunch," he said.

Lucas took Cora Lee and Ruby each by the elbow and ushered them down a side street where the booths were less crowded. Midway down the sidewalk, a middle-aged, balding man with a greasy combover stood on a milkcrate speaking to a small crowd that had gathered around him. The trio stopped to listen.

"The mothers of this town, of this state, want an end to the unholy activities that take place in these pagan temples of iniquity," he yelled as he swung his open hand toward a small dance emporium nearby. "Indecent gyrating and shimmying to scandalous jazz music while other couples clutch and squirm together in darkened corners! These cabarets of carnal obscenity are unbearable in our community and must be shut down for the benefit of everyone. We must protect our youth from this vile corruption!"

"I suppose, like all you soapbox do-gooders, you're one of those blasted prohibitionists opposed to a man having a beer or a tot of whiskey, too!" yelled a man in the crowd.

The speaker closed his mouth in a scowl and turned to the man. "Sir," he said in a lower voice. "I do, indeed, support our Bone-Dry Law, and I'm proud that Arkansas has led the rest of the nation by our fine example. I'm happy that our entire great country will soon enjoy the blessings of sobriety when the new Prohibition law takes effect. It should have become the law of the land immediately rather than having to wait until January to become enforceable."

His voice rose again as he continued, "Two years ago, I was a gin-rotted ruin, a hollow-hearted, empty shell of a creature not even fit to be called a man. I was a red-nosed, bleary-eyed, stumbling bum with no future but the gutter." Beating his chest with his fist, he asked, "What do you think brought about this change in me?"

Ruby snorted and shouted, "Who says there's been any change?"

The crowd roared with laughter and began to move off leaving the self-righteous orator to himself.

"Nasty old do-gooders!" Lucas fumed. "Why can't they mind their own bee's wax and stay out of

other folks' business? Passin' that 'bone-dry law!'
What's it to them if a man has a drink after an honest,
twelve-hour day's work? Who'd have voted to keep a
man from drinkin' if we want? Same ones a'wantin'
to give women the vote, I reckon. What man wants his
wife out at the votin' hall and not home cookin' and
cleanin' fer him? Who asked 'em, huh?"

Cora Lee nodded and hoped her silent agreement
would end the tirade. Ruby, however, seemed to enjoy
the drama and sought to goad him on.

"Why not let women have the vote? I'd think
you'd be fer that, bein' a modern man?"

"Why, what good does it do? A woman votin' the
same as her husband is just an echo of his opinion. If
she votes against him, then she's completely undone
and erased a man's rightful vote!

"The country'll go to ruin if a bunch of petticoats
start tryin' to run things. They don't have the brains
fer it. What self-respectin' woman wants to get down
and grub in the dirty arena of politics, anyway? It ain't
somethin' a polite female should wanna wallow
around in! I certainly won't never allow any wife of
mine to vote, even if the law is changed!"

Ruby laughed and Cora Lee squirmed at the
vehemence of Lucas' speech.

"Well, folks, this is where I take off," Ruby said
and unlatched herself from Lucas' hand. "I ain't much
interested in street fair food fer lunch, and, as they
say, 'three's a crowd.' Cora Lee, I'll see ya later."

Ruby turned and walked away. Cora Lee turned to Lucas and said, "I think I should go back with her."

"Now, don't be a spoil sport, gal. The afternoon is still young, and you promised to have lunch with me. Here," he said, pulling her along, "let's take this shortcut over to the area where the food vendors are."

Lucas pulled Cora Lee into an alley. The tall buildings on each side of the backstreet blocked out the sunlight making the way gloomy and dark. A rivulet of oily water dripped into a drainage grate near a group of garbage cans by a recessed doorway, the sound echoing on the walls of the buildings on either side. The air was dank and heavy, and Cora Lee suddenly found it hard to breathe. Anxiously, she looked over her shoulder, and a chill went up her spine as she realized there were no other people in the alley. She was alone with Lucas.

There were only a few more yards to go. Cora Lee tried to quicken her step, but Lucas had a firm hold on her elbow. She trembled, and she tried her best to keep him from sensing her growing unease.

As they neared the end of the alley, she tripped on a raised piece of broken concrete in their path. Lucas' grip on her arm tightened, and he pulled her up close to him. His arm went around her like a vise that could break her spine with the smallest squeeze.

Cora Lee's head snapped up. She gasped and held her breath for the space of a heartbeat as a sense of her old terror flashed through her mind. She thought she caught a strange expression in the shadows of his darkly handsome face. A wicked expression.

"Are you alright? You didn't hurt yerself, did ya?" His grip relaxed as he released her and gave her his arm to lean on.

Was the expression she thought she saw only a childhood memory of his teasing and tormenting? Perhaps it was only concern for her wellbeing. After all, the light in this alleyway was dim. She relaxed and hesitantly put her hand in the crook of his offered arm. "Yes, I'm fine. Thank you, Lucas."

He led her out into a bright plaza filled with canopied tables and wooden chairs. The square was surrounded by colorful booths offering different types of food and drink. The air was filled with the delightful aroma of roasted meats, baked breads, chocolate cakes, and other savory and sweet treats.

Lucas ushered Cora Lee to a table and sat her down. "I'll go and buy us somethin' to eat. How 'bout a hotdog? What would ya like to drink?" he asked.

"Just water, thanks, and a hotdog sounds swell."

A short time later, Lucas came back bearing their food and drinks. He sat down, handed Cora Lee her glass of water and a paper-wrapped hotdog, then unwrapped his own.

"Listen," he said. "There's a dance later tonight over at the tennis courts. Willie Clay and his jazz band is playin'. What say I pick you up and we go check it out? It'll be fun, huh?"

Cora Lee thought about his invitation, but decided to turn him down. "I'm sorry, Lucas. I'm working every night this week, and the thought of more dancing makes my feet hurt just thinking about it. I appreciate your offer, but I'm gonna have to say no."

Even though she now knew that Walter cared for her no more and had given himself to another, she could not yet release him from her heart. Dating Lucas still seemed disloyal and even unfaithful given that she still had such powerful feelings for Walter.

Lucas grimaced. "Of course! I do fer sure have the 'brain wilts' like you told me once. That wouldn't be any fun fer ya, would it? Maybe I can take you to the movin' picture show sometime? That way you can be off'n yer feet and enjoy some of them movie stars singin' and a'dancin' to entertain you instead!"

Cora Lee blushed as she remembered the insults she had hurled at Lucas that afternoon so many years ago on the way to the Campbell farm for Amanda's wedding. Apparently, he remembered them, too. She smiled and nodded. "I reckon I'll think about it. I might have a night off next week, and me and Ruby can go with you."

It wouldn't be an actual date if Ruby came along, she thought. *And maybe by next week I'll get over my feelings for Walter some.*

The idea of 'getting over' Walter was painful, and she suppressed an audible moan. *How will I ever get over him?*

The rest of the afternoon passed quickly, and Lucas behaved like a perfect gentleman. Cora Lee wondered if she should let down her guard, if holding the past against this man was treating him unfairly. He had apologized for his boyhood actions. She should forgive him as the Good Book taught Christians to do. Shouldn't she?

CHAPTER 21

As the calendar crawled its way through August, the long, steamy summer days lent themselves to fewer daytime outings and more activities at night. Tea rooms and 'speakeasy' dance halls enjoyed a brisk business as folks emerged from their sweltering homes to enjoy cooler evening temperatures. Cora Lee was soon able to repay Ruby the money she had borrowed to buy new clothes, and she had a growing nest egg put aside, as well.

"We should be able to rent us a little house or an apartment soon so you can bring Micah home to live with us." Cora Lee, wearing only a light-weight batiste nightgown, sat cross-legged on her bed in front of an electric fan running on the windowsill. The room was like an oven, and she wiped the sweat off of her face as she studied the 'For Rent' section of a newspaper that was spread out in front of her.

Ruby sat at the dressing table in her chemise. The heat in the room was almost suffocating. She sighed and dabbed a little scented toilet water on her temples and wrists then picked up a paper fan and waved it at her face.

"I guess we better start lookin' fer somethin'. The home has only given me 'til the end of this month to come take him, or they's gonna have to send him to the orphanage. I don't want that, but I don't know how I'll manage to care for him and pay fer rent and food and other bills."

"Oh, don't you worry about that!" Cora Lee jumped off the bed and went to Ruby. "I have it all planned out! We'll split the week and dance three nights each. That way, we'll have income from a whole week's work 'tween us, and you'll be able to spend time with Micah, too! We can even take in washing and ironing if we need extra money."

Ruby twisted her face into a rueful smile. "You think we can manage it?"

"Sure! Look here," Cora Lee grabbed the paper on her bed. "See this? Here's a little two-bed, furnished house with a parlor and a kitchenette for rent, and it's only twenty-five dollars a month. With groceries and electric and other expenses, why, I reckon we'll do fine. We're payin' sixteen dollars a month between us for this room. We have some savings, too."

Ruby knitted her brow. "You sound awful sure 'bout that, but it might be doable," she said hesitantly.

"Lemme think on it a day or two. Maybe we can go see the place on Sunday afternoon."

"I'm gonna work extra hard, Ruby. I know we can make this work!" Cora Lee gave her friend an enthusiastic hug which Ruby shook off.

"Look," Ruby warned. "Don't go gettin' worked up. I need to figure things out on my own 'fore I go leapin' and jumpin' into somethin' like that."

The two girls did a brisk business that night, and both of them were pleased with their earnings. Cora Lee put aside almost all of her money after paying her share of the rent for the week. Ruby paid her rent and put aside the fee she owed for Micah's care for the month. It left her with nothing left over to save.

"It's just one night's take," Cora Lee soothed as Ruby fretted over her finances. "You'll make plenty again tomorrow night to put aside. Maybe Saturday afternoon we can go shopping and buy something new to wear to go see that house on Sunday!"

Ruby shook her head. "I ain't gonna be spendin' money on new clothes right now. I need to save ever nickel I can. 'Sides, I wanna go visit Micah Saturday. I'm past due on his payment fer the month. I'd like to be able to tell the nurses at the home that I can take him with me sooner than the end of the month."

The rest of the week was busy at the emporium and proved profitable for all of the dancers. Abel was pleased with the business he was doing, and he was in an uncharacteristically generous mood. He gave each of his girls an extra dollar in their pay packet. The dancers couldn't wait to spend their bonuses, but Ruby and Cora Lee put their dollars aside to save for the future.

Saturday morning, Ruby and Cora Lee took the trolly across the river and went to visit Micah. The late-August day was viciously hot, and both girls were happy to spend time in the establishment's waiting room with the baby rather than outside in the park area where previous visits had been enjoyed.

Ruby cooed and cuddled the infant until the matron entered the room and lay a blanket on the floor. Taking Micah from Ruby's arms, the woman placed him on his belly on the blanket. He lifted his head and stretched his upper body, rolled over onto his back, and studied his hands as they waved about in the air above his face.

The woman took a seat in one of the wing-back chairs beside the sofa where the two girls were sitting. "I'm happy to see that you have managed to spend a little time with your son, Miss Douglas," the woman said. "I think we need to have a serious talk at this time about your future plans. We have already made arrangements with St. Joseph's Orphanage to take him the first of next month—that's in two weeks' time. Micah will be turning six months soon, and we have already kept him much longer than we should have."

Ruby's face paled. "I understand, Matron. Believe me, I'm doin' everthin' I can to make a home fer my son. I've found a nice house to rent," she lied.

Cora Lee shot her a questioning look, but Ruby ignored her and went on. "I'm plannin' to take Micah home with me 'fore the end of the month. I brung his payment fer August," Ruby said as she handed an envelope to the woman. "Please don't think I'm abandonin' my baby. He's everthin' to me."

The matron nodded and tucked the envelope into the pocket of her apron. She leaned forward and patted Ruby on her knee. "I appreciate how important this is for you, but it's also critical for Micah to be in his permanent home. While we adhere to the modern view that keeping children with their birth mothers is usually what is best, we also believe that keeping a young child in limbo is just the opposite. Medical research is proving that a baby must bond with their parent at an early age. Left too long, that bond may never develop, and that's what we are trying to avoid for Micah. He needs a family, structure, and a permanent home."

The woman rose from the chair and walked to the table under the window. Pulling open a drawer, she withdrew a sheet of paper and gave it to Ruby.

"This is a list of items we recommend you have ready when you take the baby home. As you can see, you will need to have these items immediately. The others, the ones below the line there," the matron pointed, "will need to be on hand before he starts walking. There's a recipe for his formula on the back, but he has already transitioned to cow's milk. You won't need to prepare formula, but you will need to be sure you have an icebox to keep his milk and orange juice fresh."

Cora Lee leaned in to read the list as Ruby studied it. The number of items was extensive: cloth diapers and pins, powder, diaper cream, bottles, nipples, burp cloths, cod liver oil, blankets and quilts, long-sleeved dresses, hats, booties, mittens, thumb guard, teething serum (morphine recommended over alcohol formulary), walker, playpen, pram, crib. Cora Lee could see by Ruby's face and the way she gripped the list that she was getting upset by the magnitude of it.

"We will be giving you a handbook to help you as you get adjusted to having your baby at home with you. We recommend that you keep him on the strict sleeping and eating schedule to which he's already accustomed. He's over the colic age, but he will still be vulnerable to upset stomach if you're not careful.

"Handle him only now and then—don't coddle, don't hug and kiss excessively. A daily cuddle of five or ten minutes is the maximum. A kiss on the forehead at bedtime is acceptable or when he's done something very, very good.

"Be sure that he is kept warm and out of drafts. And remember, crying is essential to promote the development of strong lungs. He should be allowed to cry energetically several times a day."

The matron bent to pick Micah up from the floor. "Say 'bye-bye' to your mummy, Micah." Turning to Ruby, she added, "Let's hope we see her again very soon." She helped Micah wave his little hand, then carried the baby through the door and closed it behind her. She left Ruby and Cora Lee to find their way out.

Ruby was silent the entire trip back across the river. Cora Lee, anxious to help make things right, prattled nervously as she detailed their plans again.

"I'm sure we can get that house. I know it's a little expensive, but we can make it work. I know we can! And we can start right away getting what's needed."

Ruby did not reply.

****

Lucas came in to the dance emporium that night to see Cora Lee. Once again, he gave all of his tickets to her and escorted her to the talk-time area. As they sat over their spiked tea, Lucas eyed her without saying anything for a few minutes. He sat his drink on the table and leaned toward her, taking her hand in his.

"Let's go out tomorrow. This place gets old after a few nights. I wanna take ya to a place where things are really poppin'. It's a 'private club,' and a friend of mine gave me the password to get in. We can have us a grand ol' time, and you don't have to let these mugs handle ya all night. You can relax and stay off yer feet. Don't that sound good? What do ya say?"

Cora Lee, still hurting from the thought of Walter bringing home a wife from France, could think of nothing less appealing than to spend an evening out with Lucas. She had not enjoyed the time she spent with him at the street fair. She had decided to forgive his childhood assault on her, of course, but that did not mean she had to date him. She shook her head and pulled her hand away.

"I'm sorry you're bored with being here, but I understand. You go ahead and enjoy your 'poppin' place.' Ruby and me are trying to save up money to rent a little house soon. I need to stay here and work, but thank you for the offer, Lucas."

Lucas scowled, and his eyes narrowed. "Listen, Cora Lee," he said tersely. "It ain't right fer you to work all the time. Listen to me." He leaned forward and grabbed her hand, holding it in a vice-like grip. The look in his cold, blue eyes was anything but friendly. "You need to get out of this musty old dance hall and have a little fun with me."

He released her hand and sat back in his chair, sniffed and took a swig of his 'tea' before setting his cup down on the table with calculated care. "Do what I say." His voice softened, but his eyes were still hard. "It's fer yer own good, ya know."

What makes you think you know what's good for me? Cora Lee controlled the impulse to throw her retort in her 'date's' face.

"Besides," Lucas went on, "I told my friend I was bringin' a dame, and I ain't gonna show up without one. Yer goin' with me, and that's the end of it."

Cora Lee's mouth dropped open in astonishment. Did he just *order* her to do something she had politely declined to do? Who did he think he was? Who did he think *she* was? She could feel the color rising in her cheeks in indignation. Without a second thought, she sat up in her chair, straightened her shoulders, jutted her chin at him, and said between clenched teeth, "I said 'no,' and *that's* the end of it!"

She reached into her pocket and withdrew the tickets Lucas had given her to buy talk time, tossed them on the table, and stood. She walked stiffly back to the pen where she was quickly claimed for a dance by a giraffe of a man in a checked, three-piece suit.

Mavis finished the dance with her brown-suited escort and approached Lucas where he still sat fuming over Cora Lee's rejection. "Trouble in paradise?" she asked in a smug tone.

Lucas scowled, picked up his tickets, and handed them to Mavis. "Dance."

Mavis smiled, accepted the tickets, and allowed Lucas to lead her out to the floor. He maneuvered her to the center of the floor where Cora Lee was being held a little too tightly by the giraffe man. Making sure he was close enough for Cora Lee to hear, he said loudly, "Yer too fine a woman to work in a seedy joint like this, Mavis. I'd think only trollops, sluts, and trash would allow themselves to be manhandled all night by any man that comes along and can pay 'em a nickel!"

Mavis laughed gayly and tossed her head. "Well, a poor gal's gotta do what a poor gal's gotta do. Most of the dancers in here are alright. *Some* of 'em, though," she added giving Cora Lee a pointed look, "ain't from so fine a stock!"

Thankfully, the song ended, and Cora Lee was escorted back to the pen. Ruby came off of the floor and sat down beside her. "You look like ya could tear the head off a wampus cat. What happened?"

Cora Lee shook her head. "It's nothing to worry about. Lucas is the same mean, mangy dog he's always been, is all."

"Well, tigers don't change they stripes, do they? And we got better things to worry about than Lucas McDaniel. We need to dig in and start earnin' a lot more money if we're gonna be able to move into that house—or any house, fer that matter. Gettin' Micah out of that home 'fore they send him to the orphanage is all I can think about, now!"

Cora Lee agreed. "An orphanage isn't a good place to raise any child."

Ruby looked at her. "I reckon you'd know."

Cora Lee nodded, and she was able to put Lucas out of her mind for the rest of the evening. Maybe he had even lied to her about Walter's French girlfriend—or wife? Dared she hope?

The band began another tune, and both girls jumped up to claim the tickets of two customers who approached the pen. They were younger and better dressed than most of the customers who came in every night. One wore a three-piece suit and silk tie; the other wore a pin-striped, double-breasted leisure suit. They carried themselves with a cocky sort of arrogance and looked around the hall as if they were disdainful of their surroundings.

The two men pulled the girls onto the floor, and Ruby was immediately two-stepped away to a dark corner. Cora Lee lost sight of her friend across the crowded room. She twisted her head about searching for Ruby, but the man in whose arms she danced pulled her so close that movement of her upper body was almost impossible.

"Now, don't you worry none about your friend," the young man in a pin-striped leisure suit said as he nuzzled her neck. He laughed. "I'm sure she's showing ol' Larry a fine time. Why don't we move over behind that pillar?"

Cora Lee pushed against the man's chest and shook her head. "I prefer to stay out of those dark corners!"

The man pulled her back to his chest a little too roughly. "I'm sure you'd prefer to earn a lot more than these three tickets for the dance, too, wouldn't you?" He reached into his vest pocket and pulled out a silver dollar. "This is for you, doll, if you let me hold you *real* close while we dance. I'm not gonna hurt you none, just wanna have a little fun. Your friend over there don't seem to mind it."

He jerked his head toward the back of the room where Ruby was letting her dance partner have 'a little fun.' The man had his hands all over Ruby, and Cora Lee shivered at the sight. Did she really find it so easy to allow that? Was that silver dollar so valuable? More valuable than virtue, honor, and self-respect?

Cora Lee's dance partner put one hand behind her neck and slid his other hand down her back. Cupping her backside, he shoved his groin into hers. She gasped and pushed him away. The hand he had behind her neck caught in her necklace and broke the string sending buttons flying onto the dance floor.

The music paused for a mid-dance ticket break as Cora Lee stood frozen in shocked silence. Her hand flew to her neck, and she fell to her knees. She scooped up the broken necklace and loose buttons from the floor as tears blurred her vision.

The music started up again, and her dance partner walked off the floor. Cora Lee struggled to her feet with her precious mementoes clutched in her hand. Sobbing, she ran out of the room, her face burning in embarrassment and shame over the way her pin-striped dance partner had felt free to man-handle her.

But, did she deserve better, she asked herself. *Isn't this what I'm becoming, after all?*

CHAPTER 22

Walter's head rocked gently against the window as the train from Saint Louis swayed from side to side. The wheels beneath him clacked and rattled along the iron rails that carried him closer to home, and the conductor called out the name of yet another town along the route to Endurance as the train neared the station and began to slow.

His uneasy slumber, even though broken frequently by other passengers and the ticket conductor moving through the car from time to time, was the most sleep he had enjoyed for days. After going through the awful 'delousing' experience by the military on his discharge, he had collected his pay, donned a clean, if somewhat shabby and poorly mended, uniform, and started his long travels back to Bennett's Ridge.

A small ferry, overcrowded with soldiers eager for home, had taken him to a ship riding off the port of Brest, France almost two weeks ago. During the six days aboard the ship back to the United States, he had suffered badly from sea sickness that made sleep almost impossible. What little sleep he had managed had been broken by horrific nightmares that woke him shaking and drenched in cold sweats.

He had found it almost better to avoid sleeping than to suffer the dreams of battle that plagued not only himself, but many of the other men who traveled with him. Their screams and whimpers during the night rang through the ship as loudly as his own.

His ship had docked at Ellis Island, and after processing, he took a ferry from the island to New York City. A short bus ride took him to Grand Central Station where he had tried, if unsuccessfully, to nap while waiting on a train to take him to Chicago. He changed trains in Chicago and arrived in Saint Louis where he had started this last leg of his return home. After a short wait, he caught the train, finally, back to the town of Endurance.

He dozed off as the train pulled into a station and stopped, but was jolted awake by passengers shuffling to leave and others finding their seats and stowing their luggage. A woman took a seat next to him and shoved her valise under the seat in front of her.

Walter rubbed his gritty, red eyes and nodded politely to her. Shifting his feet, which were propped up on his duffle bag on the floor, he moved his legs to give the lady more room. Leaning against the window, he closed his eyes, praying for sweeter dreams to roll beneath his lids than the hideous pictures of war that often found their way there.

He no longer had a desire for adventure and travel. *Mae Clarey was right. Ain't no better place on earth than home,* he thought as memories of Cora Lee drifted through his mind. The train jerked into motion as it left the station, and he drifted off once again. He slept soundly for a time before the conductor passed through the crowded car checking tickets and marking them with his hole-punch.

"Next stop is yours, sir," the conductor woke Walter, then he moved to the next passenger.

Walter nodded, sat up straight in his seat, and rubbed his face to wipe away the cobwebs that had gathered in his head. His brain was foggy, and he was surprised to see the sun had moved well past the noon hour. As the train began to slow, excitement began coursing through his body at the thought of being home again—the thought of seeing Cora Lee again…holding her…kissing her.

As the train neared the station, Walter excused himself and waited for the woman next to him to stand and let him up. He retrieved his duffle bag and slid out of his seat into the aisle. The swaying car made standing with his bag difficult. He braced his feet in a wide stance and gripped the back of each row of seats as he lurched down the aisle to the door and waited for the train to come to a stop at the depot in Endurance.

He stepped down off the train and saw several other returning soldiers, still in uniform, gathering near the far end of the platform. Walter fought his way through passengers and the people there to greet them and joined the group, surprised to find Jacob Bennett and Roy Dale among them. Aside from his brief encounter with Lucas McDaniel in France, Walter had not seen nor heard from any of the young men from Bennett's Ridge since the end of his training at Camp Pike before being shipped overseas.

The three young men clapped each other heartily on the shoulders, hugged unashamedly, and congratulated each other on surviving the war and making it home. In a jumble, they gave brief updates about their units and where they had served and how long they had been in the trenches. Stories in more detail would be saved for times when moonshine would help to dislodge harsher memories and soften their sharp edges.

Eager to be on their way, the men walked to the steps at the end of the platform. "Silas should be here with the wagon to carry us home," Jacob said. "Can't wait to climb back into that old wagon!"

Looking around, however, Silas and his wagon were nowhere to be found. Instead, there were three open-topped Model T Ford motorcars, draped with patriotic bunting, waiting to take the returning soldiers through town in a celebratory 'Welcome Home' parade. Walter's heart sank as he realized his journey's end would be delayed yet again.

"So close, and yet so far, eh?" Jacob sighed.

"Once more into the breach, fellas," Roy Dale quipped, quoting Shakespear.

A middle-aged, portly man dressed in coattails draped with a sash that read "Mayor" across his chest and with a top hat on his head directed soldiers to cars that were soon filled to capacity. The men that were left standing were told to march along the side and wave to the crowd as the parade passed through town.

"Your family and friends wait to greet you at the fairgrounds at the end of a short parade," the mayor announced. "There'll be a ceremony with a band playing in your honor. I will be giving a welcoming speech. That will be followed by light refreshments of donuts and lemonade provided by the Ladies of the War Camp Community Support Guild. You men are expected to be on your very best behavior as befits your stations and positions as members of our military and returning heroes to our fair city."

The boys from Bennett's Ridge exchanged glances and stifled groans. "Duty calls, men," Jacob said.

"Well, I'll ketch up, fellas," Walter said. "I'm goin' back into the depot to send a telegram to Ruby down in Little Rock to tell her we're back. I'm gonna spend a few days with Ma and get rested up some. *And see Cora Lee,* he added to himself. "Then I'm plannin' to go fetch Ruby back home, if I can. Go ahead, and I'll meet up with ya at the fairgrounds."

"I'll come, too," Jacob and Roy Dale said in unison.

The young men returned to the depot office where a quick telegram was hastily composed and sent to Ruby with just two words:

"We're home."

CHAPTER 23

The women, the mothers, the decent folks in this town want to see an end to the unholy activities that take place in this pagan temple of iniquity—this den of squalor and degradation—this Sodom and Gomorrah!"

The man with the greasy combover from the street fair had set up his milkcrate outside of Abel's dance emporium and was holding a soapbox rally against the establishment. Irma Malone stood behind him with two other women. They wore sashes across their chests that read, "Ladies of Virtue League." The small crowd that had gathered around the man was growing as passersby stopped to listen.

"Indecent gyrating and shimmying to scandalous jazz music. Couples clutch and squirm together in darkened corners. Innocent young men tempted into the vilest of wickedness, against the teachings of their dear mothers, led by natural curiosity to their destruction! Drawn by the devil himself to this place where they themselves become creatures of contempt! Lounge lizards! Parlor snakes! Jazz-mad men who dance like creatures made feverish by these temptresses-for-hire!

"This sleezy gin joint, this rum-soaked hole is nothing more than a den of fallen women. Sirens who dress in scandalous attire, wear painted faces and cheap perfume, who bedeck themselves with jewels to draw a man's eye, lure them onto the rocks of eternal damnation and entrap them in sin. This cabaret of carnal obscenity is unbearable in our community! It must be closed down to protect our youth—our very society—from this revolting, unacceptable vulgarity and corruption."

Abel stood outside the doorway of his dancehall, an ugly, dangerous look clouding his face. Ruby, Cora Lee, and Edith stood next to him nervously listening to the man's tirade.

"We've heard enough," Abel growled as he turned to open the door. "Go inside 'fore these fools decide to do somethin' stupid."

The four of them went into the building, and Abel bolted the door behind them. He walked to the door of the ticket office and said, "Best go on upstairs and get ready for work. I doubt if that circus will last much longer. Too hot for those people to stand around in the sun listening to the rantings of them nuisances."

The three girls made a hasty retreat up the stairs to the third floor. Edith went with Ruby and Cora Lee to their room where some of the other dancers were congregated around the open window above the gathering below. The words of the little man were clear as his voice drifted up to them.

"What on earth is the matter with those people?" Edith wrung her hands and looked as if she might cry. "We ain't doin' nothin' ugly in here! We only dance with the fellas and talk to 'em is all."

"What's that nasty little man mean by callin' us 'fallen women?' We ain't no such thing!"

"Temptresses? The only thing I'm tempted to do is clock him one!"

"I'd like to pop him one right in the ol' lemon! The nerve! Sirens, indeed!"

One of the girls picked up a flower pot that sat on the windowsill and was about to throw it out the window at the crowd below when Mavis' shrill voice cut through the room like an ax.

"All right, ladies! That's enough standin' around. Go on back to your own rooms and start gettin' ready for work! It's gonna be a busy night."

The girls jumped and scrambled past Mavis as they hurriedly returned to their rooms. Cora Lee walked over to the window and switched on the electric fan as Mavis sat down on Ruby's bed. She pulled a folded envelope from the pocket of her dress and waved it in the air.

"Abel said this telegram came for you while you was out." She eyed the missive and slowly handed it to Ruby. Ruby snatched the paper out of her hand.

"Oooh," Mavis cooed in a mocking falsetto as she leaned back on her elbows. "Ain't you the hoity toity one, gettin' a telegram and all. Who's it from?"

"None of yer bee's wax. You delivered it to me, now get out."

Mavis stood and gave Cora Lee a leering wink. "Probably some lover boy." Laughing, Mavis sauntered out of the room, and Ruby tore at the telegram.

"It's from Walter."

Cora Lee gasped and held out her hand. Ruby handed her the telegram. Cora Lee stared at the message. The two words swam on the paper, and her vision blurred

"We're home," Ruby said. "That's all it says."

"He's brought someone back with him." Her initial rush of relief that Walter had come back safely was rapidly replaced by despair as Cora Lee realized that he had not come home alone. "Lucas said he thought Walter would be bringing back a wife from France. I guess this means that he has."

"It don't say who the 'we' is. Yer jumpin' to conclusions where ya don't have to."

Cora Lee's knees buckled, and she sat down heavily on her bed as she fought to maintain her composure. She hadn't wanted to believe that Walter was lost to her, that he had fallen in love with someone else. In her heart, she had been holding out hope that Lucas was wrong, that Walter would come back to her.

Her broken necklace seemed to be a harbinger of his loss, but she had not wanted to believe it. The paper she clenched in her fist was inescapable proof, though, that she could not now ignore. Walter was no longer hers.

And what would he want with her now, anyway? Wasn't she now a 'fallen woman,' like the soapbox man with the combover had called them all? Wasn't this a 'shameful den of iniquity?' Wasn't Lucas right when he had called her 'a trollop, slut, and trash?'

She *did* wear a dancing frock that was too short. She *had* begun to wear lipstick and rouge her cheeks. Her perfume *was* cheap, and she *did* have a jeweled headband like the one Edith wore. A man *had* made free to take crude advantage of her on the dancefloor.

Could it be true? Cora Lee wondered if she was the shameful thing that the Ladies of Virtue League claimed was sinful, indecent, and vile.

And, if so, how could she face Walter again?

CHAPTER 24

Ruby stood in the hallway leaning against the wall near her room in close conversation with Edith as Cora Lee came out of the bathroom at the end of the corridor. The two jumped apart and smiled at her as if they were guilty of some great conspiracy. Cora Lee looked at the pair questioningly as she approached them, and, when they didn't speak, slipped past them into her room. Ruby followed Cora Lee into the room as Edith walked away.

"Everything okay?" Cora Lee asked, puzzled by Ruby's strange behavior.

Ruby sat down on the chair at the vanity and picked up her hairbrush without speaking to her roommate. After taking a few swipes at her curly, red bob, she put down the brush and twisted in the chair to face Cora Lee. She cleared her throat, and Cora Lee sat down on her bed to give Ruby her full attention.

"Edith and me went to see that little house you saw in the rent ads, and it was a real dump. It didn't have furniture like the ad said except fer a couch and one kitchen chair. It didn't have no icebox, either." She cleared her throat again. "Turns out, uh, Edith's uncle has a little house that's closer to here. It's fully furnished, and it even has an icebox already. He said he'd rent it to her and me at a big discount fer just eighteen dollars a month." Ruby looked down. "I'm gonna rent that place with her instead of you."

Cora Lee sat motionless on the bed and stared at Ruby. Ruby raised her head, her jaw set in a hard line. "It'd be foolish not to fer that kind of price. I gotta do what's best fer me and Micah, and what's best is fer us to be livin' in a decent place fer the least amount of money I can manage."

Ruby turned back to the mirror, picked up her berry-colored lipstick, and ran it over her cupids-bow lips. She picked up Walter's telegram from the vanity, blotted her lipstick on it, and turned back to Cora Lee.

"I refuse to feel guilty about doin' what's best fer my baby," she said almost angrily. "I know you was countin' on us movin' in together, but I don't need ya. I've found a better deal with Edith, and she's gonna help gather up some of the stuff on that baby list that I need to get, too."

Flabbergasted, Cora Lee sat frozen as the words Ruby threw at her sunk in. She stood up slowly. "How can you just cast me aside like I don't mean anything to you? I left home and came here to help you…"

"Who said I need yer help?" Ruby cut in. "You come down here, all high and mighty, like yer better'n me. Well, ya ain't! And I don't need yer savin' me from nothin, no how. I'm makin' my own way here, makin' my life the way I want it. And I'm perfectly happy—I'm perfectly fine with the decisions I've made and the choices I'm makin'!"

"Well, I guess things are turning out as God intended, then," Cora Lee said as coolly as she could manage, trying to control the trembling in her voice. Ruby's words stung, and stung deeply.

"No," Ruby spat. "Things is turnin' out the way *I'm* intendin'. *God* ain't got nothin' to do with it."

Cora Lee gasped, her eyes wide in shock. She stood and stared at her roommate, then stiffly walked out of the room, silent lest she say something as hurtful as Ruby had flung at her. She may be able to curb her tongue, but she was unable to control the hurt, disappointment and anger building inside her.

Although she had only been away from her home in the mountains for a little over three months, it could have been an eternity. So much about herself had changed, and Bennett's Ridge was a whole world away now. She didn't think she still had a belonging place there, and Ruby had decided that she and Micah were not part of her future or her purpose. Without a purpose, without a friend, without Walter, she had no belonging place here, either.

And did she want to 'belong' here in what she was beginning to see as the seedy, sordid dancehall life she was making for herself?

She leaned against the wall in the hallway. Her head was reeling. She was unmoored, unsteady, adrift.

I *need a glass of special tea—only without the tea.*

She made her way, unsteadily, down the hall and down the stairs to the ballroom and bar, empty of dancers and drinkers at this time of day. Abel looked up as she entered and said nothing as she almost stumbled to the bar and sat down on one of the high stools. He reached behind him, took down a small glass, and took a silver flask out of his hip pocket. Unscrewing the lid from the flask, he poured a shot of gin into the glass.

"Okay, spill it. What's eatin' on ya?" He slid the drink to her, his heavy brow furrowed in concern as he returned the flask to his pocket. "You ain't sick are ya? Can't have a sick horse in my stable."

Cora Lee shook her head and took a swallow of the gin enjoying the slow, punishing burn it kindled in her throat and stomach. "I'm leaving here, I guess," she said as she sat her half-empty glass on the bar. "Ruby and Edith are moving out together, and seems I don't have any reason to stay now. I was only here to help Ruby, but she just told me she 'got a better deal' with Edith." The pain of that admission burned hotter than the liquor swimming in her stomach. "They're moving into a house without me."

"And that's a blow to ya?" Abel clearly found Cora Lee's distress unjustified. "What difference does it make if Ruby needs ya or not? You're a good dancer, the customers like ya, and you make good money here, don't ya? What do you need her for?"

Cora Lee looked at Abel, unable to explain her feelings of isolation, of homelessness, of abandonment. She had become useless to anyone on this earth, and she didn't know who she was or what she was turning into. The world was spinning away from her and leaving her in some soulless void.

She had managed to remake the button necklace she wore again at her neck. Her fingers sought and found the charms, but found no solace there. The loved ones represented by those disks were either dead, or, in Walter's case, had chosen to spend their lives with someone else. She was completely alone.

"See here," Abel said, "I don't want you to leave, but it ain't good for business to have one of my gals mopin' around the place. I don't want you to stay if ya ain't happy." He looked around and chuckled. "If you don't think this place is 'somethin' wonderful,' or your own little slice of Heaven."

Cora Lee put on a sad smile. "Oh, I don't think Heaven is some amusement park full of Ferris wheels, carousels and candy. I just know that it isn't a dancehall full of sad men and handsy dancers, either. I think Heaven is more like birdsong and sunshine—the shade of an oak tree…"

"Well, that's what you had 'fore ya came here, weren't it? So, why'd ya leave? Why not go back?"

"I've got no place there anymore. There's nobody to go back to there."

"You gotta make your own place in the place you wanna be wherever that may turn out to be. Stiffen your lip, put some starch in your shirt, and carve out your own spot; don't let anybody push you out of it."

Cora Lee shrugged. "Somebody else told me that, too," she said, thinking of the advice Ruby's mother had once given her. "But, I have no idea what 'my own spot' might even look like, now. I don't think I know how to do that."

"What do you mean ya don't know how? You done that here, didn't ya? Nobody moved aside to make room for ya here, did they?

"Ruby did," Cora Lee mumbled and shrugged. "Without her, I'd have never made it here, would I?"

Abel scoffed. "Ruby? Ruby don't do nothin' for nobody lessen it benefits Ruby. What you done here, you done by yourself. You can do the same anywhere. I don't want you to quit, but if you decide to leave, you'll do fine wherever you end up. Don't let nobody else make that decision for ya or push ya out of where ya wanna be." Abel stretched out his hand and touched the rim of Cora Lee's glass. "And you don't need this stuff to help ya decide, either."

He pulled the glass away and drank what was left in it. He walked to the sink where he rinsed the glass and set it on the sideboard. Cora Lee let his words sink in, and she decided he was right about the gin.

Still, she needed something to help pull her mind out of the tailspin it was in. She didn't want to return to her room. She couldn't face Ruby, yet—not until she had worked through the disappointment and hurt that was overwhelming her.

And not until she came to terms with the shame of realizing she was really nothing more than a dancehall floozy. She had been able to justify her actions when they were taken to help Ruby. She couldn't now excuse what she was becoming—what she'd become—when Ruby was no longer her purpose.

"I'm gonna take a walk. I need some fresh air and to think for a bit to figure out what I'm gonna do."

Abel nodded as he came back and stood in front of her. "Be back here in time to get ready for work—if you're still wantin' a job here. If not," he pulled a rag from the pocket of his apron and wiped at the spot on the bar where her glass had been, "there's a north-bound train that leaves about eight o'clock tonight."

CHAPTER 25

The town of Endurance was just coming to life for the day when the train pulled into the depot, the rising sun illuminating the street and buildings with its soft glow. A man in a white apron pulled racks of produce out onto the sidewalk in front of the general store; a short, older woman unlocked the door of a small haberdashery nearby; a stable boy brushed down a horse outside the big, double doors of the blacksmith's barn.

Cora Lee drew in a lung full of sweet mountain air as she stepped off the train and walked onto the open platform at the station. The cool, early-morning breeze was a welcome change from the oppressive, late-summer heat and muggy, dank humidity she'd left behind in Little Rock. Thankful that her long journey was almost at an end, she only needed to hire someone to carry her to the ridge road. From there, she'd have a manageable walk back to her home on Bennett's Ridge.

If she was lucky, she might even run into Mr. Oakley or Joshua on one of their frequent trips to town and ask for a ride back with them once they finished their business. With a wry smile, she wondered if they would recognize her now. She had to admit, mentally looking herself over, she had changed a great deal in the few months she'd been away.

Instead of a straw bonnet tied under her chin, she had a narrow, blue scarf wrapped around her head and tied beneath her bobbed hair. Her blue-and-pink checkered, shift-style dress was loose fitting and had a dropped waist. The fashionably-short hem of her box-pleated skirt exposed lower legs clad in sheer silk hose rather than heavy cotton stockings, and she wore low Mary Jane heels rather than the button-up boots she'd left home in.

But, the change in her was more than in the clothes she wore. It was more than skin—or clothes—deep. It reached the very core of her. The things she had lost were not only friends and a sense of purpose; she had lost the future she had envisioned for herself as Walter's wife and the mother of his children. She no longer believed she was worthy of being anyone's wife or mother, anyway.

Her behavior over the last few months as a dime-a-dance girl had seemed excusable on her mission to help Ruby and rescue Micah. Without that goal, without that justification, she could only see a future in remaining at the dance emporium as the shameful, vile siren calling men to sinful destruction that the soapbox man and the Ladies of Virtue League had called her. The thought of that touched her soul, broke her heart, and it had altered the way she saw herself.

She left her home an unsure, timid girl and returned a more confident, but now directionless, woman with no friends, no fiancé, and no future. *I've changed.* And with that thought came the memory of Ada Campbell's words, *"Change is just a way of life. Nothin' and nobody stays the same ferever."*

The dawning, bright sky of morning didn't match the gloom in her heart. The pleasure of her homecoming didn't lift the shame she carried over her experiences as a dancehall floozy at the Something Wonderful—*something awful*—Dance Emporium.

She consoled herself that, despite Ruby's rude rejection of her help and friendship, Cora Lee had managed to do some good for her friend, anyway. She had left half of her savings from her dancehall job in an envelope under Ruby's pillow with a note wishing her nothing but happiness. The money she had earned seemed tainted, and Cora Lee only kept the amount she had left home with and the price of her train ticket back to Endurance.

Picking up her valise, she stepped off the platform onto the street and looked around for a possible carriage or wagon to hire. Not seeing one, she decided to walk to the general store across the road and ask if any such conveyance might be available anywhere in town. As she started across the road, though, she spied a small church sitting next to the store and decided to stop in there first. *Perhaps a few moments spent in prayer in God's house will help me*, she thought.

Cora Lee pushed the heavy, red-painted door of the little church open, and walked inside. A plaque hung on the wall inside that read, *"Trust in Him at all times; ye people; Pour out your heart before Him: God is a refuge for us." – Psalm 62:8"* She ran her fingers over the words, comforted by God's offer of protection.

Walking into the nave, she took a seat in one of the pews at the back. Inside was cool and quiet. Dust motes danced in shafts of softly-colored sunlight that spilled dimly through three stained-glass windows on the eastern wall. The air was heavy with the scent of old wood and fresh lemon oil mixed with the faint scent of something earthy and sweet. She bowed her head and listened for the voice of the Savior.

No words, no reassuring message came to her.

After a time, she lifted her head and sighed. "I guess I've gotten too far away. That'll be my purpose now." she decided. "Getting close to You, again, Father."

She sat for a long while letting the peace that surrounded her soak into her soul. Granny Mae's words echoed in her mind. *"The Bible says we're to forget the things behind us and reach for the things to come. Trust in God, do yer best, and you'll be fine."*

She bowed her head and confessed her sins. In that moment, she opened her heart and received the grace of God through her Savior, Jesus Christ, accepting His forgiveness for the sins and shortcomings of her past. Here, in Christ, she was finally, at last, able to find her true "belongin' place."

"Amen," she said softly as the weight of her burden shifted and rolled off of her soul.

She stood, picked up her valise, and walked out of the church feeling clean, renewed in Grace, and ready to face God's plan for her life with a joyful heart. She had forgiven Walter for finding someone else to love and share his life with. She was determined that when she ran into him and his wife, she would be welcoming and kind.

Be polite. Be helpful. Be happy for him, she told herself. It became her new inner mantra, and repeating it helped her believe that she would be able to bear the pain of seeing him with another woman. *Will I ever be able to bear that pain?*

Turning back to the general store, she was brought up short by the sight of a wagon parked in front of the mercantile. The green paint and yellow trim were faded now, but the black lettering was still clear. A bright smile flooded her face, and Cora Lee hurried to the front of the store as Peddler Man Dan emerged.

She threw herself into his arms, happy to see her old friend from years ago. He was older, his long, stringy-black hair now thinning and streaked with grey. A few feathers and beads were missing from his vest. His face, wrinkled now, had taken on a sickly, ashen color, but he was still the same boisterous, good-natured fellow she remembered from her childhood.

"Well!" the man exclaimed. "It's my little friend from up on the ridge!" He stepped back and looked Cora Lee up and down with exaggerated amazement on his face. "At least, I think it is. You've grown, ain't ya? Cut yer hair? And ain't ya dressed fancified!"

Cora Lee nodded and smiled. "Yes, it's me, for sure. I guess I have changed quite a bit, but you haven't changed much. We've missed you coming around. How come you to stop your route with us up on the ridge?"

"Well, after the Great Sickness, I had to cut back on the area I traveled. Weren't allowed to trade fer a bit durin' the quarantine last year. Then—well, I reckon I got a little old and a little tired, so I don't do as much as I used to. Say! What's a little ol' mountain gal like you doin' down here in town all alone?"

Cora Lee laughed. "I just came back from Little Rock on the train this morning. I was hoping to hire a ride back to the ridge road, but there doesn't seem to be anyone to hire. I reckon I'm gonna have to walk."

"Nah! Don't even think it!" he cut her off. "Hop up on ol' Dan's wagon. I'll take ya most of the way. I generally only trade as far as the timber camp up at the bend, but I can go on past there and take ya to the cut-off at the ridge road. The old mule can't pull the wagon up that steep path to the ridge, no more, but we'd be glad to take ya that far, at least!"

"Oh! That'd be perfect. Thank you!"

Dan took Cora Lee's valise and stored it under the bench seat. He gave her a hand as she climbed up on the wagon. He swung up next to her, took his seat on the bench, clicked his tongue and gently slapped the mule's rump with his reigns. As the wagon lurched forward, Dan broke out in a boisterous hymn.

Jesus called his first disciples
By the sea of Galilee
Yes, Jesus preached the gospels
And said 'Come follow me'

Cora Lee gave him a sidelong glance and joined in with a grin. They sang their way out of town and past the farms that lay in the folds of the foothills.

As they approached the river, the road turned northward toward the lumber mill and logging site located near Endurance. The sound of rushing water grew louder, and Cora Lee caught glimpses of the river here and there through the woods on the right side of the road.

"That there's the Big River—biggest river in Missouri," Dan said. "The loggin' camp up ahead is owned by a company called Grandin." He shook his head and snorted in disgust. "They's about took all the pine trees out of Missouri they can get they hands on. They's cuttin' oak, too."

The chaotic clamor of men shouting, trees crashing to the ground, logs colliding as they slid down a flume into the mill pond, and a giant saw ripping trees into lumber in the mill house broke through the sound of the river and pierced the peaceful serenity of the pair's trip. Cora Lee plugged her ears until they passed the din of the mill.

"That cut off there leads to the tent encampment where the loggers and they families live. I reckon I'll take ya on up to the ridge road and then do my business here on the way back." Dan said.

"You know, I was born in my pa's wagon in a logging camp," Cora Lee said, relieved to be moving away from the noise and back into the quiet of the countryside around them. "I never knew my ma or pa, 'cause they died when I was still little."

Dan nodded. "I knew yer ma from the many times I traded up on the ridge. You look a lot like how I remember her. She used to love to trade rocks and pine cones and little things she'd find in the woods fer ribbons and bows and such. I'd make a show of how 'valuable' her trades was. And they was valuable, too. They wasn't worth any money, of course, but they sure are a blessin' to me, now, in the way of bein' a treasured collection of sweet memories."

He reached into a pocket on his vest and withdrew a milky-white, rounded pebble that was about the size of a wild grape. He handed it to Cora Lee.

"Yer ma give me this when she was about ten or so. I keep it on me as a good luck charm, and to remind me of happy times past."

Cora Lee studied the rock, noting it's almost luminescent purity. "I've seen these around on the ground a bunch, but I never thought about picking one up to keep for a good luck charm. It's funny to know that my ma would see beauty and value in it enough to trade for a hair ribbon." She handed the stone back to Dan. "Thank you for sharing that story."

Dan nodded and tucked the rock back into his vest pocket. The rest of the ride from town to the cut-off at Bennett's Ridge passed pleasantly, and Cora Lee was sorry when the trip seemed to end too soon.

When Dan pulled the wagon to a stop, Cora Lee climbed down from her seat and pulled her suitcase from under it. Looking up at her old friend, she smiled. "Thank you so much for bringing me, Mr. Dan. You lifted my spirits as well as saving me from a long walk."

"Glad to do it, missy." He reached into another pocket on his vest and pulled out a stick of peppermint candy. "Now, don't ya go fergettin' yer ol' friend, Peddler Man Dan." He smiled a sad little smile. "I ain't likely to be back this way. I'm growin' too old fer this life. I reckon I'll soon be layin' under a shade tree in Heaven enjoyin' my final reward and fishin' on the cool, green banks of the river Jordan."

Cora Lee was startled by his words. She took the gift and nodded. "Like I said a long time ago, Mr.

Dan," she said. "You'd be kind of hard to forget. You've made your mark in this life, and you'll be making a sizeable dent in the next one, too, I'm sure."

Could she say the same about herself? As Dan slapped the mule with the reins and the wagon lurched away, Cora Lee gave a little wave and faced the path that led to the ridge road. She bent to remove her shoes and silk stockings and, barefoot and bare-legged, walked on.

As she crested the hill and approached the old cemetery on her left, she stopped. She set her shoes, stockings, and suitcase by the road, pushed through the turnstile gate, and walked to her grandmother's final resting place.

Sheltered under an ancient hickory tree, the wooden marker at the grave had weathered the Ozark sun and rains well. The lettering on it was still clearly readable.

Mae Murphy Clarey, Wife of Nelson
1845 –1917
Rest in Peace.

The earth covering Mae's plot had settled and sunk, and Cora Lee made a mental note to ask Joshua to bring more dirt to fill it in. Lying next to her grandmother were the graves of her grandfather, Nelson, and four other Clarey's—her four uncles, she assumed. Three other tiny plots were marked only by three little crosses with no names on them.

Cora Lee brushed leaves and twigs away from their plots wishing she'd had the opportunity to have met all of them, then moved among the other, newer gravesites. She stood for a moment over each one silently remembering the loved ones and friends who lay there. She was relieved to see that no new graves had been dug in the months that she'd been away.

When she found the plot where Alice lay, she dropped to her knees. "Hello, my dear friend," she whispered. "How I miss your happy chatter and your bright smile!" Pretty Alice. Always chattering and excited over a new beau or with a plan to win one with some charm or conjure.

Cora Lee rolled from her knees to one hip, curled her legs around her, and settled more comfortably on the ground. "You'd be surprised by all the ways that the big, wide world is changing—so fast it's a wonder anyone can keep up with it at all."

After a quiet moment, she went on. "You might find it funny if you could see me, too. You see, I set off on a 'big adventure' to find Ruby Douglas and be of some use to someone in this world. All I managed to do, though, was to lose myself and be no use to anyone, at all. Now I've come back feeling about as dumb as a branch-water looby. Granny always said 'a man shouldn't go back on his raisin',' and she was right. I did, and it didn't work out worth a lick."

She heaved a sigh and got up from the ground. She left the cemetery and continued on her way to her cabin grateful that the winding dirt road was empty.

No other travelers came within earshot or into view, and it was as if the whole world belonged only to her. Suddenly, she couldn't wait to take off the dress she was wearing and be back in the old, homespun skirt and button-up blouse she'd left hanging on a wall-peg at home.

Quickening her step, she was surprised to see smoke coming out of the chimney at Old Man McDaniel's place. She hated to think of such a nice farm going to ruin and was glad it appeared that Lucas had either sold or rented the place to a new family.

As she passed the Dobson farm, she made plans to come back by soon and check on Robert to learn how he was doing after his medical discharge from the army. Dora Oakley and he had seemed like a good match, so perhaps they would marry and start their own family someday.

Across the road from Robert Dobson's place, she could hear the steady rhythm of an ax ringing out in the air. She supposed Silas was somewhere nearby cutting wood. She was saddened by the thought of that quiet, taciturn man living by himself. He and Walter had worked so hard to build that beautiful home. Was it just a silent, empty and sad shell now without Amanda in it?

Memories of her sweet teacher and friend played in her mind. Amanda had been so kind to her after her granny's passing. She wondered if their son, Junior, had come back home to live with Silas, or was he still living with the older Bennetts?

Her steps slowed at the Campbell farm. She stopped at the gate almost ready to shout a greeting at the house, then walked on. In her mind, she could still see Alice skipping out of the door onto the porch and down the steps, full of life and ready for fun.

As Cora Lee shook her head and walked on, she came to the far edge of Alice's farm. The blackberry bushes that grew over the fence there were heavy with late-summer fruit.

I'll ask Mr. Campbell if I can harvest some to put up jam. I probably need to pick Granny's peaches, too, so they don't rot on the tree, she thought as she continued down the road, rounded the bend and approached the cut-off to the river.

And there he was.

Standing where she had seen him for the first time so many years ago on her walk to visit the Campbells with Granny Mae. He'd been hacking at a bush with a stick, wearing shabby clothes, black hair falling into his golden-brown eyes. Now, he stood in that same spot with his back to her—so tall, so straight.

So very *real*.

CHAPTER 26

Cora Lee's feet froze in place. She stood as still and rigid as the hills that rose around them. Her lungs refused to exhale, and her eyes refused to blink. She stared at Walter, her heart pounding like a drum in her chest, her face draining of color and then flooding with crimson heat. She wanted to run back the way she had just come, and she wanted to run into his arms at the same time. She wanted to pretend that he had not forgotten her, that he had not married another, that he was still hers.

Walter turned and met her eyes. The air around her became as thick as honey so that it was difficult to breathe. The world seemed to fade away. Her head swam, and, suddenly, Walter was the only thing she could see.

He started toward her as a brilliant smile lit up his handsome face, then it melted away in a look of confusion as he came closer.

"Cora Lee," he said, unsure of her reaction and stopping a short distance away. He lifted a hand as if to touch her, then dropped it at his side.

Hearing her name on his lips, the sound of his voice, was her undoing. Her eyes filled with tears, and her hands trembled as she quickly brushed them away. She shook her head to clear it. How could she bear being so close to him, loving him as she did, and with the knowledge that he would never be hers?

Be polite. Be helpful. Be happy for him, she repeated the chant that had played over and over in her head since she left the church in Endurance. She forced her face into a calm, icy mask and tried to throw up a wall between the emotions raging in her heart and the man who stood only a few yards away.

She drew a breath and shook her head again. Setting down her valise and laying her stockings and shoes on top of it, she managed to paste a smile on her face. *How did I do that?* She took a step toward him. *How are my legs moving?*

"Walter." *Is that my voice? So calm, so distant, so polite?* Her voice only shook a little as she made a monumental effort to control it. "How very nice to see you've made it home safe. We were all so worried…"

Her platitudes were cut off as he moved toward her, took her in his arms and smothered her words with a deep, desperate kiss.

292

Cora Lee put her hand between them and tried, unsuccessfully, to push him away. "Walter, so much has happened since you left. I've changed—grown. So have you. You've been through so much, too. And—what," she almost choked on the words. "What about your beautiful French wife? I'm anxious to meet her."

Walter startled and gasped as if she had doused him in ice water. He released her and stepped back.

"Wife? What're ya talkin' about? What 'wife?'"

Her face creased in confusion. "Lucas said you met someone in France. He said you were probably married—and you sent that telegram?"

"I never 'met someone in France,' and I sure never got married. I never even—Oh! well, I went to lunch with a shop girl once, but not really by my choosin' or 'cause I was steppin' out with her or anythin' like it."

Walter paused, and a light switched on in his face. "Oh, phooey! Lucas told you that? We run into each other by chance when I was walkin' that shop girl back from lunch. She'd sorta latched onto me. She were pretty, Cora Lee, but she weren't you. I didn't never meet up with her again, and I sure as sun melts butter never married the gal."

His words weren't clear. She forced her face to remain carefully blank, frozen in the mask of indifference she had worked so hard to perfect. *What is he saying? He isn't married?*

Walter moved close again and stood inches away from the girl he loved. "I promise, yer the only gal I ever wanted—the only one I thought of since I left the night I asked ya to wait fer me. Yer the picture I carried in my heart through all them long months since I left home. There ain't never been nobody else. There never could be."

"But, what about the telegram you sent Ruby? You said, 'We're home.' What 'we' did you mean?"

"I was with Jacob Bennett and Roy Dale! Them two got back to Endurance on the same train as me, and we met up at the station there. That's who the 'we' was. Nobody else weren't with me."

Cora Lee stared at him while his words finally began to make sense. A thrill ran through her as she realized that Walter was free, that he still loved her.

The thrill was quickly overtaken by anger at the realization that Lucas had lied to her, could have so meanly tried to poison the sweet, steadfast love she had for Walter. It was almost unbelievable that even Lucas could have been so ugly that he would have deliberately lied to break the friendship, the love, that was blooming in her heart for her childhood friend.

"Lucas is a suggin, mangy dog!" she exploded. "I should have never listened to a word that came out of his sorry, lying mouth!"

She turned, teeth clenched, and picked up her things. Anger toward Lucas, mixed with an overwhelming feeling of relief and an upsurge of passionate love for Walter, swirled through her body in a confused, upending mix. She didn't want Walter to see her in such an unflattering state, and she fought to get her emotions under control.

She marched off toward her cabin. Walter hastily followed. The two of them arrived at Mae's gate, and Cora Lee stopped. Dazed by a storm of emotions sweeping through her heart, she needed some time to gather herself so she could think clearly.

"Let's not go in yet," she said. "I'm too addlepated by all this."

She put down her things and turned to walk around the house with Walter staying close behind. They climbed to the wooded spot on the small rise behind the cabin where Cora Lee had spent so many peaceful hours when she was growing up. The walk served to calm her anger with Lucas and allowed her to begin to process all that Walter had told her.

"Sit with me here a bit," she invited as she found a spot beneath her favorite oak tree. She needed a few more moments to clear her head, sort through the knowledge that Walter hadn't married, that he said he still loved her. She needed time to be with him, look at him, touch him, and to accept the reality that he was truly here with her.

"You don't have to go home right away, do you?" she asked hopefully.

Walter shook his head and dropped to the ground near her. He took off his hat, pulled his knees up, and wrapped his arms around his legs. He didn't take his eyes off of her face.

"I wrote you some letters. Did you get them?"

Walter nodded. "I got two."

"Well, I sent more than two. How come you never wrote back or even sent a note to your ma?"

Walter shrugged and shifted his seat uneasily. "I don't write too good. Didn't wanna ask nobody to write fer me. I thought about home—about you—ever day, though, and I kept yer letters in my pocket."

He pulled the letters from his shirt and stared at them for a moment. "Maybe you'll read 'em to me sometime, and let me know what the other ones said?"

Cora Lee smiled. "Sure, Walter. I can do that."

The hills around them were familiar and comforting. They sat for a while in silence in the sun-dappled arbor, content to be in each other's company after so long a separation. This was the place where they had once, a long age ago, shared a happy hour in song. The memory seemed a lifetime and, yet, only a moment ago.

"How is your mother?" Cora Lee broke the silence. "Will you let her know I'll come visit soon as I can?"

"Ma's doin' good. She's anxious to know 'bout Ruby, though. She told me you went down there to see 'bout her—to see 'bout her and that baby." The thought of Ruby having and keeping the boy was painful, and the emotion showed on Walter's face.

"You don't have to be disappointed in her, Walter. Micah is lovely! He's as cute as he can be, and healthy, and Ruby loves him with all her heart. She's got a friend, Edith, who's helpin' her out with him.

Ruby loves living in the city—it suits her. I know they're gonna do fine down there."

Walter said nothing, and Cora Lee continued after giving him a few minutes to process her words.

"You should go and visit her someday soon. It'll put your mind at ease about her situation, and I know she'll want to see you."

He spoke then. "I ain't ever gonna leave you again, Cora Lee. I've had enough of bein' away from you to last fer a lifetime."

Cora Lee smiled at him, reached out and squeezed his hand. "I'm not going anywhere, Walter."

Although the sun was past the noon hour, there was no urgency to be anywhere but in each other's company. Cora Lee studied Walter's face in the golden-green shadows of their shady sanctuary. Time and trouble had etched lines into his young face, and there was a sadness in his eyes that had not been there before.

"Was it very bad for you over there?" she asked and lay her hand on his arm.

Walter hesitated. Brief visions of the horrors of war flashed in his head like flickering images from an old kinetoscope he had once seen while he was still in France. He forced himself to shut the images down.

"Oh, lots of it was just boredom, and bugs, and mud, and waitin' around. Bad times were awful bad, though. I try not to think about it."

Silence grew again between them, and Cora Lee did not break it with more questions. She let Walter's thoughts fill the space. After a quiet pause, he continued, "It may seem strange to you, but I didn't so much mind seein' the bodies of dead men. It was the wounded that got to me–not so much the blood and innards, but the screams and cryin'—the pain on their faces and hearin' the moanin' and dyin' men callin' fer their mothers.

"The worst was the gas, but you don't need to hear nothin' 'bout that." He turned his face away and cleared his throat then turned back to her and continued. "Women don't fight fer a reason, and they sure don't need to hear 'bout it, neither."

Cora Lee looked into Walter's golden-brown eyes where shadows of things that he would never speak of lay. Would her love be enough to lead him out of the dark valley of his war-torn memories? Would her faith be strong enough to help lead him to the still waters of God's everlasting peace?

Gently, she leaned toward him still softly touching his arm. "'After the wind an earthquake, but the Lord was not in the earthquake. After the earthquake a fire, but the Lord was not in the fire. And after the fire came a gentle whisper,'" she quoted from I Kings. "You're home now. That 'gentle whisper,' the healing breath of God, is here for you. It's here for us both."

Walter looked into her eyes as if searching for something. After a moment, his face relaxed in a slight smile, and he nodded.

A soft breeze rustled the leaves of the oak tree above them and swirled around the couple as they sat together in contented silence. Cora Lee's heart began to swell. She knew, in that moment, that God had brought her to this place in this exact way, working, again, in His mysterious ways to show her His plan for her life and, hopefully, for Walter's life, too.

"So what's next for you, Walter? Are you going to stay? Farm? Maybe—travel?" She sincerely hoped he wasn't planning to leave again. She held her breath as she waited for his answer.

"I took some mechanics classes over in France. Workin' on engines and machines is somethin' I got good at, and I like doin' it. I saved up most of my pay, and I was thinkin' I'd set up an automobile and engine repair shop down in town. I think I could make a good livin' at it. Someday soon, I might even be able to buy a house with a yard. What would ya think about that?"

Cora Lee smiled. "Why, Walter! I think that would be a grand idea! If you like doing that kind of work, it'd help folks out when things broke down, and it sounds like it'll pay well. You should sure do it."

She bit her lip and looked away from him. *He's thinking of moving away from here. But Endurance isn't very far away, and his mother is still here. I'll still see him sometimes, I think.*

"I'd surely hope to see you, though, from time-to-time. Will you stop in when you come back home to see your ma?"

Rising, Walter stuck out his hand. Cora Lee took his hand, and he pulled her up into his arms.

"Cora Lee, yer everthin' that's 'home' to me. I want you to go with me, of course! I know I had a fire in me to leave this place, and I was driven to find adventure in my life. It took going away to make me understand that 'adventure' ain't always found in travelin' to new places or meetin' new people. Comin' to learn that I have a path in life laid out fer me, learnin' what that path is, and makin' peace with that has been an adventure in itself."

She nodded, and he went on. "I know now, Cora Lee, that yer my path. Yer my adventure. I want you to be my wife; I want us to share that path and build that future, that life, together."

She sucked in a breath in gladness at his proposal. Then dismay engulfed her as thoughts of all the mistakes of her recent past flooded her mind. Would this man be able to love her if he knew all the things she had done? Would he still want her if he knew of her 'adventures' while they were apart? She had accepted the forgiveness of God, but she owed it to Walter to tell him the truth so he could decide if he still wanted her.

"Walter," she began, her voice trembling in uncertainty as she began her confession. "I'm not the girl you left behind. I've done many…"

"Don't," he cut her off. "It don't matter, not a bit. What matters is that we're here, together, now, in this moment. If you feel ya need to tell me about that, there's time for that in our future, and I'll be willin' to listen. What matters now is that we've made our peace with the Almighty, and we're ready to start fresh. We're new people, and the past is gone. Tell me yer ready to make a future with me, 'cause I am ready to make my life with you."

She didn't answer as his words swirled in her mind, and she tried to make sense of them. Her face knitted in confusion. *What is he saying? What does he mean?*

"But, maybe you don't wanna leave here?" Her silence and the look on her face confused him.

"Maybe the home you have up here on the ridge is where ya wanna stay?" He searched her face as he waited for her answer.

Her eyes shimmered. He brushed a tear from her cheek with his thumb. She closed her eyes almost unable to bear the weight of his touch on her face.

She cleared her throat and answered, "Because I found a belonging place in the mountains—because I found security and safety here, and because this is where I thought I left my heart—this is where I ran back to. I realize, though, my heart isn't in this place."

Cora Lee looked around and indicated their surroundings with a sweep of her hand. She brought her hand to rest on Walter's chest and was surprised to feel his heart pounding beneath his shirt. She raised her face to his.

"My heart, my future, my everything is here. Wherever you are, that's where I want to be."

A barely audible revelation, a quiet love note delivered in the hush of a golden afternoon to the orchestra of a late-August wind combing softly through the trees. Walter heard the words and hoped he could trust them. He wrapped her hand in his, tightened his other arm around the girl that he loved, and drew her closer to him.

"Tell me ya love me as I love you," he whispered, his voice rough with longing. "I need to hear ya say it."

Cora Lee met the eyes of her friend, the eyes of a man she had loved for most of her life. "My heart isn't in the mountains of the Missouri Ozarks," she croaked. "It isn't in some far-off city."

Her voice sounded like that of a woman dying of thirst. "My heart is right here, Walter. My heart, my home has always been and will always be with you. I love you, Walter."

READING GROUP GUIDE

Characters:

1. Who was your favorite character? Why?
2. Did you relate to any of these characters? Why or why not?
3. How well did the author develop each of the characters in the novel?
4. Were there any characters that you would have liked to see play a larger part in the story? In what way?
5. If you could invite any one of the characters to dinner, who would it be?

Plot and Themes:

6. What are central themes of the story?
7. How well developed were they?
8. What was unique about the storyline and setting?
9. Would this make a good movie? Why or why not?

<u>Romance:</u>

10. Was the love story in this book realistic?
11. Was the love story in this book well-balanced?
12. Would you have liked to see other couples'
    romances develop? Who?
13. Were you satisfied with the level of "heat"
    between Cora Lee and Walter?

<u>Settings:</u>

14. The story takes place in three main locations—
    Bennett's Ridge, Missouri; Brest, France; and
    Little Rock, Arkansas. How well did the
    author bring these settings to life?
15. The majority of the book was set in the period
    between 1912 and 1919, a time of great
    societal change. Which character do you think
    was able to adapt best?

<u>Pacing:</u>

16. Did any part of the story seem rushed?
17. Did any part of the story seem to drag?
18. Was the ending paced well?

<u>Personal Opinions:</u>

19. Did you highlight any passages?
20. Did any part upset or frustrate you?
21. Did any part change your opinion about anything?
22. Would you recommend this book to others?
23. What kind of readers do you think would like this book? Young adult? New adult? History lovers? Romance readers?

ACKNOWLEDGMENTS

The germination of this book began many years ago when my father opened up to us about his childhood—a particularly difficult and unstable one. His mother, my grandmother, was born in the Ozark mountains, orphaned at a very young age, passed around by neighbors as she grew up, and finally made her way to Little Rock, Arkansas as a young girl in the 1920s.

I have always wondered how my grandmother survived. I regret that she passed away when I was sixteen, and that I had not thought to learn about her past from her own stories. From Dad, I learned that she, like Cora Lee and Ruby, among other jobs, worked in a dime-a-dance hall as a girl.

Dad was born in 1929, and spent several years at St. Joseph's Orphanage in Levy, a suburb of North Little Rock. My grandmother divorced my grandfather when Dad was in third grade, so he and his brother had a particularly rough time growing up during the Depression. Despite the challenges and disadvantages they faced, both boys became amazingly successful in their careers and wonderful men, husbands, and fathers. I am indebted to my dad and my uncle for sharing what they remembered of their mom with me.

Much of the dialogue, too, were words and expressions used by my grandmother during my childhood, and so it was her voice in my head as Granny Mae was speaking.

Although this story is completely fictionalized, and it is not meant in any way to parallel the journey that my grandmother took, her story is the seed that planted this novel. I thank her for that.

I am grateful for the backing of my sisters who have been so wonderful during my struggle with writer's block, writer's doubt, writer's euphoria, and writer's incessant need at times to never shut up about my Work in Progress. Thank you, ladies, for your help and patience.

I am especially thoughtful of my sister, Deborah, who had such an eye for detail. She could spot a misspelling or an errant comma from a mile away. I am sad she did not live to see the finished work she had such an important hand in.

My writers' group, Write On Waxahachie, which I found soon after moving to this beautiful city, has given me so much encouragement. I am appreciative of your honesty, your keen eyes, your joyous comradery, your warm friendship, and your enthusiastic support.

Much research has gone into each detail of this manuscript. Being a history lover, I enjoyed the research as much as I loved writing it into the fabric of this tale. Old newspaper advertisements and books from the time were wonderful for immersion into the era.

Last but not least, I am truly thankful to those of you who have chosen to read this novel. Thank you! Thank you! Thank you!

Blessings,

Rebecca Cathey
www.rebeccacatheyauthor.com

ABOUT THE AUTHOR

Rebecca Cathey started writing short stories and poetry as soon as she learned to draw her letters correctly as a first grader at Maxie Speer Elementary in Arlington, Texas, where she lived with her family.

She earned her Bachelor of Sciences degree in History graduating summa cum laude from Texas Wesleyan University in Ft. Worth, Texas.

She is a hobbyist personal historian and memoirist and has won awards for her memoir essay, *Tender Treasures*, and two of her short stories, *Love Songs* and *Green Eyes*.

She currently resides in Waxahachie, Texas.

Visit her online at www.rebeccacatheyauthor.com.

www.ingramcontent.com/pod-product-compliance
Lightning Source LLC
Chambersburg PA
CBHW010514100726
47903CB00009B/2741